THE END OF THE DREAM...

He caught his breath at the slim, graceful delicacy of her body; then he snatched her close to him, and his mouth lost its gentleness as he kissed her hungrily.

Feverishly, she unbuttoned his shirt, pressing little kisses to his flesh as she revealed it. She had never caressed him so freely before, but she did so now, discovering with delight the curling hair that roughened his chest and ran in a narrow line down his abdomen.

She wanted only his touch, his love. "Oh, Nikolas, please... Being your wife will be heaven!"

He stiffened, pulling away from her. "I've never mentioned marriage to you, Jessica. I'm not that big a fool."

LINDA HOWARD

ALL THAT GLITTERS

Silhouette® Books

Published by Silhouette Books New York

SILHOUETTE BOOKS
300 East 42nd St., New York, N.Y. 10017

ALL THAT GLITTERS

Copyright © 1982 by Linda Howard

All rights reserved. Except for use in any review, the reproduction
or utilization of this work in whole or in part in any form by any
electronic, mechanical or other means, now known or hereafter
invented, including xerography, photocopying and recording, or in
any information storage or retrieval system, is forbidden without
the permission of the publisher, Silhouette Books, 300 E. 42nd St.,
New York, N.Y. 10017

ISBN: 0-373-48270-1

Published Silhouette Books 1982, 1993

All the characters in this book have no existence outside the
imagination of the author and have no relation whatsoever to
anyone bearing the same name or names. They are not even
distantly inspired by any individual known or unknown to the
author, and all incidents are pure invention.

®: Trademark used under license and registered in the United States
Patent and Trademark Office and in other countries.

Printed in the U.S.A.

To Gary

Chapter One

Charles said bluntly, without warning, "Constantinos arrived in London this morning."

Jessica looked up, her mind blank for a moment, then she realized what he had said and she smiled ruefully. "Well, you did warn me, Charles. It seems you were right." Not that she had ever doubted him, for Charles's instincts in business were uncanny. He had told her that if she voted her stock in ConTech against the Constantinos vote, she would bring down on her head the wrath of the single largest stockholder and chairman of the board, Nikolas Constantinos, and it appeared that once again Charles had been exactly right. The vote on the Dryden issue had been yesterday. Despite Charles's warnings, she had voted against the takeover and her vote had carried the majority. Less than twenty-four hours later, Constantinos had arrived in London.

Jessica had never met him, but she had heard enough horror tales about him to count herself lucky in that respect. According to gossip, he was utterly ruthless in his business dealings; of course, it stood to reason that he would not have achieved his present position of power by being meek and mild. He was a billionaire, powerful even by Greek standards; she was only a stockholder, and she thought humorously that it was a case of overkill for him to bring out his heavy artillery on her, but it looked as though no problem was too small for his personal attention.

Charles had pointed out that she could have voted for the takeover and saved herself a lot of trouble, but one of the things that Robert had taught her in the three years of their marriage was to stand up for herself, to trust her instincts and never to sell herself short. Jessica had felt that the move against Dryden was underhanded and she voted against it. If Constantinos was unable to accept that she had the right to vote her stock as she wanted, then he would just have to learn to deal with it. Regardless of how much power he wielded, she was determined not to back down from her stand, and Charles had found that she could be very stubborn when she set her mind to something.

"You must be very careful around him," Charles instructed her now, breaking into her thoughts. "Jessica, my dear, I don't believe you realize just how much pressure the man can bring to bear on you. He can hurt you in ways you've never imagined. Your friends can lose their jobs; mortgages can be called in on their homes; banks will cease doing business with you. It can even extend to such small things as repairs to your auto being delayed or seats on flights suddenly becoming unavailable. Do you begin to see, my dear?"

Disbelievingly, Jessica stared at him. "My word, Charles, are you serious? It seems so ludicrous!"

"I regret that I am very serious. Constantinos wants things done his way, and he has the money and the power to ensure that they are. Don't underestimate him, Jessica."

"But that's barbaric!"

"And so is Constantinos, to a degree," said Charles flatly. "If he gives you the option of selling your stock to him, Jessica, then I strongly urge you to do so. It will be much safer for you."

"But Robert—"

"Yes, I know," he interrupted, though his voice took on a softer tone. "You feel that Robert entrusted that stock to you, and that he would have voted against the Dryden takeover, too. Robert was a very dear and special man, but he's dead now and he can't protect you. You have to think of yourself, and you haven't the weapons to fight Constantinos. He can demolish you."

"But I don't want to fight him," she protested. "I only want to carry on as I always have. It seems so silly for him to be upset over my vote—why should he take it so personally?"

"He doesn't take it personally," explained Charles. "He doesn't have to. But you've gone against him and you'll be brought into line, regardless of what he has to do to accomplish it. And don't think that you can appeal to his better nature—"

"I know," she broke in, her soft mouth curving into a smile. "He doesn't have one!"

"Exactly," said Charles. "Nor can he be feeling very charitable toward you; your record in voting against him, my dear, is very nearly perfect."

"Oh, dear," she said wryly. "I hadn't realized. But at least I'm consistent!"

Charles laughed unwillingly, but his cool eyes gleamed with admiration. Jessica always seemed in control of herself, capable of putting things into their proper perspective and reducing crises to mere annoyances, though he feared that this time she was in over her head. He didn't want her hurt; he never again wanted to see the look in her eyes that had been there after Robert's death, the despair, the pain that was too deep for comforting. She had recovered, she was a strong woman and a fighter, but he always tried to protect her from any further hurt. She had borne enough in her young life.

The phone rang and Jessica got up to answer it, her movements, as always, lithe and as graceful as a cat's. She tucked the receiver against her shoulder. "Stanton residence."

"Mrs. Stanton, please," said a cool, impersonal male voice, and her sharp ear caught the hint of an accent. Constantinos already?

"This is Mrs. Stanton," she replied.

"Mrs. Stanton, this is Mr. Constantinos's secretary. He would like to see you this afternoon—shall we say at three-thirty?"

"Three-thirty?" she echoed, glancing at her wristwatch. It was almost two o'clock now.

"Thank you, Mrs. Stanton," said the voice in satisfaction. "I will tell Mr. Constantinos to expect you. Good day."

The click of the receiver made her take the phone from her ear and stare at it in disbelief. "Well, that was cheeky," she mused, hanging up the instrument. It was possible that he had taken her echo of the time as an affirmation, but her instincts told her otherwise. No, it was simply that she was not expected to make any protest, and it wouldn't have mattered if she had.

"Who was that, my dear?" asked Charles absently, gathering up the papers he had brought for her signature.

"Mr. Constantinos's secretary. I've been summoned into the royal presence—at three-thirty this afternoon."

Charles's elegant eyebrows rose. "Then I suggest you hurry."

"I've a dental appointment at four-fifteen," she fretted.

"Cancel it."

She gave him a cool look and he laughed. "I apologize, my dear, and withdraw the suggestion. But be careful, and try to remember that it would be better to sell the stock than to try to fight Constantinos. I have to go now, but I'll ring you later."

"Yes, 'bye," she said, seeing him out. After he had gone, she dashed upstairs and took a shower, then found herself dawdling as she selected her dress. She was unsure what to wear and stood examining the contents of her wardrobe for long moments; then, in swift impatience with herself, she took down a cool beige jersey dress and stepped into it. It was classically simple and she wore it with four-inch heels to give her enough height to make her look more than a child.

She wasn't very tall, and because she was so fragile in build she tended to look about sixteen years old if she didn't use a host of little tricks to add maturity to her appearance. She wore simple clothing, pure in cut, and high heels whenever possible. Her long, thick, tawny hair she wore twisted into a knot at the back of her neck, a very severe hairstyle that revealed every proud, perfect line of her classically boned face and made her youth less obvious. Too much makeup would have made her look like a child playing grown-up, so she wore only subtle shades of eye shadow, naturally tinted lipsticks, and a touch of peach blusher. When she looked into the mirror, it was to check that her hair was subdued and her expression cool and reserved; she never saw the allure of long, heavily lashed green eyes or the provocative curve of her soft mouth. The world of flirtations and sexual affairs was so far removed from her consciousness that she had no concept of herself as a desirable woman. She had been a child when Robert had taken her under his protective wing—a sullen, self-conscious, suspicious child—and he had changed her into a responsible adult, but he had never attempted to teach her anything about the physical side of marriage and she was as untouched today at the age of twenty-three as she had been when she was born.

When she was ready, she checked the clock again and found that she had three-quarters of an hour to reach the ConTech building, but in the London traffic she would need every minute of that time. She snatched up her bag and ran downstairs to check on her dog, Samantha, who was very pregnant. Samantha lay in her bed, contentedly asleep even though her sides were grotesquely swollen by the puppies she carried. Jessica made certain there was water in her dish, then let herself out and crossed to her car, a sleek dark green sports model. She loved its smooth power and now she needed every ounce of it as she put it through its paces.

The traffic signals were with her and she stepped out of the lift on the appropriate floor of the ConTech building at precisely three-twenty-nine. A receptionist directed her to the royal chambers and she opened the heavy oak door at the appointed time.

A large room stretched before her, quietly furnished with chocolate-brown carpeting and chairs upholstered in brown and gold. Set to one side of massive double doors was a large desk, and seated at that desk was a slim, dark man who rose to his feet as she entered.

Cool dark eyes looked her up and down as she crossed the room to him, and she began to feel as if she had violated some law. "Good afternoon," she said, keeping all hint of temper out of her voice. "I am Mrs. Stanton."

The dark eyes swept over her again in a manner that was almost contemptuous. "Ah, yes. Please be seated, Mrs. Stanton. I regret that Mr. Constantinos has been delayed, but he will be free to see you shortly."

Jessica inclined her head and selected one of the comfortable chairs, sitting down and crossing her graceful legs. She made certain that her face remained expressionless, but inside she was contemplating scratching the young man's eyes out. His manner set her teeth on edge; he had a condescending air about him, a certain nastiness that made her long to shake the smug look off his face.

Ten minutes later she wondered if she was expected to cool her heels here indefinitely until Constantinos deigned to see her. Glancing at her watch, she decided to give it another five minutes, then she would have to leave if she was to be on time for her dental appointment.

The buzzer on the desk sounded loudly in the silence and she looked up as the secretary snatched up one of the three telephones on his desk. "Yes, sir," he said crisply, and replaced the receiver. He removed a file from one of the metal cabinets beside him and carried it into the inner sanctum, returning almost immediately and closing the double doors behind him. From all indications, it would be some time yet before Constantinos was free, and the five minutes she had allowed were gone. She uncrossed her legs and rose to her feet.

Coolly uplifted eyebrows asked her intentions.

"I have another appointment to keep," she said

smoothly, refusing to apologize for her departure. "Perhaps Mr. Constantinos will call me when he has more time."

Outraged astonishment was plain on the man's face as she took up her bag and prepared to leave. "But you can't go—" he began.

"On the contrary," she interrupted him, opening the door. "Good day."

Anger made her click her heels sharply as she walked to her car, but she took several deep breaths before she started the engine. No sense in letting the man's attitude upset her, perhaps enough to cause an accident, she told herself. She would shrug it off, as she had learned to do when she had been battered with criticism following her marriage to Robert. She had learned how to endure, to survive, and she was not going to let Robert down now.

After her dental appointment, which was only her annual checkup and took very little time, Jessica drove to the small dress shop just off Piccadilly that her neighbor Sallie Reese owned and operated, and helped Sallie close up. She also looked through the racks of clothing and chose two of the new line of evening gowns that Sallie had just stocked; perhaps because she had never had anything pretty when she was growing up, Jessica loved pretty clothes and had no resistance to buying them, though she was frugal with herself in other matters. She didn't wear jewelry and she didn't pamper herself in any way, but clothing—well, that was another story. Robert had always been amused by her little-girl glee in a new dress, a pair of jeans, shoes; it really didn't matter what it was so long as it was new and she liked it.

Remembering that made her smile a little sadly as she paid Sallie for the gowns; though she would never stop missing Robert, she was glad that she had brought some laughter and sunshine into the last years of his life.

"Whew, it has been a busy day," sighed Sallie as she totaled up the day's revenue. "But sales were good; it wasn't just a case of a lot of people window-shopping. Joel will be ecstatic; I promised him that he could buy that fancy stereo he's had his heart set on if we had a good week."

Jessica chuckled. Joel was a stereo addict, and he had been moaning for two months now about a marvelous set that he had seen and just had to have or his life would be blighted forever. Sallie took all of his dire predictions in stride, but it had been only a matter of time before she agreed to buy the new stereo. Jessica was glad that now her friends could afford a few luxuries without totally wrecking their budget. The dress shop had turned their fortunes around, because Joel's income as an accountant was just not enough nowadays to support a young family.

When Robert had died, Jessica had found herself unable to live in the luxurious penthouse without him and she had left it, instead buying an old Victorian house that had been converted into a duplex and moving into the empty side herself. Joel and Sallie and their twin five-year-old hellions, who went by the names of Patricia and Penelope, lived in the other side of the old house and the two young women had gradually become good friends. Jessica learned how Sallie had to scrimp and budget and make all of their clothing herself, and it was Sallie's needlework that had given Jessica the idea.

The Reeses had not had the capital to open a shop, but Jessica had, and when she found the small, cozy shop off Piccadilly, she leaped on it. Within a month it was remodeled, stocked, and in business with the name of SALLIE'S RAGS on the sign outside.

Patty and Penny were in kindergarten and Sallie was happily installed in her shop, making some of the clothing herself and gradually expanding until now the shop employed two salesgirls full time, besides Sallie herself, and another woman who helped Sallie with the sewing. Before the first year was out, Sallie had repaid Jessica and was flushed with pride at how well it had turned out.

Sallie was now rounding quite nicely with a third little Reese, but she and Joel no longer worried about expenses and she was ecstatic about her pregnancy. She was fairly blooming with good health and high spirits, and even now, when she was tired, her cheeks had a pink color to them and her eyes sparkled.

After they had closed up, Jessica drove Sallie by to pick up Patty and Penny, who stayed late on Friday nights with their baby-sitter, as that was the night Sallie closed out the week. The twins were in school for the best part of the day, and when summer holidays came, Sallie intended to stay home from the shop with them, as her pregnancy would be advanced by then. When Jessica pulled up outside the baby-sitter's home, both of the little girls ran to the car shrieking "Hello, Auntie Jessie! Have you any candy for us?" That was a standard Friday-night treat and Jessica had not forgotten. As the girls mobbed her, Sallie went laughing to pay the sitter and thank her, and by the time she came back with her hands full of the girls' books and sweaters, Jessica had them both settled down in the car.

Sallie invited Jessica to eat dinner with them, but she declined because she did not like to intrude too much on the family. Not only was she rather reserved herself, but she sensed that Sallie wanted to be with Joel to celebrate the good news of the week's business in the shop. It was still new enough to them that it was a thrill, and she didn't want to restrain them with her presence.

The phone started ringing just as she opened the door, but Jessica paused for a moment to check on Samantha before she answered it. The dog was still in her basket, looking particularly peaceful, and she wagged her tail in greeting but did not get up. "No pups yet?" asked Jessica as she reached for the phone. "At this rate, old girl, they'll be grown before they get here." Then she lifted the phone on the kitchen extension. "Mrs. Stanton speaking."

"Mrs. Stanton, this is Nikolas Constantinos," said a deep voice, so deep that the bass notes almost growled at her, and to her surprise the accent was more American than Greek. She clutched the receiver as a spurt of warmth went through her. How silly, she chided herself, to melt at the sound of a faint American accent just because she was American herself! She loved England, she was content with her life here, but nevertheless, that brisk sound made her smile.

"Yes, Mr. Constantinos?" she made herself say, then wondered if she sounded rude. But she would be lying if she said something trite like "How nice it is to hear from you" when it wasn't nice at all; in fact, it would probably be very nasty indeed.

"I would like to arrange a meeting with you tomorrow, Mrs. Stanton," he said. "What time would be convenient for you?"

Surprised, she reflected that Constantinos himself did not seem to be as arrogant as his secretary; at least he had *asked* what time would be convenient, rather than *telling* her what time to present herself. Aloud she said, "On Saturday, Mr. Constantinos?"

"I realize it is the weekend, Mrs. Stanton," the

deep voice replied, a hint of irritation evident in his tone. "However, I have work to do regardless of the day of the week."

Now that sounded more like what she had expected. Smiling slightly, she said, "Then any time is convenient for me, Mr. Constantinos; I haven't any commitments for tomorrow."

"Very well, let's say tomorrow afternoon, two o'clock." He paused, then said, "And, Mrs. Stanton, I don't like playing games. Why did you make an appointment with me this afternoon if you did not intend to keep it?"

Stung, she retorted coldly, "I didn't make the appointment. Your secretary phoned me and told me what time to be there, then hung up before I could agree or disagree. It rushed me, but I made the effort and waited for as long as I could, but I had another appointment to keep. I apologize if my effort was not good enough!" Her tone of voice stated plainly that she didn't care what his opinion was, and she didn't stop to think if that was wise or not. She was incensed that that cockroach of a secretary had *dared* to imply that she was at fault.

"I see," he said after a moment. "Now it is my turn to apologize to you, Mrs. Stanton, and *my* apology is sincere. That will not happen again. Until tomorrow, then." The phone clicked as he hung up.

Jessica slammed the phone down violently and stood for a minute tapping her foot in controlled temper, then her face cleared and she laughed aloud. He had certainly put her in her place! She began almost to look forward to this meeting with the notorious Nikolas Constantinos.

When Jessica dressed for the meeting the next day, she began early and allowed herself plenty of time to change her mind about what she would wear. She tried on several things and finally chose a severely tailored dull-gold suit that made her look mature and serious, and this she teamed with a cream-colored silk shirt. The muted gold picked up the gold in her tawny hair and lightly tanned skin, and she didn't realize the picture she made or she would have changed immediately. As it was, she looked like a golden statue come to life, with gleaming green jewels for eyes.

She was geared up for this meeting; when she walked into the outer office at two o'clock, her heart was pounding in anticipation, her eyes were sparkling, and her cheeks were flushed. At her entrance the secretary jumped to his feet with an alacrity that told her some stinging comments had been made concerning his conduct. Though his eyes were distinctly hostile, he escorted her into the inner office immediately.

"Mrs. Stanton, sir," he said, and left the office, closing the doors behind him.

Jessica moved across the office with her proud, graceful stride, and the man behind the desk rose slowly to his feet as she approached. He was tall, much taller than the average Greek, and his shoulders strained against the expensive cloth of his dark gray suit. He stood very still, watching her as she walked toward him, and his eyes narrowed to slits. She reached the desk and held out her hand; slowly her fingers were taken, but instead of the handshake she had invited, her hand was lifted and the black head bent over it. Warm lips were pressed briefly to her fingers, then her hand was released and the black head lifted.

Almost bemused, Jessica stared into eyes as black as night beneath brows that slashed across his face in a straight line. An arrogant blade of nose, brutally hard cheekbones, a firm lip line, a squared and stubborn chin, completed the face that was ancient in its structure. Centuries of Greek heritage were evident in that face, the face of a Spartan warrior. Charles had been right; this man was utterly ruthless, but Jessica did not feel threatened. She felt exhilarated, as if she was in the room with a tiger that she could control if she was very careful. Her heartbeat increased and her eyes grew brighter, and to disguise her involuntary response, she smiled and murmured, "Are you trying to charm me into voting my shares the way you want before you resort to annihilation?"

Amazingly, a smile appeared in response. "With a woman, I always try charm first," he said in the deep tones that seemed even deeper than they had last night over the phone.

"Really?" she asked in mock wonder. "Does it usually work?"

"Usually," he admitted, still smiling. "Why is it that I have the feeling, Mrs. Stanton, that you'll be an exception?"

"Perhaps because you're an unusually astute man, Mr. Constantinos," she countered.

He laughed aloud at that and indicated a chair set before his desk. "Please sit down, Mrs. Stanton. If we are to argue, let us at least be comfortable while we do it."

Jessica sat down and said impulsively, "Your accent is American, isn't it? It makes me feel so much at home!"

"I learned to speak English on a Texas oil field," he said. "I'm afraid that even Oxford couldn't erase the hint of Texas from my speech, though I believe it was thought by my instructors that my accent is Greek! Are you from Texas, Mrs. Stanton?"

"No, but a Texas drawl is recognizable to any American! How long were you in Texas?"

"For three years. How long have you been in England, Mrs. Stanton?"

"Since shortly before I married, a little over five years."

"Then you were little more than a child when you married," he said, an odd frown crossing his brow. "I'd assumed that you would be older, at least thirty, but I can see that's impossible."

Lifting her dainty chin, Jessica said, "No, I was a precocious eighteen when I married." She began to tense, sensing an attack of the type that she had endured so many times in the past five years.

"As I said, little more than a child. Though I suppose there are countless wives and mothers aged eighteen, it seems so much younger when the husband you chose was old enough to be your grandfather."

Jessica drew back and said coldly, "I see no reason to discuss my marriage. I believe our business concerns stocks."

He smiled again, but this time the smile was that of a predator, with nothing humorous in it. "You're certainly correct about that," he allowed. "However, that issue should be solved rather easily. When you sold your body and your youth to an old man of seventy-six, you established the fact that monetary gain ranks very high on your list of priorities. The only thing left to discuss is: how much?"

Chapter Two

Years of experience had taught Jessica how to hide her pain behind a proud, aloof mask, and she used that mask now, revealing nothing of her thoughts and feelings as she faced him. "I'm sorry, Mr. Constantinos, but you seem to have misjudged the situation," she said distantly. "I didn't come here to accept a bribe."

"Nor am I offering you a bribe, Mrs. Stanton," he said, his eyes gleaming. "I'm offering to buy your stock."

"The shares aren't for sale."

"Of course they are," he refuted her silkily. "I'm willing to pay more than market value in order to get those stocks out of your hands. Because you are a woman, I've given you certain allowances, but there is a limit to my good nature, Mrs. Stanton, and I'd advise you not to try to push the price any higher. You could find yourself completely out in the cold."

Jessica stood and put her hands behind her back so he couldn't see how her nails were digging into her palms. "I'm not interested at any price, Mr. Constantinos; I don't even want to hear your offer. The shares aren't for sale, now or at any other time, and especially not to you. Good day, Mr. Constantinos."

But this man was no tame secretary and he did not intend to let her leave until he had finished with his business. He moved with a lithe stride to stop her and she found her path blocked by a very solid set of shoulders. "Ah, no, Mrs. Stanton," he murmured softly. "I can't let you leave now, with nothing settled between us. I've left my island and flown all the way to England for the express purpose of meeting you and putting an end to your asinine notions, which are wreaking havoc with this company. Did you think that I'd be put off by your high-and-mighty airs?"

"I don't know about my high-and-mighty airs, but your king-of-the-mountain complex is getting on my nerves," Jessica attacked, her voice sarcastic. "I own those shares, and I vote them as I think I should. The Dryden takeover was underhanded and stank to the heavens, and I voted against it. I would do it again if the issue arose. But a lot of other people voted against it as well, yet I notice that it's *my* stock you want to buy. Or am I only the first of the group to be brought into line?"

"Sit down, Mrs. Stanton," he said grimly, "and I will attempt to explain to you the basics of finance and expansion."

"I don't wish to sit down—"

"I said *sit!*" he rasped, and abruptly his voice was harsh with menace. Automatically Jessica sat down, then despised herself for not facing him and refusing to be intimidated.

"I am *not* one of your flunkies," she flared, but did not get up. She had the nasty feeling that he would push her down if she tried to leave.

"I am aware of that, Mrs. Stanton; believe me, if you were one of my employees, you would have learned long ago how to behave yourself," he retorted with heavy irony.

"I consider myself quite well-behaved!"

He smiled grimly. "Well-behaved? Or merely cunning and manipulative? I don't imagine it was very difficult to seduce an old man and get him to marry you, and you were smart enough to select a man who would die shortly. That set you up very nicely, didn't it?"

Jessica almost cried aloud with the shock of his words; only her years of training in self-control kept her still and silent, but she looked away from him. She could not let him see her eyes or he would realize how deeply vulnerable she was.

He smiled at her silence. "Did you think that I didn't know your history, Mrs. Stanton? I assure you, I know quite a lot about you. Your marriage to Robert Stanton was quite a scandal to everyone who knew and admired the man. But until I saw you, I never quite understood just how you managed to trap him into marriage. It's all very clear now; any man, even an old one, would jump at the chance to have your lovely body in his bed, at his convenience."

Jessica quivered at the insult and he noticed the movement that rippled over her skin. "Is the memory less than pleasing?" he inquired softly. "Did you find the payment more than you'd expected?"

She struggled for the composure to lift her head, and after a moment she found it. "I'm sure my private life is no concern of yours," she heard herself say coolly, and felt a brief flare of pride that she had managed that so well.

His black eyes narrowed as he looked down at her and he opened his mouth to say more, but the phone rang and he swore under his breath in Greek, then stepped away from her to lift the phone to his ear. He said something in harsh, rapid Greek, then paused. His eyes slid to Jessica.

"I have an urgent call from France, Mrs. Stanton. I'll only be a moment."

He punched a button on the phone and spoke a greeting, his language changing effortlessly to fluent French. Jessica watched him for a moment, still dazed with her inner pain, then she realized that he was occupied and she seized her chance. Without a word, she got to her feet and walked out.

She managed to control herself until she was home again, but once she was safely enclosed by her own walls, she sat down on the sofa and began to sob softly. Was it never to end, the nasty comments and unanimous condemnations of her marriage to Robert? Why was it automatically assumed that she was little more than a prostitute? For five years she had borne the pain and never let it be known how it knifed into her insides, but now she felt as though she had no defenses left. Dear God, if only Robert hadn't died!

Even after two years she could not get used to not sharing amusing thoughts with him, to not having his dry, sophisticated wisdom bolstering her. He had never doubted her love, no matter what had been said about their December-May marriage, and she had always felt the warmth of his support. Yes, he had given her financial security, and he had taught her how to care for the money he willed to her. But

he had given her so much more than that! The
material things he had bestowed on her were small in
comparison to his other gifts: love, security, self-
respect, self-confidence. He had encouraged her
development as a woman of high intelligence; he had
taught her of his world of stocks and bonds, to trust
her own instinct when she was in doubt. Dear, wise
Robert! Yet, for his marriage to her he had been
laughed at and mocked, and she had been scorned.
When a gentleman of seventy-six marries a gorgeous
young girl of eighteen, gossips can credit it to only
two things: greed on her part, and an effort to revive
faded appetites on his.

It hadn't been that way at all. Robert was the only
man she had ever loved, and she had loved him
deeply, but their relationship had been more that of
father to daughter, or grandfather to granddaughter,
than of husband to wife. Before their marriage
Robert had even speculated on the advantages of
adopting her, but in the end he'd decided that there
would be fewer legal difficulties if he married her.
He wanted her to have the security she'd always
lacked, having grown up in an orphanage and been
forced into hiding herself behind a prickly wall of
sullen passivity. Robert was determined that never
again would she have to fight for food or privacy or
clothing; she would have the best, and the best way
to secure that way of life for her was to take her as
his wife.

The scandal their marriage had caused had rocked
London society; vicious items concerning her had
appeared in the gossip columns, and Jessica had
been shocked and horrified to read several accounts
of men who had been "past lovers of the enterprising
Mrs. S." Her reaction had been much the same as
Robert's: to hold her head even higher and ignore

the mudslingers. She and Robert knew the truth of the marriage, and Robert was the only person on earth whom she loved, the only person who had ever cared for her. Their gentle love endured, and she had remained a virgin throughout their marriage, not that Robert had ever given any indication that he wished the situation to be different. She was his only family, the daughter of his heart if not his flesh, and he schooled her and guided her and went about settling his financial affairs so they could never be wrested out of her control. And he trusted her implicitly.

They had been, simply, two people who were alone in the world and had found each other. She was an orphan who had grown up with a shortage of any type of love; he was an old man whose first wife had died years before and who now found himself without family in his last years. He took in the wary young girl and gave her every comfort, every security, even marrying her in an effort to make certain she never wanted for anything again. Jessica, in turn, felt a flood of love for the gentle, elderly man who gave her so much and asked for so little in return. And he had loved her for bringing her youth and beauty and bright laughter into the fading years of his life, and had guided her maturity and her quick mind with all the loving indulgence of a father.

While Robert had been alive, their scarcity of friends had not really bothered her, though she had suffered under the cuts she had received. There were a few real friends, like Charles, and they had been sufficient. But now Robert was gone and she lived alone, and the poisonous barbs she still received festered in her mind, making her ache and lie awake at night. Most women refused to speak to her and men acted as if she was fair game, and the fact that she kept quietly to herself was evidently not enough to change anyone's opinion of her. Thinking about it now, she acknowledged that, outside of Charles and Sallie, she had no friends. Even Sallie's Joel was a bit stiff with her, and she knew that he disapproved.

It wasn't until the shadows of early evening had darkened the room that she roused from her dejected seat on the sofa and went slowly upstairs to stand under the shower. She felt deadened, and she stayed under the needlelike spray for a long time, until the hot water began to go, then she got out, dried off, and dressed in a pair of faded old jeans and a shirt. Listlessly she brushed her hair out and left it loose on her shoulders, as it usually was when she was at home. Only when she was going out did she feel the need for the more severe hairstyle, to give her an older look, and she would not be going anywhere tonight. Like an animal, she wanted only to find a dark corner and lick her wounds.

When she went into the kitchen, she found Samantha moving about restlessly in her basket; as Jessica watched, frowning, the dog gave a sharp little whine of pain and lay down. Jessica went over and stroked the silky black head. "So, it looks like tonight is the night, my girl! Not before time, either. And if I remember correctly, it was on a Saturday that you ran away from me and got yourself in this fix, so I suppose it's poetic justice."

Samantha didn't care about philosophy, though she licked the gentle hand that stroked her. Then she laid her head down and began that sharp whining again.

Jessica stayed in the kitchen with the dog, and as time wore on and no puppies were born, she began to get worried, for Samantha appeared to be in distress. Was something wrong? Jessica had no idea what kind of four-legged Romeo Samantha had met; was it possible that she had mated with a larger breed and now the puppies were too big to be born? Certainly the little black dog was very swollen.

She rang over to Sallie's side of the house, but the phone rang endlessly and she hung up. Her neighbors were out. After chewing her lip indecisively for a moment, Jessica took the phone directory and began looking for the vet's number. She didn't know if Samantha could be moved while she was in labor, but perhaps the vet made house calls. She found the number and reached for the phone, which rang just as she touched it. She gave a startled cry and leaped back, then she grabbed up the receiver. "Mrs. Stanton."

"This is Nikolas Constantinos."

Of course it was, she thought distractedly. Who else had such a deep voice? "What do you want?" she demanded.

"We have unfinished business—" he began.

"It will just have to stay unfinished," she broke in. "My dog is having puppies and I can't talk to you. Good-bye, Mr. Constantinos." She hung up and waited a second, then lifted the receiver again. She heard a dial tone as she checked the vet's number again, then began dialing.

Half an hour later she was weeping in frustration. She could not get her vet, or any other, on the phone, probably because it was Saturday night, and she was sure that Samantha was going to die. The dog was yelping in agony now, squirming and shuddering with the force of her contractions. Jessica felt appallingly helpless, and grief welled up in her so that the tears streamed down her cheeks.

When the doorbell rang, she scrambled to answer it, glad to have some company, even if the caller knew nothing about dogs. Perhaps it was Charles, who was always so calm, though he would be as useless as she. She jerked the door open and Nikolas Constantinos stepped in as if he owned the house, closing the door behind him. Then he swung on her and she had a glimpse of a grim, angry face before his expression changed abruptly. He took in her jean-clad figure, her mane of hair and tear-streaked face, and he looked incredulous, as if he didn't believe it was really her. "What's wrong?" he asked as he produced a handkerchief and offered it to her.

Without thinking, Jessica took it and scrubbed at her cheeks. "It—it's my dog," she said thinly, and gulped back fresh tears. "I don't think she can have her puppies, and I can't get a vet on the phone. . . ."

He frowned. "Your dog is really having puppies?"

For answer, she burst into a fresh flow of tears, hiding her face in the handkerchief. Her shoulders shook with the force of her sobs, and after a moment she felt an arm slide about her waist.

"Don't cry," Constantinos murmured. "Where is she? Perhaps I can help."

Of course, why not? She should have thought of that herself; everyone knew billionaires were trained in animal husbandry, she told herself hysterically as she led the way into the kitchen.

But despite the incongruity of it, Nikolas Constantinos took off his jacket and slung it over the back of a chair, removed the gold studs from his cuffs and slid them into his pants pocket, then rolled up the sleeves of his white silk shirt. He squatted on his heels beside Samantha's bed and Jessica knelt next to him, because Samantha was inclined to be snappy with strangers even when she was in the best of moods. But Samantha did not offer to snap at him, only watched him with pleading, liquid eyes as he ran his hands gently over her swollen body and examined her. When he had finished, he stroked Samantha's head gently and murmured some Greek words to her that had a soft sound to them, then he turned his head to smile reassuringly at Jessica. "Everything seems to be normal. We should see a pup any minute now."

"Really?" Jessica demanded, her excitement spiraling as her fears eased. "Samantha is all right?"

"Yes, you've worried yourself to tears for nothing. Hasn't she had a litter before?"

Ruefully Jessica shook her head, explaining, "I've always kept her in before. But this time she managed to slip away from me and, well, you know how it goes."

"M'mmm, yes, I know how it goes," he mocked gently. His black eyes ran over her slim build and made her aware that he had a second meaning for his statement. He was a man and he looked on her as a woman, with a woman's uses, and instinctively she withdrew from his masculine appraisal. But despite that, despite everything he had said to her that afternoon, she felt better now that he was here. Whatever else he was, the man was capable.

Samantha gave a short, sharp yelp and Jessica turned anxiously to her dog. Nikolas put his arm about Jessica's shoulders and pulled her against his side so that she felt seared by the warmth of his body. "See, it's beginning," he murmured. "There's the first pup."

Jessica knelt there enthralled, her eyes as wide and wondrous as a child's, while Samantha produced five slick, squirming little creatures, which she nudged one by one against the warmth of her belly. When it became obvious that Samantha had finished at five, when all of the squeaking little things were snuggled against the furry black belly and the dog was lying there in tired contentment, Nikolas got to his feet and drew Jessica to hers, holding her for a moment until the feeling had returned to her numb legs.

"Is this the first birth you've witnessed?" he asked, tilting her chin up with his thumb and smiling down into her dazed eyes.

"Yes . . . wasn't it marvelous?" she breathed.

"Marvelous," he agreed. The smile faded from his lips and he studied the face that was turned up to him. When he spoke, his voice was low and even. "Now everything is fine; your tears have dried, and you are a lucky young woman. I came over here determined to shake some manners into you. I advise you not to hang up on me again, Jessica. My temper is"—here he gave a shrug of his wide shoulders, as if in acceptance of something he could not change—"not calm."

Half-consciously she registered the fact that he had used her given name, and that his tongue had seemed to linger over the syllables, then she impulsively placed her hand on his arm. "I'm sorry," she apologized warmly. "I wouldn't have done it if I hadn't been so worried about Samantha. I was trying to call the vet."

"I realize that now. But at the time I thought you were merely getting rid of me, and very rudely, too. I wasn't in a good mood anyway after you had walked out on me this afternoon. But when I saw you . . ." His eyes narrowed as he looked her up and down again. "You made me forget my anger."

She stared at him blankly for a moment before she realized that she hadn't any makeup on, her hair was tumbled about her shoulders, and worse than that, she was barefoot! The wonder was that he had even recognized her! He had been geared up to smash a sophisticated woman of the world, and instead he had found a weeping, tousled girl who did not quite reach his shoulder. A blush warmed her cheeks.

Nervously she pushed a strand of hair away from her face. "I—ummm—I must look a mess," she stammered, and he reached out and touched the streaked gold of her hair, making her forget in midsentence what she had been saying.

"No, you don't look a mess," he assured her absently, watching the hair slide along his dark fingers. "You look disturbingly young, but lovely for all your wet lashes and swollen lids." His black eyes flickered back to hers. "Have you had your dinner yet, Jessica?"

"Dinner?" she asked vaguely, before she mentally kicked herself for not being faster than that and assuring him that she had indeed already had her meal.

"Yes, dinner," he mocked. "I can see that you haven't. Slip into a dress and I'll take you out for dinner. We still have business to discuss and I think it would be wiser if the discussion did not take place in the privacy of your home."

She wasn't certain just what he meant by that, but she knew better than to ask for an explanation. Reluctantly she agreed. "It will take me about ten minutes," she said. "Would you like a drink while I'm dressing?"

"No, I'll wait until you can join me," he said.

Jessica ran upstairs and washed her face in cold water, which made her feel immensely better. As she applied her makeup, she noticed that her mouth was curved into a little smile and that it wouldn't go away. When she had completed her makeup, she took a look at herself and was disturbed by the picture she presented. Because of her bout of weeping, her lids were swollen, but with eye shadow and mascara applied, they looked merely sleepy and the irises gleamed darkly, wetly green, long Egyptian eyes that had the look of passions satisfied. Her cheeks bloomed with color, natural color, because her heart was racing in her breast, and she could feel the pulse throbbing in her lips, which were still smiling.

Because it was evening, she twisted her hair into a swirl atop her head and secured it with a gold butterfly clasp. She would wear a long dress, and she knew exactly which one she wanted. Her hands were shaking slightly as she drew it out of the closet, a halter-necked silk of the purest white, almost glittering in its paleness. She stepped into it and pulled the bodice up, then fastened the straps behind her neck. The dress molded itself to her breasts like another skin, then the lined silk fell in graceful folds to her feet—actually, beyond her feet, until she stepped into her shoes. Then the length was perfect. She slung a gold gauze wrap over her arm and she was ready, except for stuffing a comb and lipstick into a tiny evening bag—and remembering at the last minute to include her house key. She had to descend the stairs in a more dignified manner than she had gone up them, for the delicate straps of her shoes were not made for running, and she was only halfway down when Nikolas appeared from the living room and came to stand at the foot of the stairs, waiting for her. His gleaming eyes took in every inch of her in the shimmering white silk and she shivered under the expression she could see in them. He looked . . . hungry. Or . . . what?

When she reached the bottom step, she stopped and looked at him, eye to eye, but still she could not decide just what it was that glittered in those black depths. He put his hand on her arm and drew her down the last step, then without a word took the gold wrap and placed it about her bare shoulders. She quivered involuntarily under his touch, and his gaze leaped up to hers; this time it was all she could do to meet it evenly, for she was disturbed by her response to the lightest touch of his fingers.

"You are . . . more than beautiful," he said quietly.

What did that mean? She licked her lips uncertainly and his hands tightened on her shoulders; a quick glance upward revealed that his gaze had fastened on her tongue. Her heart leaped wildly in response to the look she saw, but he dropped his hands from her and stepped back.

"If we don't go now, we won't go at all," he said, and she knew exactly what that meant. He wanted her. Either that, or he was putting on a very good act, and the more she thought about it, the more such an act seemed likely. Hadn't he admitted that he always tried his charm on a woman in order to get his own way?

He certainly must want those shares, she mused, feeling more comfortable now that she had decided that he was only putting on the amorous act in order to get around her on the shares. Constantinos in a truly amorous mood must be devastating to a woman's senses, she thought, but her own leaping senses had calmed with the realization of what he was up to and she was once more able to think clearly. She supposed she would have to sell the shares; Charles had advised it, and she knew now that she would certainly not be able to continuously defy this man. She would tell him over dinner that she was willing to sell the shares to him.

He had turned out all of the lights except for a dim one in the kitchen for Samantha, and now he checked to make certain the door was locked behind them. "Haven't you any help living in with you?" he asked, frowning, his hand sliding under her elbow as they walked to his car.

"No," she replied, amusement evident in her voice. "I'm not very messy and I don't eat very much, so I don't need any help."

"But that means you're alone at night."

"I'm not frightened, not with Samantha. She sets up a howl at a strange footstep, and besides, Sallie and Joel Reese are in the other side, so I'm not really alone."

He opened the door of the powerful sports car he was driving and helped her into the seat, then went around to his side. She buckled her safety belt, looking with interest at the various dials and gauges. This thing looked like the cockpit of an airplane, and the car was at odds with what she had expected of him. Where was the huge black limousine with the uniformed chauffeur? As he slid into his seat and buckled up, she said, "Do you always drive yourself?"

"No, but there are times when a chauffeur's presence isn't desirable," he said, smiling a little. The powerful engine roared into life and he put the car into gear, moving forward with a smooth rush of power that pushed her back into her seat.

"Did you sell the country estate?" he asked from out of nowhere, making her wonder just how much he did know about her. More than just that vicious gossip, evidently; but he had known Robert before their marriage, so it was only natural that he should know about Robert's country home.

"Robert sold that a year before he died," she said steadily. "And after he died, I let the penthouse go; it was far too big and costly for just me. My half-house is just large enough."

"I would have thought a smaller apartment would have been better."

"I really don't like apartments, and then, there was Samantha. She needs room to run, and the neighborhood is friendly, with a lot of children."

"Not very glamorous," he commented dryly, and her ire rose a bit before she stifled it with a surge of humor.

"Not unless you think lines of drying laundry are glamorous," she agreed, laughing a little. "But it's quiet, and it suits me."

"In that dress, you look as if you should be surrounded by diamonds and mink, not lines of laundry."

"Well, what about you?" she asked cheerfully. "You in your silk shirt and expensive suit, squatting down to help a dog have puppies?"

He flashed her a look that glinted in the green lights from the dash. "On the island, life is much simpler than in London and Paris. I grew up there, running wild like a young goat."

She had a picture of him as a thin young boy, his black eyes flashing as he ran barefoot over the rough hills of his island. Had the years and the money and the layers of sophistication stifled the wildness of his early years? Then, even as she formed the thought in her mind, she knew that he was still wild and untamed, despite the silk shirts he wore.

Conversation died after that, each of them concerned with their own thoughts, and it wasn't until he pulled up before a discreetly lit restaurant and a doorman came to open the doors for them that Jessica realized where he had brought her. Her fingers tightened into fists at the curl of apprehension that twisted in her stomach, but she made her hands relax. He couldn't have known that she always avoided places like this—or could he? No, it was impossible. No one knew of her pain; she had always kept her aloof air firmly in place.

Taking a deep breath, she allowed herself to be helped out of the car, then it was being driven away and Nikolas had his hand on her elbow, escorting her to the door. She would not let it bother her, she told herself fiercely. She would talk with him and eat her meal and it would be finished. She did not have to pay any attention to anyone else they might meet.

After a few dinners out after their marriage, Robert had realized that it was intensely painful to his young bride to be so publicly shunned by people who knew him, and they had ceased eating out at the exclusive restaurants he had always patronized. It had been at this particular restaurant that a group of people had literally turned their backs on her, and Robert had gently led her away from their half-eaten dinner before she lost all control and sobbed like a child in front of everyone. But that had been five years ago, and though she had never lost her horror at the thought of eating in such a place—and this place in particular—she held her head proudly and walked without hesitation through the doors being held open by the uniformed doorman.

The maître d' took one glance at Nikolas and all but bowed. "Mr. Constantinos, we are honored!"

"Good evening, Swaine; we'd like a quiet table, please. Away from the crowd."

As they followed the maître d', winding their way between the tables, Jessica recovered herself enough to flash an amused glance up at the tall man beside her. "An isolated table?" she queried, her lips twitching in a suppressed smile. "So no one will notice the mayhem?"

The black head inclined toward her and she saw

his flashing grin. "I think we can keep it more civilized than that."

The table that Swaine selected for them was as isolated as was possible on a busy Saturday night. It was partially enclosed by a bank of plants that made Jessica think of a jungle, and she half-listened for the scream of birds before she chided herself for her foolishness.

While Nikolas chose a wine, she glanced about at the other tables, half afraid that she would see a familiar face; she had noticed the little silence that had preceded them as they made their way to their table, and the hiss of rapid conversation that broke out again in their wake. Had Nikolas noticed? Perhaps she was overly sensitive, perhaps the reaction was for Nikolas rather than herself. As a billionaire, he was certainly more noticeable than most people!

"Don't you like the table?" Nikolas's voice broke in on her thoughts and she jerked her eyes back to him, to find that he wore an irritated expression on his hard, dark face as he stared at her.

"No, the table's fine," she said hastily.

"Then why are you frowning?" he demanded.

"Black memories," she said. "It's nothing, Mr. Constantinos. I just had an . . . unpleasant experience in here once."

He watched her for a moment, then said calmly, "We can leave if it bothers you."

"It bothers me," she admitted, "but I won't leave. I think it's past time I got over my silly phobias, and what better time than now, when I have you to battle with and take my mind off old troubles?"

"That's twice you have alluded to an argument between us," he commented. He leaned closer to her, his hard brown hand reaching out to touch the low flower arrangement between them. "There won't be any arguments tonight. You're far too lovely for me to want to spend our time together throwing angry words about. If you start to argue, I'll simply lean over and kiss you until you're quiet. I've warned you now, so if you decide to spit defiance at me like a ruffled kitten, I can only conclude that you want to be kissed. What do you think about that, hmmm?"

She stared at him, trying to control her lips, but they parted anyway in a delicious smile and finally she laughed, a peal of laughter that brought heads swinging in their direction. She leaned over the table, too, and said confidentially, "I think, Mr. Constantinos, that I'll be as sweet and charming as it's possible for me to be!"

His hand left the flowers and darted out to capture her wrist, his thumb rubbing lightly over the delicate blue veins on the inside of her arm. "Being sweet and charming will also get you kissed," he teased huskily. "I think that I'll be the winner regardless! And I promise you that I'll kiss you hard if you call me mister again. Try to say Nikolas; I think you'll find it isn't that difficult. Or call me Niko, as my friends do."

"If you wish," she said, smiling at him. Now was the time to tell him about the shares, before he became too serious about his charming act. "But I want to tell you that I've decided to sell the shares to you, after all, so you don't have to be nice to me if you don't want to. I won't change my mind even if you're nasty."

"Forget the shares," he murmured. "Let's not talk about them tonight."

"But that's why you asked me to dinner," she protested.

"Yes, it was, though I haven't a doubt I could have

come up with another good excuse if that one had failed." He grinned wickedly. "The little waif with the tear-streaked face was very fetching, especially as I knew a cool, maddeningly sophisticated woman was lurking behind the tears."

She shook her head. "I don't think you understand, Mr. Con—er—Nikolas. The shares are yours. There's no need to keep this up."

His lids drooped over the dark brilliance of his eyes for a moment and his hand tightened on her wrist. "Very well, let's discuss the damned shares and be finished with it, as you won't leave the subject alone. Why did you change your mind?"

"My financial advisor, Charles Welby, had already told me to sell rather than try to fight you. I was prepared to sell them, but your manner made me angry and I refused out of sheer contrariness, but as usual, Charles is right. I can't fight you; I don't want to become embroiled in boardroom politics. And there's no need for that outrageous price you mentioned, market value will do nicely."

He straightened, dropping her wrist, and he said sharply, "I have already given you an offer; I won't go back on my word."

"You'll have to, if you want the shares, because I'll accept market value only." She faced him calmly despite the flare of temper she saw in his face.

He uttered something short and harsh in Greek. "I fail to see how you can refuse such a sum. It's a stupid move."

"And I fail to see how you'll remain a billionaire if you persist in making such stupid business deals!" she shot back.

For a moment his eyes were like daggers, then laughter burst from his throat and he threw back his head in sheer enjoyment.

Oblivious of the many interested eyes on them, he

leaned forward once more to take her hand. "You are a gorgeous snow queen," he said huskily. "It was worth losing the Dryden issue to meet you. I don't think I will be returning to Greece as soon as I had planned."

Jessica's eyes widened as she stared at him. It seemed he was serious; he was actually attracted to her! Alarm tingled through her, warming her body as she met the predatory gaze of those midnight eyes.

Chapter Three

The arrival of the wine brought her a welcome relief from his penetrating gaze, but the relief was only momentary. As soon as they were alone again, he drawled, "Does it bother you that I'm attracted to you? I would have thought you would find it commonplace to attract a man's desire."

Jessica tried to retrieve her hand, but his fingers closed firmly over hers and refused to let her go. Green sparks began to shoot from her eyes as she looked up at him. "I don't think you are attracted," she said sharply. "I think you're still trying to put me in my place because I won't bow down and kiss your feet. I've *told* you that the shares are yours, now please let go of my hand."

"You're wrong," he said, his hand tightening over hers until the grip was painful and she winced. "From the moment you walked into my office this afternoon, every nerve in my body has been screaming. I want you, Jessica, and signing those shares over to me won't get me out of your life."

"Then what will?" she demanded, tight-lipped. "What is your price for leaving me alone?"

A look of almost savage anger crossed his face; then he smiled, and the smile chilled her blood. The midnight eyes raked over her face and breasts. "Price?" he murmured. "You know what the price would be, to leave you alone . . . eventually. I want to sate myself with you, burn you so deeply with my touch that you will never be free, so that whenever another man touches you, you will think of me and wish me in his place."

The thought—the image it provoked—was shattering. Her eyes widened and she stared at him in horror. "No," she said thickly. "Oh, no! Never!"

"Don't be so certain," he mocked. "Do you think I couldn't overcome any resistance you might make? And I'm not talking about forcing you, Jessica; I'm talking about desire. I could make you want me; I could make you so hungry for my lovemaking that you'd beg me to take you."

"No!" Blindly she shook her head, terrified that he might really force himself on her. She wouldn't permit that, never; she had endured hell on earth because everyone saw her as a gold-digging little tart, but she would never let herself be reduced to the level of a kept woman, a mistress, all of the ugly things they had called her. "Don't you understand?" she whispered raggedly. "I don't want to get involved with you—with any man—on any level."

"That's very interesting," he said, his eyes narrowing on her face. "I can understand that you'd find your marriage duties to an old man to be revolting, but surely all of your lovers can't have been so bad. And don't try to pretend that you went into that marriage as pure as the driven snow, because I won't believe you. An innocent wouldn't sell herself to an old man, and besides, too many men claim to have . . . known you.''

Jessica swallowed hard on the nausea that welled up in her and her head jerked up. White-faced, green eyes blazing, she spat at him, "On the contrary, Robert was an angel! It was the other men who left a bad taste in my mouth—and I think, Mr. Constantinos, that in spite of your money, you give me the worst taste of all''

Instantly she was aware that she had gone too far. His face went rigid and she had only a second of warning before the hand that held her fingers tightened and pulled, drawing her out of her chair until she was leaning over the table. He rose and met her halfway, and her startled exclamation was cut off by the pressure of his mouth, hot and hard and probing, and she had no defense against the intrusion of his tongue.

Dimly she could hear the swelling murmurs behind her, feel a flash of light against her lids, but the kiss went on and on and she was helpless to pull away. Panic welled in her, smothering her, and a whimper of distress sounded in her throat. Only then did he raise his punishing mouth, but he still held her over the table like that, his eyes on her white face and trembling lips, then he very gently reseated her and resumed his own seat. "Don't provoke me again," he said through his teeth. "I warned you, Jessica, and that kiss was a light one compared to the next one you will get."

Jessica didn't dare look up at him; she simply sat there and stared at her wine, her entire body shaking. She wanted to slap him, but more than that she wanted to run away and hide. That flash of light that she had noticed had been the flash of a camera, she knew, and she cringed inside to think of the field day the scandal sheets would have with that photo. Nausea roiled in her stomach and she fought fiercely against it, snatching up her wineglass with a shaking hand and sipping the cool, dry wine until she had herself under control again.

A rather uncomfortable-looking waiter appeared with the menus and Jessica used every ounce of concentration that she possessed in choosing her meal. She had thought of allowing Constantinos to order for her; in fact, he seemed to expect her to do so, but it had become very important that she cling to that small bit of independence. She had to cling to something when she could feel the eyes boring into her from all corners of the room, and when across from her sat a man who made man-eating tigers seem tame.

"It's useless to sulk," he said now, breaking in on her thoughts with his smooth, deep voice. "I won't allow that, Jessica, and it was only a kiss, after all. The first of many. Would you like to go sailing with me tomorrow? The weathermen are predicting a warm, sunny day and you can get to know me as we laze about all day in the sun."

"No," she said starkly. "I don't ever want to see you again."

He laughed outright, throwing back his gleaming dark head, his white teeth flashing in the dimness like a wild animal's. "You're like an angry child," he murmured. "Why don't you scream that you hate me, and stamp your feet in a temper so I may have the pleasure of taming you? I'd enjoy tussling with you, rolling about until you tired yourself out and lay quietly beneath me."

"I don't hate you," she told him, regaining some

of her composure despite his disturbing words. She even managed to look at him quite coolly. "I won't waste the energy to hate you, because you're just passing through. After the shares have been signed over, I'll never see you again, and I can't see myself shedding any tears over your absence, either."

"I can't let you continue to delude yourself," he mocked. "I'm not merely passing through; I've changed my plans—to include you. I'll be in London for quite some time, for as long as it takes. Don't fight me, my dear; it's only a waste of time that's better spent in other ways."

"Your ego must be enormous," she observed, sipping at her wine. "You seem unable to believe that I simply don't fancy you. Very well, if that's what it takes to rid myself of you, when you take me home we'll go upstairs and you may satisfy your odd little urges. It won't take much effort, and it'll be worth it to see the back of you." Even as the words left her mouth, Jessica almost jumped in amazement at herself. Dear heaven, how did she manage to sound so cool and disinterested, and say such dreadful things? What on earth would she do if he took her up on it? She had no intention of going to bed with him if she had to scream her silly head off and make a scandal that would force both of them out of the country.

His face had turned to stone as she talked and his eyes had narrowed until they were mere slits. She had the urge to throw up her arms to protect her face, even though he didn't move a muscle. At last he spoke, grinding the words out between his teeth. "You cold little bitch, you'll pay for that. Before I'm finished with you, you'll regret opening your mouth; you'll apologize for every word. Go upstairs with you? I doubt I'll wait that long!"

She had to get out, she had to get away from him. Without thinking, she clutched her bag and said, "I have to go to the ladies—"

"No," he said. "You aren't going anywhere. You're going to sit there until we've eaten, then I'll drive you home."

Jessica sat very still, glaring at him, but her hostility didn't seem to bother him. When their meal was served, he began to eat as if everything was perfectly calm and normal. She chewed on a few bites, but the tender lamb and stewed carrots turned into a lump in her throat that she couldn't swallow. She gulped at her wine, and there was a flash of a camera again. Quickly she set down her glass and paled, turning her head away.

He missed nothing, even when it seemed that he wasn't paying attention. "Don't let it upset you," he advised coolly. "The cameras are everywhere. They mean nothing; it's merely something to fill the space in their empty little tabloids."

She didn't reply, but she remembered the earlier flash, when he had been kissing her so brutally. She felt ill at the thought of that photo being splashed all over the gossip pages.

"You don't seem to mind being the target of gossip," she forced herself to say, and though her voice was a bit strained, she managed the words without gulping or bursting into tears.

He shrugged. "It's harmless enough. If anyone is really interested in who I had dinner with, or who stopped by our table for a moment's conversation, then I really have no objection. When I want to be private, I don't go to a public place."

She wondered if he had ever been the subject of such vicious gossip as she had endured, but though the papers were always making some mention of him closing a deal or flying here and there for conferences, sometimes with a vague mention of his latest "lovely," she could recall nothing about his private life. He had said that he lived on an island. . . .

"What's the name of the island where you live?" she asked, for that was a subject as safe as any, and she dearly needed something that would allow her time to calm herself.

A wicked black brow quirked upward. "I live on the island of Zenas, which means Zeus's gift, or, more loosely translated, the gift of the gods. I'm using the Greek name for the god, of course; the Roman version is Jupiter."

"Yes," she said. "Have you lived there for long?"

The brow went higher. "I was born there. I own it."

"Oh." Of course he did; why should he live on someone else's island? And she had forgotten, but now she remembered, what he had said about growing up wild on the island. "Is it a very large island? Does anyone else live there, or is it just you alone on your retreat?"

He grinned. "The island is roughly ten miles long, and as much as five miles wide at one place. There is a small fishing village, and the people graze their goats in the hills. My mother lives in our villa year round now; she no longer likes to travel, and of course, there's the normal staff in the villa. I suppose there are some two hundred people on the island, and an assortment of goats, chickens, dogs, a few cows."

It sounded enchanting, and she forgot her troubles for a moment as she dreamed about such a quiet, simple life. Her eyes glowed as she said, "How can you bear to leave it?"

He shrugged. "I have many interests that require my time and attention, and though I'll always look on the island as my home, I'm not quite a hermit.

The modern world has its attractions, too." He raised his wineglass to her and she understood that a large amount of the world's attraction was in its women. Of course, on a small Greek island the young women would be strictly supervised until they wed, and a healthy man would want to relieve his more basic urges.

His gesture with the wineglass brought her attention back to her own wineglass, and she saw that it was nearly empty. "May I have more wine?"

"No," he refused smoothly. "You've already had two glasses, and you've merely pushed your food around on your plate instead of eating it. You'll be drunk if you continue. Eat your dinner, or isn't it the way you like it? Shall I have it returned to the kitchen?"

"No, the food is excellent, thank you." What else could she say? It was only the truth.

"Then why aren't you eating?"

Jessica regarded him seriously, then decided that he was a big boy and he should certainly be able to handle the truth. "I'm not exactly enjoying myself," she told him. "You've rather upset my stomach."

His mouth twitched in grim amusement. "You haven't upset mine, but you have without doubt upset my system in every other way! Since meeting you, I totally absolve Robert Stanton of foolishness, except perhaps in whatever overly optimistic expectations he may have had. You're an enchanting woman, even when you're insulting me."

She had never mentioned her relationship with Robert to anyone, but now she had the urge to cry out that she had loved him, that everyone was wrong in what they said of her. Only the years of practice in holding herself aloof kept her lips sealed on the wild cry of hurt, but she did allow herself to comment,

"Robert was the least foolish man I have ever met. He knew exactly what he was about at all times."

Nikolas narrowed his eyes. "Are you saying that he knew you married him only for his money?"

"I'm saying nothing of the kind," she retorted sharply. "I won't discuss my marriage with you; it's none of your business. If you're finished with your meal, I'd like to go home now."

"*I've* finished," he said, looking pointedly at her plate. "However, you've hardly even begun to eat. You need food to absorb some of the wine you've had, and we won't leave here until you eat."

"I would bolt it down without chewing if that would free me from your company," she muttered as she lifted her fork and speared a morsel of meat.

He waited until she had the meat in her mouth and was chewing before he said, "But it won't. If I remember correctly, you have invited me upstairs when I take you home. To satisfy my 'odd little urges,' I think was how you phrased it. I accept your invitation."

Jessica swallowed and attacked another piece of meat. "You must have misunderstood," she said coldly. "I wouldn't let you inside my house, let alone my bedroom."

"My apartment will do just as well," he replied, his eyes gleaming. "Or the ground, if you prove difficult about the matter."

"Now see here," she snapped, putting her fork down with a clatter. "This has gone far enough. I want you to understand this clearly: I'm *not* available! Not to you, not to any man, and if you touch me, I'll scream until everyone in London hears me."

"If you can," he murmured. "Don't you imagine that I'm capable of stifling any screams, Jessica?"

"Oh?" she demanded with uplifted brows. "Are

you a rapist? Because it would be rape, have no doubt about it. I'm not playing at being difficult; I'm entirely serious. I don't want you."

"You will," he said confidently, and she wanted to scream now, in frustration. Could he truly be so dense, his ego so invulnerable, that he simply couldn't believe that she didn't want to go to bed with him? Well, if he didn't believe that she'd scream, he'd certainly be surprised if he tried anything with her!

In one swift motion she stood up, determined not to sit there another moment. "Thank you for the meal," she said. "I believe it would be best if I took a taxi home, and I'll have Charles contact you Monday about the settlement of the shares."

He stood also, calmly laying his napkin aside. "I'm taking you home," he said, "if I have to drag you to my car. Now, do you want to make your exit in a dignified manner, or slung over my shoulder? Before you decide, let me assure you that no one will come to your aid. Money does have its uses, you know."

"Yes, I know," she agreed frigidly. "It allows some people to act like bullies without fear of retribution. Very well, shall we leave?"

He smiled in grim triumph and placed a bill on the table, and even in her anger she was startled at the amount he had laid down. She looked up in time to see him nod to the maître d', and by the time they had made their way across the room her wrap was waiting. Nikolas took the wrap and gently placed it about her shoulders, his hands lingering there for a moment as his fingers moved over her flesh. A blinding flash of light told her that this, too, had been photographed, and involuntarily Jessica shrank closer to him in an effort to hide. His hands tightened on her shoulders and he frowned as he looked down at her suddenly pale face. He looked around until he located the photographer, and though he said nothing, Jessica heard a muttered apology somewhere behind them. Then Nikolas had his arm firmly around her waist and he led her outside, where his car was just being driven up.

When the doorman and the young man who had brought the car had been settled with and Nikolas had seen that she was securely buckled into her seat, he said, "Why do you flinch whenever a flash goes off?"

"I dislike publicity," she muttered.

"It scarcely matters whether you like it or not," he said quietly. "Your actions have made certain that you will have it, regardless, and you certainly should be used to it by now. Your marriage made quite a lot of grist for the mill."

"I'm aware of that," she said. "I've been called a bitch to my face and a lot worse to my back, but that doesn't mean that I've ever become accustomed to it. I was eighteen years old, *Mr.* Constantinos"—she stressed the word—"and I was crucified by the press. I've never forgotten."

"Did you think no one would notice when you married a rich, elderly man of Robert Stanton's reputation?" he almost snarled. "For God's sake, Jessica, you all but begged to be crucified!"

"So I discovered," she said, her voice catching. "Robert and I ceased going out in public when it became obvious that I would never be accepted as his wife, though he didn't care on his own account. He said that he would find out who his true friends were, and there were a few. He seemed to cherish those few, and never said anything that indicated he wanted his life to be any different, at least in my hearing. Robert was endlessly kind," she finished quietly, for she found that even the memories of

Robert helped to calm her. He had seen life so clearly, without illusions and with a great deal of humor. What would he think about this predatory man who sat beside her now?

He drove in silence and she leaned her head back and closed her eyes, tired and rather drained. All in all, it had been a long day, and the worst part was still to come, unless he decided to act decently and leave her alone. But somehow she doubted that Nikolas Constantinos ever acted in any way except to please himself, so she had best brace herself for war.

When he pulled up in the drive on her side of the house, she noticed thankfully that Sallie and Joel were home and were still awake, though her watch told her that it was ten-thirty. He cut off the engine and put the keys in his pocket, then got out and came around to open her door. He leaned in and helped her to gather her long skirt, then all but lifted her out of the car. "I'm not an invalid," she said tartly as his arm slid about her waist and pulled her against his side.

"That's why I'm holding you," he explained, his low laughter brushing her hair. "To prevent you from running."

Fuming helplessly, Jessica watched as he took the key from her bag and opened the door, ushering her inside with that iron arm at her back. She ignored him and marched into the kitchen to check on Samantha. She knelt and scratched the dog behind the ears, receiving a loving lick on the hand in return. A puppy squeaked at being disturbed and it too received a lick of the warm tongue, then Jessica was startled as two hard hands closed over her shoulders and pulled her to her feet.

She had had enough; she was tired of him and his arrogance. She exploded with rage, hitting at his face and twisting her body in his grasp as he tried to hold her against him. "No, damn you!" she cried. "I told you I won't!"

Samantha rose to her feet and gave a growl at seeing her mistress treated so roughly, but the puppies began to cry in alarm as she left them and she turned back to look at her offspring. By that time Nikolas had swept Jessica off her feet and into his arms and was back through the kitchen door with her, shouldering it shut behind him. He wasn't even breathing hard as he captured her flailing arms, and that made her even angrier. She arched her back and kicked in an effort to wiggle out of his arms; she hit out at that broad chest, and when that failed to stop him, she opened her mouth to scream. Swiftly he forced her head against his shoulder and her scream was largely muffled by his body. Blinded and breathless with fury, she gave a strangled cry as he suddenly dropped her.

Soft cushions broke her fall, then her body was instantly covered by his hard weight as he dropped down on her and pinned her. "Damn you, be still," he hissed, stretching a long arm up over her head. For a sickening moment she thought he would slap her, and she caught her breath, but no blow fell. Instead, he switched on the lamp at the end of the sofa and a soft light bathed the room. She hadn't realized where they were until he turned on the lamp and now she looked about her at the comfortable, sane setting of her living room. She turned her head to look up with bewilderment into the furious dark face above her.

"What's the matter with you?" he barked.

She blinked. Hadn't he been attacking her? He had certainly been manhandling her! Even now his heavy legs pressed down on hers and she knew that her skirt was twisted above her knees. She moved restlessly under him and he let his weight down more heavily on her in warning. "Well?" he growled.

"But . . . I thought . . . weren't you attacking me?" she asked, her brow puckering. "I thought you were, and so did Samantha."

"If I *had* been attacking you, the situation was reversed before I got very far," he snapped. "Damn you, Jessica, you don't know how tempting you are—and how infuriating—" He broke off, his black eyes moving to her lips. She squirmed and turned her head away, a breathless little "No" coming from her, but he captured her head with a hand on each side of her face and turned her mouth back to him. He was only a breath away and she tried to protest again, then it was too late. His hard mouth closed over her soft one, forcing her lips open, and his warm, wine-fragrant breath filled her mouth. His tongue followed, exploring and caressing her inner mouth, flicking at her own tongue, sending her senses reeling.

She was frightened by the pressure of his big, hard body over hers and for a moment her slim hands pushed uselessly at his heavy shoulders. But his mouth was warm and he wasn't hurting her now, and she had never before been kissed like this. For a moment—only one moment, she promised herself—she allowed herself to curve in his arms, to respond to him and kiss him back. Her hands slid over his broad shoulders to clasp about his neck, her tongue responded shyly to his; then she no longer had the option of returning his caresses or not. He shuddered and his arms tightened painfully about her and his mouth went wild, ravaging, sucking her breath hungrily from her body. He muttered something, thickly, and it took her dazed mind a minute to realize he had spoken in French and to translate the words. When she did, her face flamed and she tried to push him away, but still she was helpless against him.

He slid one hand under her neck and deftly unhooked the halter strap of her bodice. As his mouth left hers and trailed a fiery path down her neck, she managed a choked "No," to which he paid no attention at all. His lips moved the loosened straps of her bodice down as he planted fierce kisses along her shoulder and collarbone, licking the tender spot in the hollow of her shoulder until she almost forgot her rising fear and quivered with pleasure, clutching his ribs with helpless hands. He became impatient with the straps, still in the way of his wandering mouth, and jerked roughly at them, intent on baring her to the waist, and panic erupted in Jessica with the force of a volcano.

With a strangled cry she twisted frantically in his arms, holding her bodice up with one arm while, with the other, she tried to force his head away from her. He snarled in frustration and jerked her arm above her head, reaching for the material of her dress with his other hand. Her heartbeat came to a standstill and with superhuman effort she pulled her hand free, beating at his back. "No!" she cried out, nearly hysterical. "No, Nikolas, don't; I beg you!"

He stilled her words with the forceful pressure of his mouth, and she realized in a jolt of pure terror that she couldn't control him; he was bent on taking her. A sob erupted from her throat and she released her bodice to beat at him with both hands, crying wildly and choking out the muffled words, "No! No. . . ." He raised his lips from hers and she moaned, "Please! Nikolas! Ah, don't!"

The savage movements of his hands stopped and he lay still, his breath heaving raggedly in his chest. She shook with sobs, her small face drenched with tears. He groaned deep in his throat and slid off the sofa, to kneel beside it and rest his black head on the cushion beside her. Silence fell on the room again and she tried to choke back her tears. Hesitantly she put her hands on his head, sliding her fingers through his thick hair, not understanding her need to comfort him but unable to resist the impulse. He quivered under the touch of her hands and she smelled the fresh sweat on his body, the maleness of his skin, and she realized how aroused he had been. But he had stopped; he hadn't forced her, after all, and she could feel all of her hostility draining away. For all her inexperience she knew enough about men to know that it had been quite a wrench for him to become so aroused and then stop, and she was deeply grateful to him.

At length he raised his head, and she gasped at the strained, grim expression on his face. "Straighten your dress," he said thickly, "or it may be too late yet."

Hastily she hooked her straps back into place and pushed the skirt down over her legs. She would have liked to sit up, but with him so close it would have been awkward, so she remained lying against the cushions until he moved. He ran his hand wearily through his hair. "Perhaps it's just as well," he said a moment later, getting to his feet. "We made no preparations, and I know I couldn't have— Was that what frightened you, Jessica? The thought of the risk we'd have been taking with an unwanted pregnancy?"

Her voice was husky when she spoke. "No, it . . . it wasn't that. You just . . . frightened me." She sat up and wiped at her wet cheeks with the palms of her hands. He looked at her and grimly produced the handkerchief that she had used earlier, to dry her eyes when he had first arrived—was it only a few hours ago? She accepted the square of linen and dried her face, then gave it back to him.

He gave a short, harsh laugh. "So I frightened you? I wanted to do a lot of things to you, but frightening you wasn't one of them. You're a dangerous woman, my dear, deadly in your charm. You leave a man aching and empty after you've pulled away." He inhaled deeply and began to button his shirt, and only then did she notice that somehow his jacket had been discarded and his shirt unbuttoned and pulled loose from his pants. She had no memory of opening his shirt, but only she could have done it, for his hands had been too busy on her to have accomplished it.

His face still wore that taut, strained look and she said in a rush, "I'm sorry, Nikolas."

"So am I, my dear." His dark gaze flickered to her and a tight little smile touched his mouth. "But you're calling me Nikolas now, so something has been accomplished." He tucked his shirt inside his pants and dropped down on the sofa beside her. "I want to see you again, and soon," he said, taking her hand. "Will you come sailing with me tomorrow? I promise that I won't rush you; I won't frighten you as I did tonight. I'll give you time to get to know me, to realize that you'll be perfectly safe with me. Whoever frightened you of men should be shot, but it won't be like that with me. You'll see," he said encouragingly.

Safe? Would she ever be safe with this man? She strongly doubted it, but he had been nicer than she would have expected and she didn't want to make him angry, so she tempered her words. "I don't think so, Nikolas. Not tomorrow. It's too soon."

His mouth pressed into an ominous line, then he sighed and got to his feet. "I'll call you tomorrow, and don't try anything foolish like trying to hide from me. I'd only find you, and you might not like the consequences. I won't be put off like that again. Do you understand?"

"I understand that you're threatening me!" she said spiritedly.

He grinned suddenly. "You're safe so long as you don't push me, Jessica. I want you, but I can wait."

Jessica tossed her head. "It could be a long wait," she felt compelled to warn.

"Or it could be a short one," he warned in his turn. "As I said, I'll call you tomorrow. Think about the sailing; you'd like it."

"I've never been sailing; I don't know the first thing about it. I could be seasick."

"It'll be fun teaching you what you don't know," he said, and he meant more than sailing. He leaned over and pressed a warm kiss to her mouth, then drew away before she could either respond or resist. "I'll let myself out. Good night, Jessica."

"Good night, Nikolas." It felt odd to be saying good night to him as if those moments of passion and terror had never happened. She watched as he picked up his jacket from the floor and walked out, his tall, lean body moving with the wild grace of a tiger. When he was gone, the house felt empty and too quiet, and she had a sinking feeling that Nikolas Constantinos was going to turn her life upside down.

Chapter Four

$\mathcal{D}$espite feeling edgy when she went to bed, Jessica slept deeply and woke in a cheerful frame of mind. She had been silly to let that man work her into a state of nerves, but she would try to avoid him in the future. Charles could handle all the details of selling the stock.

Humming to herself, she fed Samantha and praised the puppies to their proud mother, then made toast for herself. She had not acquired the English habit of tea, so instead she drank coffee; she was lingering over the second cup when Sallie rapped on the window of the back door. Jessica got up to unlock the door and let her in, and she noticed the worried frown that marred Sallie's usually smiling face. Sallie held a folded section of newspaper.

"Is anything wrong?" asked Jessica. "But before you tell me, would you like a cup of coffee?"

Sallie made a face. "Coffee, my girl? You're not

civilized yet! No, Jess, I think you should see this. It's a nasty piece, and just when all of that business was beginning to die down. I wouldn't have brought it over, Joel thought I shouldn't, but—well, you'll be hit with it when you go out, and I thought it would be better for you to see it privately."

Jessica held out her hand wordlessly for the paper, but she already knew what it was. Sallie had folded it to the gossip and society pages, and there were two photographs there. One, of course, was of Nikolas kissing her. She noticed dispassionately that it was a good picture, Nikolas so dark and strong, she much slighter in build, their mouths clinging together over the table. The other photo was the one taken when they had been leaving and Nikolas had had his hands on her shoulders, looking down at her with an expression that made her shiver. Raw hunger was evident in his face in that photo, and remembering what had happened when he brought her home made her wonder anew that he had stopped when she became frightened.

But Sallie was pointing to the column under the photos and Jessica sat down at the table to read it. It was a witty, sophisticated column, tart in places, but at one point the columnist became purringly vicious. Nausea welled in her as she skimmed over the lines of print:

London's notorious Black Widow was observed spinning her web over another helpless and adoring victim last night; the elusive Greek billionaire Nikolas Constantinos appeared to be completely captivated by the Widow's charm. Can it be that she has exhausted the funds left to her by her late husband, the esteemed Robert Stanton? Certainly Nikolas is able to maintain her in her accustomed style, yet from all reports this man may not be as easy to capture as she found her first husband. One wonders just who will be the victor in the end. The Widow seems to stop at nothing—but neither does her chosen prey. We will observe with interest.

Jessica dropped the paper onto the table and sat staring blindly across the room. She shouldn't let it bother her; she had been expecting this to happen. And certainly she should be accustomed to it, after five years, but it seemed that rather than becoming hardened, she was more sensitive now than she had been years ago. Then she had had Robert to buffer her, to ease the pain and make her laugh, but now she had no one. Any pain she suffered was suffered alone. The Black Widow—that phrase had been coined immediately after Robert's death, and it had stuck. Before that they had at least referred to her by name. The cutting little bits had always been nasty but stopped short of libel, not that she would ever have pursued the matter. The publicity involved in a suit would have been even nastier, and she would rather live a quiet life, with her few friends and small pleasures. She would even have returned to the States if it hadn't been for Robert's business interests, but she wanted to see to them and use the knowledge Robert had given her. Robert would have wanted that, too, she knew.

Sallie was watching her anxiously, so Jessica pulled a deep, shuddering breath into her lungs and forced herself to speak. "Well, that was certainly a vicious bit, wasn't it? I had almost forgotten how really rotten it can be. . . . But I won't make the mistake of going out again. It isn't worth it."

"But you can't hide away all your life," protested Sallie. "You're so young; it isn't fair to treat you like—like a leper!"

A leper—what an appalling thought! Yet Sallie wasn't so wrong, even though Jessica had yet to be stoned out of town. She was still welcome in very few homes.

Sallie cast about for a different subject, for although Jessica was trying to act casual about the whole matter, her face had gone pale and she looked stricken. Sallie jabbed the photo in the newspaper and said, "What about this dish, Jess? He's a gorgeous man! When did you meet him?"

"What?" Jessica looked down and two spots of color came back to her cheeks as she gazed at the photo of Nikolas kissing her. "Oh . . . actually, I only met him yesterday."

"Wow! He certainly is a fast worker! He looks the strong, masterful type, and his reputation is mind-boggling. What's he like?"

"Strong, masterful, and mind-boggling," Jessica sighed. "Just like you said. I hope I don't have to meet with him again."

"You've mush in your head!" exclaimed Sallie indignantly. "Honestly, Jess, you are unbelievable. Most women would give their right arm to go out with a man like that, rich *and* handsome, and you aren't interested."

"But then, I'm wary of rich men," Jessica replied softly. "You've seen an example of what would be said, and I don't think I could go through that again."

"Oh! I'm sorry, love," said Sallie. "I didn't think. But—just think! Nikolas Constantinos!"

Jessica didn't want to think of Nikolas; she wanted to forget the entire night. Looking at her friend's pale, closed face, Sallie patted her shoulder and slipped away. Jessica sat for a time at the table, her mind blank, but when she stood up to place her cup and saucer in the sink, it suddenly became more than she could handle and the tears fell freely.

When the bout of weeping ended, she was exhausted from the force of it and she wandered into the living room to lie down on the sofa, but that reminded her of Nikolas lying there with her, and instead she collapsed into a chair, pulling her feet up into the seat and wrapping her robe about her legs. She felt dead, empty inside, and when the phone rang, she stared at it dumbly for a long moment before she lifted the receiver. "Hello," she said dully.

"Jessica. Have you—"

She took the receiver away from her ear when she heard the deep voice, and listlessly let it drop back onto the cradle. No, she couldn't talk to him now; she hurt too deeply.

When the doorbell pealed some time later, she continued to sit quietly, determined not to answer it, but after a moment she heard Charles's voice call out her name and she got to her feet.

"Good morning," she greeted him while he eyed her sharply. She looked beaten.

"I read the paper," he said gently. "Go upstairs and wash your face and put on some clothes, then you can tell me about it. I intended to call you yesterday, but I had to go out of town, not that I could have done anything. Go on, my dear, upstairs with you."

Jessica did as she was told, applying cold water to her face and smoothing the tangles from her hair, then changing out of her nightgown and robe into a pretty white sundress with tiny blue flowers on it. Despite her numbness, she was glad that Charles was there. With his cool lawyer's brain he could pick at her responses until they were all neatly arranged where she could understand them, and he would analyze her feelings. Charles could analyze a rock.

"Yes, much better," he approved when she entered the living room. "Well, it is rather obvious that my fears for you were misplaced; Constantinos was obviously quite taken with you. Did he mention the Dryden issue?"

"He did," said Jessica, and even managed a smile for him. "I'm selling the stock to him, but don't imagine everything was sweetness and light. We get along like the proverbial cats and dogs. His comments on my marriage make that gossip column seem mild in comparison, and I have walked out on him and hung up on him once each—no, I've done it twice; he called this morning and I didn't want to talk to him. It would be best if I don't see him again, if you could handle all of the details of the stock transaction."

"Of course I will," replied Charles promptly. "But I feel certain you're underestimating your man. From that photo in the newspaper, he's attracted to more than your ConTech stock."

"Yes," admitted Jessica, "but there's no use. I couldn't live with that type of publicity again, and he attracts reporters and photographers by the dozens."

"That's true, but if he doesn't want something to be published, it isn't published. His power is enormous."

"Are you trying to argue his side, Charles?" Jessica asked in amazement. "Surely you understand that his attraction is only temporary, that he's only interested in an affair?"

Charles shrugged. "So are most men," he said dryly. "In the beginning."

"Yes, well, I'm *not* interested. By the way, the shares are going for market value. He offered much more than that, but I refused it."

"I see Robert's standards there," he said.

"I'll sell the stock to him, but *I* won't be bought."

"I never thought you would. I wished myself a fly

on the wall during your meeting; it must've been diverting," he said, and smiled at her, his cool, aristocratic face revealing the dry humor behind his elegant, controlled manner.

"Very, but it stopped short of murder." Suddenly she remembered and she smiled naturally for the first time since reading that horrid gossip column. "Charles, Samantha had her puppies last night, five of them!"

"She took time enough," he observed. "What will you do with five yelping puppies about the house?"

"Give them away when they're old enough. There are plenty of children in the neighborhood; it shouldn't be that difficult."

"You think so? When have you last tried to give away a litter of unknown origin? How many females are there?"

"How should I know?" she demanded, and laughed. "They don't come with pink and blue bows around their necks, you know."

Charles grinned in return and followed her into the kitchen, where she proudly displayed the pups, all piled together in a little heap. Samantha watched Charles closely, ready to nip if he came too near her babies, but he was well aware of Samantha's tendencies and kept a safe distance from her. Charles was too fastidious to be an animal lover and the dog sensed this.

"I see you've no tea made," he commented, looking at the coffeepot. "Put the water on, my dear, and tell me more about your meeting with Constantinos. Did it actually become hot, or were you teasing?"

Sighing, Jessica ran water from the tap into a kettle and put it on the stove. "The meeting was definitely unfriendly, even hostile. Don't let the photo of that kiss fool you, Charles; he only did that

as a punishment and to make me shut up. I can't—"
She started to say that she couldn't decide if she
trusted him or not, but the ring of the doorbell
interrupted her and she stopped in her tracks, a chill
running up her spine. "Oh, glory," she gulped.
"That's him now; I know it is! I hung up on him, and
he'll be in a raging temper."

"I'll be brave and answer the door for you while
you make the tea," offered Charles, searching for an
excuse to get to Constantinos before he could upset
her even more. That shattered look was fading from
her eyes, but she was still hurt and vulnerable and
she wasn't up to fending off someone like Constantinos. Jessica realized why Charles offered to get the
door; he was the most tactful man in the world, she
thought as she set out the cups and saucers for tea.
And one of the kindest, always trying to shield her
from any unpleasantness.

She stopped in her tracks, considering that. Why
hadn't Charles offered to meet with Constantinos
and work out the deal on the shares rather than
letting her go herself? The more she thought about
it, the more out of character it seemed. A wild
suspicion flared and she dismissed it instantly, but it
crept back. Had Charles deliberately thrown her
into Nikolas's path? Was he actually *matchmaking*?
Horrors! What had he been thinking of? Didn't he
know that Nikolas Constantinos, while very likely to
ask her to be his mistress, would never even consider
marriage? And Charles certainly knew her well
enough to know that she would never consider
anything but!

Marriage? With Nikolas? She began to shake so
violently that she had to put the tray down. What
was wrong with her? She had only met the man
yesterday, yet here she was thinking that she would
never settle for less than being his wife! It was only

that he was physically attractive to her, she told herself desperately. But Jessica was nothing if not honest with herself and she knew immediately that she was hiding from the truth. It wasn't only a physical attraction that she felt for Nikolas. She had seen a great many men who were handsome and physically appealing to her, but none that she had wanted as she had wanted Nikolas last night. Nor would she have been so receptive to Nikolas's caresses if her mind and emotions hadn't responded to him, too. He was brutal and ruthless and maddeningly arrogant, but she sensed in him a masculine appreciation for her femininity that tore down her barriers of hostility. Nikolas wanted her. That was fairly obvious, and she could have resisted that, had she not been aware that he delighted in her sharp mind and equally sharp tongue.

All in all, she was dangerously attracted to him, even vulnerable to falling in love with him, and that realization was a blow that surpassed the unpleasant shock of that vicious gossip column. White-faced, trembling, she stared at the kettle of boiling water, wondering what she was going to do. How could she avoid him? He was not a man to accept no for an answer, nor was she certain that she could say no to him, anyway. Yet to be in his company was to invite even greater pain, for he would not offer marriage and she would not be satisfied with less.

Eventually the shrill whistle of the kettle drew her mind back to the present and she hurriedly turned the heat off and poured the water over the tea. She had no idea if Nikolas would drink tea and decided that he wouldn't, so she poured coffee for him and also for herself; then, without allowing herself time to think about it, she picked up the tray and carried it through to the living room before she could lose all her courage.

Nikolas was lounging on the sofa like a big cat, while Charles had taken a chair; they both got to their feet as she entered, and Nikolas stepped forward to take the heavy tray from her hands and place it on the low table. She shot him a wary glance from under her lashes, but he didn't look angry. He was watching her intently, his gaze so penetrating that she shivered. He immediately noted her reaction and a sardonic half-smile curved his mouth. He put his hand on her arm and gently forced her to a seat on the sofa, then took his place beside her.

"Charles and I have been discussing the situation," he said easily, and she started, shooting a desperate look at Charles. But Charles merely smiled and she could read nothing from his expression.

"What situation?" she asked, reaching for some hidden well of calmness.

"The position our relationship will put you in with the press," he explained smoothly as she handed Charles's tea across to him. By some miracle she kept from dropping the cup and saucer, though she felt her entire body jerk. When Charles had rescued his drink, she turned a pale face up to Nikolas.

"What are you saying?" she whispered.

"I think you know, my dear; you're far from stupid. I'll take certain steps that will make it plain to all observers that I don't feel I need the press to protect me from you, and that any long noses poked into my private life will rouse me to . . . irritation. You won't have to worry any longer about being the subject of a nasty Sunday-morning column; in fact, after I finish convincing the press to do as I want, all sympathy will probably swing to you."

"That's quite unnecessary," she said, lowering her lashes as she offered a cup of coffee to him. She felt confused; it had not occurred to her that Nikolas might use his influence to protect her, and rather than feeling grateful, she withdrew into a cool reserve. She didn't want to be indebted to Nikolas and drawn further into his sphere of influence. The paper had gotten it all wrong; he was the spider, not she! If she allowed it, he would weave silken threads all about her until she was helpless against him.

"I'll be the judge of that," Nikolas snapped. "If you'd told me last night why you were so upset about that damned photographer, I could have prevented both the column and the photos from being printed. Instead, you let your pride stand in the way, and look what you've endured, all for nothing. Now I know the extent of the situation and I'll act as I think best."

Charles said mildly, "Be reasonable, Jessica. There's no need for you to endure spiteful gossip. You've suffered it for five years; it's time that state of affairs was ended."

"Yes, but . . ." She halted, for she had been about to say, But not by *him,* and she wasn't certain enough of Nikolas's temper to risk it. She took a deep breath and began again. "What I meant was, I don't see the need for any intervention, because there won't be another opportunity for this to happen. I'd have to be a fool to allow myself to get into that situation after what happened last night. I'll simply live here as quietly as possible; there's no need for me to frequent places where I'd be recognized."

"I won't allow that," Nikolas put in grimly. "From now on, you'll be by my side when I entertain or when I go out. People will meet you, get to know you. That's the only sure way of forever stifling the gossip, to let these people become acquainted with you and find out that they like you. You *are* a likable little wench, despite your damnable temper."

71

"Thank you!" she returned smartly, and Charles grinned.

"I could kick myself for missing your first meeting," he put in, and Nikolas gave him a wolfish grin.

"The first wasn't as interesting as the second," he informed Charles dryly. "And the third meeting isn't beginning all that well, either. It'll probably take me all day to convince her not to be obstinate over the matter."

"Yes, I can see that." Charles winked and replaced his empty cup on the tray. "I'll leave you to it, then; I've some work to do."

"Call me tomorrow and we'll settle about the shares," said Nikolas, getting to his feet and holding out his hand.

Jessica's warning sirens went off. "The shares are already settled," she said in fierce determination. "Market value only! I told you, Nikolas, I won't sign the papers if you try to buy me off with a ridiculously high price!"

"I shall probably break your neck before the day is out," returned Nikolas genially, but his eyes were hard. Charles laughed aloud, something very rare for him, and Jessica glared at him as he and Nikolas walked to the door. They exchanged a few low words and her suspicions flared higher. Then Nikolas let him out and returned to stand before her with his hands on his hips, staring down at her with an implacable expression on his hard face.

"I meant what I said," she flared, scrambling to her feet to stand before him and braving the volcanic heat of his eyes.

"So did I," he murmured, raising his hand and absently stroking her bare shoulder with one finger, his touch as light and delicate as that of a butterfly. Her breath caught and she stood very still until the caress of that one finger drove her beyond control and she began to tremble. The finger moved from her shoulder to her throat, then up to press under her chin and raise her face to his. "Have you decided if you want to go out on the boat with me?" he asked as his eyes slipped to her mouth.

"I—yes. I mean, yes, I've decided, and no, I don't want to go," she explained in confusion, and the corners of his mouth lifted in a wry smile.

"Then I suggest we go for a drive, something to keep me occupied. If we stay here all day, Jessica, you know what will happen, but the decision is yours."

"I haven't invited you to stay at all, much less all day!" she informed him indignantly, pulling away from him.

His arm dropped to his side and he watched sharply as the color rose in her cheeks. "You're afraid of me," he observed in mild surprise. Despite her brave, defiant front, there had been a flash of real fear in her eyes, and he frowned. "What is it about me that frightens you, Jessica? Are you afraid of me sexually? Have your experiences with men been so bad that you fear my lovemaking?"

She stared numbly at him, unable to formulate an answer. Yes, she was afraid of him, as she had never before feared any other human being. He was so lawless—no, not that. He made his own laws, his influence was enormous; he was practically untouchable by any known power. She already knew that her emotions were vulnerable to him and that she had no weapons against him at all.

But he was waiting for an answer, his strong features hardening as she moved involuntarily backward. She gulped and whispered wildly, "You—you wouldn't understand, Nikolas. I think that a woman would be in very good hands with you, so to speak, wouldn't she?"

"I like to think so," he drawled. "But if it isn't that, Jessica, what is it about me that makes you as wary as a frightened doe? I promise I won't slaughter you."

"Won't you?"

The whispered, shaking words had scarcely left her mouth before he moved, closing the distance between them with two lithe strides and capturing her as she gave an alarmed cry and tried to dart away. His left arm slid about her waist and pulled her strongly against him, while his right hand caught a fistful of her tawny hair and pulled firmly on it until her face was tilted up to his.

"Now," he growled, "tell me why you're afraid."

"You're hurting me!" she cried, anger chasing away some of her instinctive fear. She kicked at his shins and he gave a muffled curse, releasing her hair and scooping her up in his arms instead. Holding her captive, he sat down on the sofa and pinned her squirming body on his lap. The struggle was woefully unequal and in only a moment she was exhausted and subdued, lying quietly against the arm that was so hard and unyielding behind her back.

He chuckled. "Whatever you're afraid of, you're definitely not afraid to fight me. Now, little wildcat, tell me what bothers you."

She was tired, too tired to fight him right now, and she was beginning to understand that it was useless to fight him, in any event. He was determined to have everything his way. Sighing, she turned her face into his shoulder and inhaled the warm, earthy male scent of him, slightly sweaty from their struggle. What could she tell him? That she feared him physically because she had known no man, that it was a virgin's instinctive fear? He would never believe that; he would rather believe the tales that many men had made love to her. And she couldn't

74

tell him that she feared him emotionally, that she was far too vulnerable to his power, or he would use that knowledge against her.

Then an idea struck her. He had given it to her himself. Why not let him believe that she had been so mistreated that she feared all men now? He had seemed receptive to that idea. . . .

"I don't want to talk about it," she muttered, keeping her face turned into his shoulder.

His arms tightened about her. "You have to talk about it," he said forcefully, putting his mouth against her temple. "You have to get it out in the open, where you can understand it."

"I—I don't think I can," she said breathlessly, for his arms were preventing proper breathing. "Give me time, Nikolas."

"If I must," he said into her hair. "I won't hurt you, Jessica; I want you to know that. I can be very considerate when I get what I want."

Yes, he probably could, but he was thinking only of an affair while she was already beginning to realize that her heart was terrifyingly open, his for the taking—except that he didn't want it. He wanted only her body, not the tender emotions she could give him.

His hands were moving restlessly, one stroking over her back and bare shoulders, the other caressing her thigh and hip. He wanted to make love, *now*, she could feel the desire trembling in his body. She groaned and said, "No, Nikolas, please. I can't—"

"I could teach you," he muttered. "You don't know what you're doing to me; a man isn't a piece of rock!"

But he was, pure granite. Her slim body arched in his arms as she tried to slip away from him. "No, Nikolas! No!"

He opened his arms as if he was freeing a bird and

she slid from his lap to the floor, sitting on it like a child, her head resting on the sofa. He sighed heavily. "Don't wait too long," he advised, his deep voice hoarse. "Run upstairs and do whatever you have to do before we go for a drive. I have to get out of here or there won't be any waiting."

He didn't have to tell her a second time. On trembling legs she ran upstairs, where she combed her hair and put on makeup, then changed her shoes for modest heels. Her heart was pounding wildly as she returned downstairs to him. She hardly knew him, yet he was gaining a power over her that was frightening. And she was helpless to prevent it.

When she approached him, he stood and pulled her close with a masterful arm, and his hard warm mouth took hers lazily. When he released her, he was smiling, and she supposed he had reason to smile, for her response had been as fervent as it was involuntary.

"You'll be a blazing social success," he predicted as he led her to the door. "Every man will be at your feet if you continue to look so fetching and to blush so delightfully. I don't know how you can manage a blush, but the how really doesn't matter when the result is so lovely."

"I can't control my color," she said, miffed that he should think her capable of faking a blush. "Would you rather your kisses had no effect on me?"

He looked down at her and gave her a melting smile. "On the contrary, my pet. But if it's excitement that brings the flush to your cheeks, I shall know when you are becoming aroused and will immediately whisk you away to a private place. You must tell me all of your little signals."

She managed a careless shrug. "Before you whisk me away to be ravished, I suggest that you first make certain I'm not in the midst of a fight. Anger brings on the same reaction, I'm told. And I don't imagine that even your backing will smooth away all the rocks!"

"I want to know about any rocks that stub your toe," he said, and his voice grew hard. "I insist on it, Jessica. I won't have a repeat of the sort of trash I read this morning, not if I have to muzzle every gossip columnist in London!"

To her horror, it did not sound like an empty threat.

Chapter Five

*W*hen the doorbell rang, Jessica went very still. Nikolas put his hand on her waist and squeezed gently, then that hand urged her inexorably toward the door. Involuntarily she resisted the pressure and he looked down at her, his hard mouth curving into a dry smile. "Don't be such a little coward," he mocked. "I won't let the beasts eat you, so why not relax and enjoy it?"

Speechless, she shook her head. In the few days that she had known Nikolas Constantinos he had taken her life and turned it upside down, totally altered it. This morning he had given his secretary a list of people to call and invite to his penthouse that night, and naturally everyone had accepted. Who turned down Constantinos? At four o'clock that afternoon Nikolas had called Jessica and told her to dress for the evening, he would pick her up in two hours. She had assumed that they would be dining out again, and though she hadn't looked forward to it, she had realized the futility of resisting Nikolas. It wasn't until he had her at his penthouse that he had told her of his plans.

She was angry and resentful that he had done all of this without consulting her, and she had scarcely spoken to him since her arrival, which seemed to bother him not at all. But underneath her anger she was anxious and miserable. Though well aware that, with Nikolas backing her, no one would dare be openly cold or hostile, she was sensitive enough that it didn't really matter if their dislike was hidden or out in the open. She knew it was there, and she suffered. It didn't help that Nikolas's secretary, Andros, was there, his contempt carefully hidden from Nikolas but sneeringly revealed to her whenever Nikolas wasn't looking. It had developed that Andros was a second cousin to Nikolas, so perhaps he felt he was secure in his position.

"You're too pale," observed Nikolas critically, pausing with his hand on the handle to open the door. He bent and kissed her, hard, deliberately letting her feel his tongue, then straightened away from her and opened the door before she could react in any way other than the delicate flush that rose to her cheeks.

She wanted to kick him, and she promised herself that she would have his hide for his arrogant action, but for now she steeled herself to greet the small clusters of people who were arriving. Stealing a glance at Nikolas, she saw that his hard masculine lips wore a light coat of her lipstick and she blushed anew, especially when several of the sharp-eyed women noted it also, then darted their glances to her own lipstick as if matching the shades. Then he stretched out one strong hand and pulled her closer to his side, introducing her as his "dear friend and business partner, Jessica Stanton." The dear friend description brought knowing expressions to many faces, and Jessica thought furiously that he might as well have said *"chère amie,"* for that was how everyone was taking it. Of course, that was Nikolas's intention, but *she* did not plan to fall meekly in with his desires. When the second half of his introduction sank in, everyone immediately became very polite where for a moment she had sensed a direct snub. *Chère amie* was one thing, but business partner was another. He had made it obvious, with only a few well-chosen words, that he would take any insult to Jessica as an insult to himself.

To her surprise and discomfiture, Nikolas introduced one tall, smartly dressed blonde as a columnist, and by the pressure of his fingers she knew that this was the gossip columnist who had written that vicious little bit about her for the Sunday paper. She greeted Amanda Waring with a calm manner that revealed nothing, though it took all of her self-control to manage it. Miss Waring glared at her for a fraction of a second before assuming a false smile and mouthing all of the conventional things.

Her attention was jerked back to Nikolas by the spectacle of a stunning redhead sliding a silken arm about his muscular neck and stretching up against him to kiss him slowly on the mouth. It wasn't a long kiss, nor a deep one, but nevertheless it fairly shouted of intimacy. Jessica went rigid as an unexpected and unwelcome flame of jealousy seared her. How dare that woman touch him! She quivered and barely restrained herself from jerking the woman away from him, but if Nikolas himself hadn't released the woman's arm from his neck and stepped back from her, she might still have created a scene. The glance Nikolas gave her was as apologetic as one could expect from him, but the effect was ruined by the gleam of amusement in the midnight depths of his eyes.

Deliberately Nikolas drew his handkerchief out of his pocket and wiped the redhead's coral-beige lipstick from his mouth, something he hadn't done when he had kissed Jessica. Then he took Jessica's hand and said, "Darling, I'd like you to meet an old friend, Diana Murray. Diana, Jessica Stanton."

Lovely dark blue eyes turned on Jessica, but the expression in them was savage. Then the soft lips parted in a smile. "Ah, yes, I do believe I've heard of you," Diana purred.

Beside her, Jessica felt Nikolas turn as still as a waiting panther. She tightened her fingers on his hand and responded evenly, "Have you? How interesting," and turned to be introduced to Diana's escort, who had been watching with a guarded expression on his face, as if he didn't want to become involved.

Despite Nikolas's bombshell, or perhaps because of it, the room was fairly humming with conversation. Andros was moving from group to group, quietly taking over some of the duties of the host, thereby freeing Nikolas for the most part. For a while Nikolas steered Jessica about from one small knot of people to another, talking easily, bringing her into the conversations and making it obvious by his possessive hand on her arm or the small of her back that she was his, and had his support. Then, callously, she felt, he left her on her own and went off to talk business.

For a moment she was panic-stricken and she looked about, hunting for a corner seat. Then she met Andros's cold, smiling look and knew that he expected her to make a fool of herself. She took a firm grip on her wavering nerves and forced herself to approach a small group of women who were laughing and discussing a current comedy play. It wasn't until she had joined the group that she saw it contained Amanda Waring. Immediately a little silence fell over the women as they looked at her, assessing her position and wondering just how far good manners went.

She lifted her chin and said in a calm voice, "Isn't the lead role played by that actress Penelope something-or-other who was such a smash in America last year?"

"Penelope Durwin," supplied a plumpish, middle-aged woman after a moment. "Yes, she was nominated for their best-actress award, but she seems to like live theater better than films."

"Aren't you an American?" asked Amanda Waring in a velvet little voice, watching Jessica with her icy eyes.

"I was born in America, yes," said Jessica. Was this to become an interview?

"Do you have any plans to return to America to live?"

Jessica stifled a sigh. "Not at this time; I like England and I'm content here."

Conversation ceased for a stiff moment, then Amanda broke the silence again. "Have you known Mr. Constantinos long?" Whatever Amanda's personal feelings, she was first and foremost a columnist, and Jessica was good copy. More—Jessica was fantastic copy! Aside from her own notorious reputation, she was apparently the current mistress of one of the world's most powerful men, an elusive and sexy Greek billionaire. Every word that Jessica said was newsworthy.

"No, not for long," Jessica said neutrally, and then a different voice broke into the circle.

"With a man like Nikolas, it doesn't take long,

does it, Mrs. Stanton?" purred a soft, openly hostile voice. Jessica quivered when she heard it and turned to look at Diana, meeting the woman's impossibly lovely blue eyes.

For a long moment Jessica looked at her quietly and the silence became so thick that it was almost suffocating as they all waited to see if a scene would develop. Jessica couldn't even summon up anger to help her; if anything, she pitied this gorgeous creature who watched her with such bright malice. Diana so obviously adored Nikolas, and Jessica knew how helpless a woman was against his charm, and his power. When the silence was almost unbearable, she replied gently, "As you say," and turned back to Amanda Waring. "We met for the first time this past Saturday," she said, giving the woman more information than she had originally intended, but she would be foolish to let the woman's antagonism live when she could so easily put it down.

Her ploy worked. Miss Waring's eyes lit, and hesitantly the other women rejoined the conversation, asking Jessica if she had any plans to visit Mr. Constantinos on his island. They had heard it was fabulous; was he leaving England soon; was she going with him? In the midst of answering their questions Jessica saw Diana leave the group, and she gave an inward sigh of relief, for she had felt that the woman was determined to provoke a scene.

After that, the evening was easier. The women seemed to unbend a little as they discovered that she was a rather quiet, perfectly well-behaved young woman who did not act in the least as if she coveted their husbands. Besides, with Nikolas Constantinos to control her, they certainly felt safe. Though he kept himself to the knot of men discussing business, every so often his black eyes would slide to Jessica's slim figure, as if checking on her. Certainly his alert gaze convinced any unattached male that it would be wise not to approach her.

Only once, when Jessica slipped away for a moment to check her hair and makeup, did she feel uneasy. She saw Diana talking very earnestly to Andros, and even as she watched, Andros flicked her a cool, contemptuous look that chilled her. She hurried away to Nikolas's bedroom and stood for a moment trying to calm her accelerated heartbeat, telling herself that she shouldn't be alarmed by a look. Heavens, she should be accustomed to such looks!

A knock on the door made her shake off her misgivings and she turned to open the door. Amanda Waring stood there. "May I disturb you?" she asked coolly.

"Yes, of course; I was just checking my hair," said Jessica, standing back for the woman to enter. She noticed Amanda looking around sharply at the furnishings, as if expecting black satin sheets and mirrors on the ceilings. In fact, Nikolas was rather spartan in his tastes and the large bedroom seemed almost bare of furniture. Of course, the huge bed dominated the room.

"I wanted to speak with you, Mrs. Stanton," began Amanda. "I wanted to assure you that nothing you said will be repeated in my column; Mr. Constantinos has made it clear that my job hangs in the balance, and I'm not a fool. I stand warned."

Jessica gasped and swung away from the mirror where she had been smoothing her hair. Horrified, she stared at Amanda, then recovered herself enough to say frostily, "He did *what?*"

Amanda's thin mouth twisted. "I'm sure you know," she said bitterly. "My editor told me this morning that if another word about the Black

Widow appeared in my column, it would not only mean my job, I would be blacklisted. It took only a phone call from Mr. Constantinos to the publisher of the newspaper to accomplish that. Congratulations, you've won."

Jessica's lips tightened and she lifted her chin proudly. "I must apologize for Nikolas, Miss Waring," she said in calm, even tones, determined not to let this woman guess her inner turmoil. "I assure you that I didn't ask him to make the gesture. He has no use for subtlety, has he?"

In spite of the coldness in the woman's eyes, her lips quirked a bit in humor. "No, he hasn't," she agreed.

"I'm sorry he's been so nasty. I realize you have a job to do, and of course I'm fair game," Jessica continued. "I'll have to talk with him—"

The door opened and Nikolas walked in, staring coldly at Amanda Waring. "Miss Waring," he said forbiddingly.

Immediately Jessica knew that he had seen the columnist enter the room after her and had come to her rescue. Before he could say anything that would alienate the woman even more, she went to him and said coolly, "Nikolas, have you really threatened to have Miss Waring dismissed if she prints anything about me?"

He looked down at her and his lips twisted wryly. "I did," he admitted, and his glance slashed to Amanda. "I won't have her hurt again," he said evenly, but his tone was deadly.

"I'm perfectly capable of taking care of myself, thank you, Nikolas," Jessica said tartly.

"Of course you are," he said indulgently, as if she was a child.

Furious, Jessica reached out for his hand and dug

her nails into it. "Nikolas—*no*. I won't stand by and watch you throw your weight around for my benefit. I'm not a child or an idiot; I'm an adult, and I won't be treated as if I don't have any sense!"

Little gold flames lit the blackness of his eyes as he looked down at her, and he covered her hand with his free one, preventing her nails from digging into him any longer. It could have looked to be a loving gesture, but his fingers were hard and forceful and held hers still. "Very well, darling," he murmured, carrying her hand to his mouth. After pressing a light kiss on her fingers, he raised his arrogant black head and looked at Amanda.

"Miss Waring, I won't mind if your column mentions that the lovely Jessica Stanton acted as my hostess, but I won't tolerate any more references to the Black Widow, or to Mrs. Stanton's financial status. For your information, we have just completed a business deal that was very favorable to Mrs. Stanton, and she has not, is not, and never will be in need of funds from anyone else."

Amanda Waring was not a woman to be easily intimidated. She lifted her chin and said, "May I quote you on that?"

Suddenly Nikolas grinned. "Within reason," he said, and she smiled back at him.

"Thank you, Mr. Constantinos . . . Mrs. Stanton," she added after a moment, glancing at Jessica.

Amanda left the room and Nikolas looked down at Jessica with those little gold lights still dancing in his eyes. "You're a little cat," he drawled lazily. "Don't you know that now you'll have to pay?"

Not at all frightened, Jessica said coolly, "You deserved it, for acting like a bully."

"And you deserve everything you get, for being such a provocative little tease," he said, and effortlessly pulled her into his arms. She tried to draw away and found herself helpless against his iron strength.

"Let me go," she said breathlessly, trying to twist away from him.

"Why?" he muttered, bending his head to press his burning lips into the hollow of her shoulder. "You're in my bedroom, and it would take only a slight tug to have this gown around your ankles. Jessica, you must have known that this gown would heat the blood of a plaster saint, and I've never claimed to be that."

She would have been amused at his statement if the touch of his mouth on her skin hadn't sent ripples of pleasure dancing through her veins. She was glad that he liked her gown. It *was* provocative; she knew it and had worn it deliberately, in the manner of a moth flirting with the flame that will singe its wings. It was a lovely gown, made of chiffon in alternating panels of sea green and emerald, swirling about her slim body like waves, and the bodice was strapless, held up only by the delicate shirring above her breasts. Nikolas was right, one tug would have the thing off, but then, she hadn't planned on being alone with him in his bedroom. She saw his head bend down again and she turned her mouth away just in time. "Nikolas, stop it! You have guests; you can't just disappear into the bedroom and stay there!"

"Yes, I can," he said, capturing her chin with one strong hand and turning her mouth up to his. Before she could reply again he had opened his mouth over hers, his warm breath filling her. His tongue probed, teasing her into response, and after a moment she forgot her protests, going up on tiptoe to strain against his hard body and offer him completely the sweetness of her mouth. Without hesitation he took it, his kisses becoming wilder and deeper as he hungrily tasted her. He groaned into her mouth and his hand began to slide up her ribs. It wasn't until his strong fingers cupped one soft breast that she realized his intentions and once again cold fear put out the fires of her own desire. She shuddered and began trying to twist out of his embrace; his arm tightened painfully about her and he arched her slim body against him, his mouth ravaging.

Jessica stiffened and cried out hoarsely, "No, please!"

He swore in Greek and pulled her back into his arms as she tried to get away from him, but instead of forcing his caresses on her, he merely held her tightly to him for a moment and she felt the thunderous pounding of his heart against her. "I won't force you," he finally said as he pressed kisses onto her temple. "You've had some bad experiences, and I can understand your fear. But I want you to understand, Jessica, that when you come to me, I won't leave you unsatisfied. You can trust me, darling."

Weakly she shook her head. "No, you don't understand," she muttered. "Nikolas, I—" She started to tell him that she had never made love, that it was fear of the unknown that made her shrink from him, but he laid a finger against her lips.

"I don't want to know," he growled. "I don't want to hear of another man's hands on you. I thought I could bear it, but I can't. I'm too jealous; I never want to hear you talk about another man."

Jessica shook her head. "Oh, Nikolas, don't be so foolish! Let me tell you—"

"No," he snapped, gripping her shoulders and shaking her violently.

Growing angry, Jessica jerked away from him and threw her head back. "All right," she rejoined tartly. "If you want to be such an ostrich, by all means go bury your head. It doesn't matter to me what you do!"

He glared at her for a moment, then his tense broad shoulders relaxed and his lips twitched with barely suppressed laughter. "It matters," he informed her mockingly. "You just haven't admitted it to yourself yet. I can see that I'll have to destroy your stubbornness as I'll destroy your fear, and in the same way. A few nights of lovemaking will turn you into a sweet, docile little kitten instead of a spitting wildcat."

Jessica stepped around him to the door, her tawny head high. As she opened the door, she turned and said coolly, "You're not only a fool, Nikolas, you're an arrogant fool."

His soft laughter followed her as she returned to the gathering, and she caught the knowing glances of several people. Diana looked furious, then turned her back in a huff. Sighing, Jessica wondered if Nikolas included Diana in many of his entertainments. She hoped not, but had the feeling that her hopes would be disappointed.

From that evening on, Nikolas completely took over her life. Almost every evening he took her to some small party or meeting, or out to dine in the poshest, most exclusive restaurants. She hardly had any free time to spend with Sallie, but that practical young woman was delighted that her friend was going out more and that no other vicious items about her had appeared in the press. Amanda Waring often mentioned Jessica's name in tandem with Nikolas's, and even hinted that the prolonged presence of the Greek in London was due entirely to the charms of Mrs. Stanton, but she made no mention of the Black Widow or of Jessica's reputation.

Even Charles was delighted that Nikolas had taken over, Jessica often thought broodingly. She felt as if a trusted friend had deserted her, thrown her into the lion's den. Didn't Charles really understand what Nikolas wanted of her? Surely he did; men were men, after all. Yet more and more it seemed that Charles deferred to Nikolas in decisions concerning her assets, and even though she knew that Nikolas was nothing short of a financial genius, she still resented his intrusion into her life.

She was bitterly disappointed but not really surprised when, shortly after Nikolas's takeover of her affairs, Charles gave her some papers to sign and told her they concerned minor matters only. She had trusted him implicitly before, but now some instinct made her read carefully through the papers while Charles fidgeted. Most of the papers did concern matters of little importance, but included in the middle of the stack was the document selling her shares in ConTech to Nikolas for a ridiculously high price and not the market price she'd insisted on. Calmly she pulled the paper out and put it aside. "I won't sign this," she told Charles quietly.

He didn't have to ask what it was. He gave her a wry smile. "I was hoping you wouldn't notice," he admitted. "Jessica, don't try to fight him. He wants you to have the money; take it."

"I won't be bought," she told him, raising her head to give him a level look. "And that's what he's trying to do, buy me. Surely you have no illusions about his intent?"

Charles studied the tips of his impeccable shoes. "I have no illusions at all," he murmured. "That may or may not be a sad thing. Unvarnished reality has little to recommend it. However, being the realist I am, I know that you haven't a prayer of besting Constantinos in this. Sign the papers, my dear, and don't wake sleeping tigers."

"He's not sleeping," she mocked. "He's only lying in wait." Then she shook her head decidedly. "No, I won't sign the papers. I'd rather not sell the stock at all than let him think he's got me all bought and paid for—or I'll sell to a third party. At market price those shares will be snapped up in a minute."

"And so will you," Charles warned. "He doesn't want those stocks in anyone else's hands."

"Then he'll have to pay me market price." She smiled, her green eyes taking on a glint of satisfaction. Just once, she thought, she had the upper hand on Nikolas. Why hadn't she thought of threatening to sell the shares to a third party before now?

Charles left with the paper unsigned and Jessica knew that he would inform Nikolas immediately. She had an engagement with Nikolas that night to attend a dinner with several of his business associates, and she toyed with the idea of simply leaving town and standing him up rather than argue with him, but that would be childish and would only postpone the inevitable. She reluctantly showered and dressed, choosing with care a gown that didn't reveal too much of her; she knew that she could trust Nikolas's thin veneer of civilization only so far. Yet the modest gown was provocative in its own way, the stark severity of the black cloth against her pale gold skin a perfect contrast. Staring at her reflection in the mirror, she thought with wry bitterness of the Black Widow tag and wondered if anyone else would think of it.

As she had half-expected, Nikolas was a full half-hour early, perhaps hoping to catch her still dressing and vulnerable to him. When she opened the door to him, he stepped inside and looked down at her with such grimness in his black eyes that she was startled, even though she'd been expecting him to be angry.

The door was hardly closed behind him when he took her wrist and pulled her against him, dwarfing her with his size and strength. "Why?" he gritted softly, his head bent down so close to hers that his breath was warm on her face.

Jessica knew better than to struggle against him; that would only fan his anger. Instead, she made herself lie pliantly against him and answered him evenly, "I told you what I'd accept, and I haven't changed my mind. I have my pride, Nikolas, and I won't be bought."

The black eyes snapped angrily at her. "I'm not trying to buy you," he snarled, his hands moving to her slim back in a caressing movement that was the direct opposite of the anger she sensed in him. Then his arms wrapped about her, welding her to his hard frame, and he dipped his head even closer to press swift, light kisses on her upturned mouth. "I only want to protect you, to make you so secure that you'll never again have to sell your body, even in marriage."

Instantly she went rigid in his arms and she flashed him a glance that scorched. "Beware of Greeks bearing gifts," she retorted hotly. "What you mean is, you want to ensure that you're the only buyer!"

His arms tightened until she gasped for breath and pushed against his shoulders in protest. "I've never had to buy a woman!" he ground out between clenched teeth. "And I'm not buying you! When we make love, it won't be because money has passed between us but because you want me as much as I want you."

Desperately she turned her head away from his

approaching mouth and gasped out, "You're hurting me!" Instantly his arms loosened their hold and she gulped in air, her head dropping to rest on his chest. Was there nothing she could say that would make him understand her point of view?

After a moment he put her away from him and drew a folded paper from the inner pocket of his jacket. Spreading it open, he placed it on the hall table and produced a pen, which he held out to her. "Sign it," he ordered softly.

Jessica put her hands behind her back in the age-old gesture of refusal. "Market value only," she insisted, her eyes holding his calmly. She played her last ace. "If you don't want them, I'm certain there are other buyers who would be glad to get those shares at market value."

He straightened. "I'm sure there are," he agreed, still in that soft, calm voice. "And I'm also certain that if you sell that stock to anyone but me, you'll regret it later. Why are you being so stubborn about money? The amount of money you sell the stock for will in no way influence the outcome of our relationship. That's already been decided."

"Oh, has it?" she cried, clenching her small fists in fury at his arrogance. "Why don't you just go away and leave me alone? I don't want anything from you, not your money, not your protection, and certainly not *you!*"

"Don't lie to yourself," he said roughly, striding forward to lace his arms about her and hold her to him. She flung her head back to deny that she was lying; that was the only chance he needed. He bent his black head, and his mouth closed over hers. His kiss wasn't rough but moved seductively over her lips, inviting her response and devastating her, sucking away her breath and leaving her weak in his arms. Her eyes closed, her lips opened helplessly to his mastering tongue, and she let him kiss her as deeply as he wished until she lay limply against him. His tenderness was even more dangerous than his temper, because her response to him was growing more passionate as she became accustomed to him and she sensed her own capitulation approaching. He was no novice when it came to women, and he knew as well as she did that the need he stirred in her was growing stronger.

"Don't lie to me, either," he muttered against her mouth. "You want me, and we both know it. I'll make you admit it." His mouth came down again to fit completely against her lips, and he took full possession of them, molding them as he wanted. He began to touch her breasts, deliberately asserting his mastery over her, trailing his fingertips lightly over the upper curves and leaving a growing heat behind. Jessica made a whimpering sound of protest, muffled by his mouth; she gasped under his onslaught, searching desperately for air, and he gave her his heated breath. Now his hand slid boldly inside her gown and cupped the round curves in his palm. At his intimate caress, Jessica felt herself drowning in the sensual need he aroused, and she gave in with a moan, twining her arms around his neck.

Swiftly he bent and slid his arm under her knees, lifting her and carrying her to the lounge, where he placed her on the sofa and eased down beside her, never ceasing the drugging kisses which kept her under his sensual command. She moved restlessly, her hands in his hair, trying to get closer to him, aching with a need and emptiness which she didn't understand but couldn't ignore.

Triumph glittered in his eyes as he moved to cover

her with his body, and Jessica opened her eyes briefly to read the look on his face, but she saw him through a haze of desire, her senses clouded. Nothing mattered right now, if only he would keep on kissing her. . . .

His fingers had explored her satiny breasts, had teased the soft peaks into firm, throbbing proof of the effect he was having on her. Sliding his body down along hers, he investigated those tempting morsels with his lips and tongue, searing her with the heat of his mouth. Her hands left his head and moved to his shoulders, her fingers digging into the muscles which flexed with his every movement. Golden fire was spreading throughout her body, melting her, dissolving her, and she let herself sink into her own destruction. She wanted to know more, she wanted to have more of him, and she thought she would die from the pleasure he was giving her.

He left her breasts to move upward and kiss her mouth again, and now he let her feel the pressure of his entire body, the force of his arousal.

"Let me stay with you tonight," he breathed into her ear. "You want me, you *need* me, as much as I want and need you. Don't be afraid, darling; there's no need to be afraid. I'll take good care of you. Let me stay," he said again, though despite the soft words it wasn't a plea, but a command.

Jessica shuddered and squeezed her eyes tightly shut, her blood boiling through her veins in frustration. Yes, she wanted him—she admitted it—but he had some terrible ideas about her, and she found it hard to forgive him for that. As soon as he spoke, she began to recover her senses and remember why she didn't want to let him make love to her, and she turned her face away from his kisses.

If she let him make love to her, he would know as soon as he possessed her that he was wrong in his accusations; but she also knew in her bones that to go to him under those circumstances would lower her to exactly what he thought her to be now, and her standards were too high to allow that. He offered nothing but physical gratification and material gain, while she offered a heart that had been battered and was now overly sensitive to each blow. He didn't want her love, yet she knew that she loved him, against all logic and her sense of self-preservation.

He shook her gently, forcing her eyes open, and he repeated huskily, "Will you let me stay, darling? Will you let me show you how sweet it will be between us?"

"No," she forced herself to reply, her voice hoarse with the effort she was making. How would he react to a denial at this stage? He had a violent temper; would he be furious? She stared up into his black gaze, and her fear was plain for him to read, though he couldn't guess the cause. "No, Nikolas. Not . . . not yet. I'm not ready yet. Please."

He drew a deep breath, mastering his frustration, and she collapsed in intense relief as she realized that he wasn't angry. Roughly he drew her head against his shoulder and stroked her hair, and she breathed in the hot male scent of his skin and let him comfort her. "You don't have to be afraid," he insisted in a low tone. "Believe me. Trust me. It has to be soon; I can't wait much longer. I won't hurt you. Just let me show you what it means to be my woman."

But she already knew, she thought in despair. His confident masculinity lured her despite her better sense. His lovemaking would be sweet and fiery, burning away her control, her defenses, leaving her totally helpless in the face of his marauding mastery. And when he was finished, when his attention was attracted by another challenge, she would be in ashes. But how long could she hold him off, when every day increased her need of him?

Chapter Six

*H*er heels clicking as she strode into the ConTech building, Jessica strove to control her temper until she was alone with Nikolas, but the determined clatter of her heels gave her away and she tried to lighten her step. Her soft lips tightened ominously. Just wait until she saw him!

"Good afternoon, Mrs. Stanton," said the receptionist with a friendly smile, and Jessica automatically returned the greeting. In a few short weeks, Nikolas had turned her world around; people smiled and greeted her now, and everyone connected with ConTech treated her with the utmost courtesy. But recognizing his enormous influence didn't make her feel more charitable toward him; she wanted to throttle him instead!

As she left the elevator, a familiar figure exited Nikolas's office, and Jessica lifted her chin as she neared Diana Murray. Diana paused, waiting for

Jessica to approach her, and good manners forced Jessica to greet her.

"My, isn't Nikolas busy this afternoon?" purred Diana, her beautiful eyes watching Jessica sharply for any signs of jealousy.

"I don't know; is he?" countered Jessica coolly.

"It doesn't matter; he'll see me anyway."

"I'm sure he will. But give him a minute," Diana advised in a sweet voice which made Jessica long to slap her. She preferred unvarnished hostility to Diana's saccharine poison. Diana smiled and added, "Let him have time to smooth himself down. You know how he is." Then she walked away, her hips swaying with just the right touch of exaggeration. Men probably found Diana irresistible, Jessica thought savagely, and she promised herself that if Nikolas Constantinos didn't walk carefully, he was going to find a storm breaking over his arrogant head.

She thrust open the door, and Andros looked up from his never-deserted post. As always when he saw her, his eyes conveyed cold dislike. "Mrs. Stanton. I don't believe Mr. Constantinos is expecting you."

"No, he isn't," agreed Jessica. "Tell him I'm here, please."

Reluctantly Andros did her bidding, and almost as soon as he had replaced the receiver, Nikolas opened the doors and smiled at her. "Hello, darling. You're a pleasant surprise; I didn't expect to see you until later. Have you decided to sign the papers?"

This reference to his purchase of her shares only served to fan higher the flame of her anger, but she controlled herself until she had entered his office and he had closed the doors firmly behind them. Out of the corner of her eye, she saw him approaching, obviously intent on taking her in his arms, and she briskly removed herself from his reach.

"No, I haven't decided to sign anything," she said crisply. "I came here to get an explanation for this." She reached into her purse and withdrew a slim packet of papers attached with a paper clip to a creased envelope. She thrust them at him and he took them, a frown wrinkling his forehead.

"What are these?" he asked, studying the darkened green of her eyes and gauging her temper.

"You tell me," she snapped. "I believe you're the responsible party."

He removed the paper clip and rapidly scanned the papers, flipping them one by one. It took only a minute; then he replaced the paper clip. "Is anything wrong? Everything looks in order."

"I'm certain everything is in perfect legal order," she said impatiently. "That isn't the problem, and you know it."

"Then exactly what *is* the problem?" he inquired, his lashes drooping to cover the expression in his eyes, but she knew that he was watching her and saw every nuance of her expression before she, too, shuttered her face.

He hooked one leg over the corner of the desk and sat down, his body relaxed. "I don't see why you're upset," he said smoothly. "Suppose you tell me exactly what you don't like about the agreement. It hasn't been signed yet; we can always make changes. I hadn't meant for you to receive your copy by mail," he added thoughtfully. "I can only suppose that my attorney tried to anticipate my wishes, and he'll certainly hear from me on that."

"I don't care about your attorney, and it doesn't make any difference how I received this piece of trash, because I won't sign it!" she shouted at him, her cheeks scarlet with anger. "You're the most arrogant man I've ever met, and I hate you!"

The amusement that had been lurking in his eyes vanished abruptly, and when she spun on her heel and started for the door, too incensed even to yell at him, he lunged from his position on the desk to intercept her before she'd taken three steps. As his hand closed on her arm, she lashed out at him with her free hand. He threw his arm up to ward off the blow, then deftly twisted and caught that arm, too, and drew her against him.

"Let me go!" she spat, too infuriated to care if Andros heard her. She twisted and struggled, heaving herself against the iron band of his arms in an effort to break free; she was given stamina by her anger, but at last even that was exhausted. When she shuddered and dropped her head against his shoulder, he lifted her easily and stepped around the desk, where he sat down in his chair and cradled her on his lap.

Jessica felt faint, drained by her rage and the struggle with him, and she lay limply against him. His heart was beating strongly, steadily, under her cheek, and she noticed that he wasn't even breathing rapidly. He'd simply subdued her and let her tire herself out. He stretched to reach the telephone and dialed a single number, then spoke quietly. "Hold all calls, Andros. I don't want to be disturbed for any reason." Then he dropped the receiver back onto the cradle and wrapped both arms about her, hugging her securely to him.

"Darling," he whispered into her hair. "There's no need to be so upset. It's only a simple document—"

"There's nothing simple about it!" she interrupted violently. "You're trying to treat me like a high-priced whore, but I won't let you! If that's the way you think of me, then I don't want to see you again."

"I don't think of you as a whore." He soothed her. "You're not thinking clearly; all you're thinking now is that I've offered you payment for going to bed with me, and that isn't what I intended."

"Oh, no, of course it wasn't," she mocked in a bitter tone. She struggled to sit up and get away from the intimate heat of his body, but his enfolding arms tightened and she couldn't move. Tears sparkled in her eyes as she gave up and relaxed against him in defeat.

"No, it wasn't," he insisted. "I merely want to take care of you—thus the bank account and the house. I know you own the house where you live now, but admit it, the neighborhood isn't the best."

"No, it isn't, but I'm perfectly happy there! I've never asked for anything from you, and I'm not asking now. I don't want your money, and you've insulted me by asking me to sign a document swearing that I'll never make any demands against your estate for 'services rendered.'"

"I'd be extremely foolish if I didn't take steps to secure the estate," he pointed out. "I don't think you'd sue me for support, darling, but I have other people to consider and a responsibility to uphold. A great many people depend on me for their livelihood —my family as well as my employees—and I can't in good conscience do anything that might jeopardize their well-being in the future."

"Do all of your mistresses have to sign away any claims on you?" she demanded, angrily brushing away the single tear which dropped from her lashes. "Is this in the nature of a form letter, everything filled in except for the name and date? How many other women live in apartments or houses you've so kindly provided?"

"None!" he snapped. "I don't think I'm asking too much. Did you truly think I'd establish you as my mistress and leave myself vulnerable to any number of other claims? Is that why you're so angry, because I've made certain you can't get any money from me except what I freely give to you?"

He'd made the mistake of releasing her arm, and she swung wildly at him, her palm striking his face with enough force to make her hand tingle. She began to cry, tears flooding down her face while she gulped and tried to control them, and in an effort to get away from him she started fighting again. The results were the same as before: he simply held her and prevented her from landing any more blows, until she was breathless and worn out. Pain and anger mingled with her sense of helplessness at being held like that, her raw frustration at being unable to make him see how utterly wrong he was about her, and she gave up even trying to control her tears. With a wrenching sob she turned her face into his shoulder and gave in to her emotional storm.

"Jessica!" he ground out from between clenched teeth, but she barely heard him and paid no attention. A small part of her knew that he had to be furious that she'd slapped him—Nikolas wasn't a man to let anyone, man or woman, strike him and get away with it—but at the moment she just didn't care. Her delicate frame heaved with the convulsive force of her weeping. It would never end, the gossip and innuendo concerning her marriage; even though Nikolas wouldn't allow anyone else to talk about her, he still believed all of those lies himself. What he didn't seem to realize was that she could endure everyone else's insults, but she couldn't endure his, because she loved him.

"Jessica." His voice was lower now, softer, and the biting power of his fingers eased on her arms.

She felt his hands touching her back, stroking soothingly up and down, and he cuddled her closer to his body.

With tender cajoling he persuaded her to lift her face, and he wiped her eyes and nose with his handkerchief as if she were a child. She stared at him, her eyes still luminous with tears, and even through her tears she could see the red mark on his cheek where she'd hit him. With trembling fingers she touched the spot. "I—I'm sorry," she said, offering her apology in a tear-thick voice.

Without a word he turned his head and kissed her fingers, then bent his head and lifted her in the same motion, and before she could catch her breath he was kissing her, his mouth hot and wild and as hungry as an untamed animal's, tasting and biting and probing. His hand searched her breasts and moved downward to glide over her hips and thighs, on down to her knees, moving impatiently under the fabric of her dress. With a shock she realized that he was out of control, driven beyond the control of will by his own anger and the struggle with her, the softness of her body twisting and straining against him. He wasn't even giving her a chance to respond to him, and fear made her heartbeat speed up as she realized that this time she might not be able to stop him.

"Nikolas, no. Not here. No! Stop it, darling," she whispered fiercely, tenderly. She didn't try to fight him, sensing that at this stage it would only excite him more. He was hurting her; his hands were all over her, touching her where no man had ever touched before, pulling at her clothing. She reached up and placed her hands on both sides of his face and repeated his name softly, urgently, over and over until, abruptly, he was looking at her and she saw that she'd gained his attention.

A spasm crossed his face, and he ground his teeth, swearing beneath his breath. He slowly helped her to her feet, pushing her from his lap, and then got to his feet as if in pain. He stood looking at her for a moment as she swayed against the desk for support; then he cursed again and walked a few feet away, standing with his back to her while he wearily massaged the back of his neck.

She stared at his broad, muscular back in silence, too drained to say anything to him, not knowing if it was safe to do so. What should she do now? She wanted to leave, but her legs were trembling so violently that she doubted her ability to walk unaided. And her clothing was disheveled, twisted, and partially unbuttoned. With slow, clumsy fingers she restored her appearance, then eyed him uncertainly. His stance was that of a man fighting himself, and she didn't want to do anything that might annoy him. But the silence was so thick between them that she was uneasy, and at last she forced her unsteady legs to move, intending to retrieve her purse from where she'd dropped it and leave before the situation worsened.

"You aren't going anywhere," he said in a low voice, and she halted in her tracks.

He turned to face her then, his dark face set in weary lines. "I'm sorry," he said with a sigh. "Did I hurt you?"

His apology was the opposite of the reaction she had expected, and for a moment she couldn't think of a response. Then she dumbly shook her head, and he seemed to relax. He moved close to her and slid his arm around her waist, urging her close to him with gentle insistence. Jessica offered no resistance and pressed her head into the sheltering hollow of his shoulder.

"I don't know what to say," he muttered. "I want you to trust me, but instead I've frightened you."

"Don't say anything," she answered, having finally mastered her voice. "There's no need to go over it all again. I won't sign the paper, and that's that."

"It wasn't meant as an insult, but as a legal necessity."

"But I'm not your mistress," she pointed out. "So there's no need for the document."

"Not yet," he agreed. "As I said, my attorney anticipated my wishes. He was in error." His tone of voice boded ill for the poor attorney, but Jessica was grateful to the unknown man. At least now she knew exactly what Nikolas thought of her, and she preferred the painful truth to living in a dream.

"Perhaps it would be better if we didn't see each other anymore," she began, but his arm tightened around her and a scowl blackened his brow.

"Don't be ridiculous," he snapped. "I won't let you go now, so don't waste your breath suggesting it. I promise to control myself in the future, and we'll forget about this for the time being."

Lifting her head from his shoulder, Jessica gave him a bitter look. Did he truly think she could forget that he thought her the sort of woman who was available for a price? That knowledge was a knife thrust into her chest, but equally painful was the certainty that she didn't want him to vanish from her life. Whatever he had come to mean to her, the thought of never seeing him again made her feel desolate. She was risking her emotional well-being, flirting with disaster, but she could no more walk away from him now than she could stop herself from breathing.

Several weeks passed in a more restrained manner, as if he'd placed himself on his best behavior, and she managed to push away the hurt. He insisted that she accompany him whenever he went out socially, and she was his hostess whenever he entertained.

The strain on her was telling. At yet another party, she felt smothered and escaped into the coolness of the dark garden, where she sucked in deep lungfuls of fresh, sweet air; she had been unable to breathe in the smoke-laden atmosphere inside. In the weeks since she had met Nikolas, she had learned to be relaxed at social gatherings, but she still felt the need to be by herself occasionally, and those quiet times had been rare. Nikolas had the power of a volcano, spewing out orders and moving everyone along in the lava flow of his authority. She wasn't certain just where he was at the moment, but she took advantage of his lapse of attention to seek the quietness of the garden.

Just before leaving for the dinner party tonight, they'd had a flaming argument over her continued refusal to sell the stock to him, their first argument since the awful scene in his office. He wouldn't back down an inch; he was furious with her for defying him, and he had even accused her of trying to trick him into increasing his offer. Sick to death of his lack of understanding and tired of the running battle, Jessica had grabbed the paper and signed it, then thrown it to the floor in a fit of temper. "Well, there it is!" she had snapped furiously. It wasn't until he'd leaned down and picked up the paper to fold it and replace it in his pocket that she'd seen the speculative gleam in his eyes and realized that she'd made a mistake. Signing now, after he had accused her of holding out for a higher price and assured her that she wouldn't get it, had convinced him that she'd been doing exactly that all along, biding her time and hoping for a higher price. But it was too late now to do anything about it, and she had grimly conquered the tears that sprang to her eyes as the pain of his suspicions hurt her.

Strolling along the night-dewed path of white gravel, she wondered sadly if the sense of ease which had come into their relationship lately had been destroyed. He had ceased pressuring her to let him make love to her, had in fact become increasingly tender with her, as if he was at last beginning to care. The thought made her breathless, for it was like a dream come true. In a thousand ways, he spoiled her and curbed his impatient nature for her, and she no longer tried to fight her love for him. She didn't even want to any longer, so thoroughly had he taken her under his influence.

But all of that might be gone now. She should never have signed that agreement! She'd given in to his bullying tactics in a fit of temper, and all she had done was to reinforce his picture of her as a mercenary temptress. What ground she'd gained in his affections had been lost in that one moment.

Moving slowly along, her head down while she dreamed wistfully of marrying Nikolas and having his children—something not likely to happen now—it was some moments before she heard the murmur of voices. She was almost upon the couple before she realized it. She halted, but it seemed that they hadn't noticed her. They were only a dim shape in the darkness, the pale blur of the woman's gown blending into the darkness of the man's dinner jacket as they embraced.

Trying to move quietly, Jessica stepped back with the intention of withdrawing without attracting attention to herself, but then the woman gave a sharp sigh and moaned, "Nikolas! Ah, my love . . ."

Jessica's legs went numb and refused to move as strength drained away from her. Nikolas? *Her* Nikolas? She was too dazed to feel any pain; she didn't really believe it. At last she managed to turn and look again at the entwined couple. Diana. Most assuredly Diana. She had recognized that voice. And—Nikolas? The bent black head, the powerful shoulders, *could* be Nikolas, but she couldn't be certain. Then his head lifted and he muttered in English, "What's wrong, Diana? Has no one been taking care of you, as lovely as you are?"

"No, no one," she whispered. "I've waited for you."

"Were you so certain I would return?" he asked, amusement coming into his voice as he raised his head higher to look into the gorgeous upturned face.

Jessica turned away, not wanting to see him kiss the other woman again. The pain had started when she saw for certain that Nikolas was the man holding Diana so passionately, but she determinedly forced it down. If she let go, she would weep and make a fool of herself, so she tilted her chin arrogantly and ignored the vise that squeezed her chest, the knife that stabbed her insides. Behind her, she heard him call her name, but she moved swiftly across the patio and into the protection of the house and the throng of people. People smiled at her now, and spoke, and she put a faint smile on her stiff lips and made her way very calmly to the informal bar.

Everyone was getting their own drinks, so she poured herself a liberal portion of tart white wine and sipped it as she moved steadily about the room, smiling, but not allowing herself to be drawn into conversation. She could not talk to anyone just now; she would just walk about and sip her wine and concentrate on mastering the savage thrust of pain inside her. She wasn't certain how she would leave the party, whether she was strong enough to leave with Nikolas or if it would be best to call a taxi, but she would worry about that later. Later, after she had swallowed enough wine to dull her senses.

Out of the corner of her eye she saw Nikolas moving toward her with grim determination, and she swung to the left and spoke to the couple she nearly collided with, marveling that her voice could be so natural. Then, before she could move away, a strong hand closed on her elbow and Nikolas said easily, "Jessica, darling, I've been chasing you around the room trying to get your attention. Hello, Glenna, Clark . . . how are the children?"

With a charming smile he had Glenna laughing at him and telling him about her two young sons, whom it seemed Nikolas knew personally. All the time they talked, Nikolas kept a tight grip on Jessica's arm, and when she made a move to break away from him, his fingers tightened until she nearly gasped with pain. Then he was leading her away from Glenna and Clark and his fingers loosened, but not enough to allow her to escape.

"You're hurting my arm," Jessica said coldly as they wove through milling groups of laughing, chattering people.

"Shut up," he ground out between his teeth. "At least until we're alone. I think the study is empty; we'll go there."

As he literally pulled her with him, Jessica had a glimpse of Diana's face before they left the room behind, and the expression of pure triumph on the woman's face chilled her.

Pride stiffened her back, and when Nikolas closed the door of the study behind them and locked it, she turned to face him and lifted her chin to give him a haughty stare. "Well?" she demanded. "What do you want, now that you've dragged me in here?"

He stood watching her, his black eyes grim and his mouth set in a thin line that at any other time would

have made her apprehensive but now left her curiously unmoved. He had thrust his hands into his
pants pockets as if he didn't trust himself to control
his temper, but now he took them out and his eyes
gleamed. "It always amazes me how you can look
like a queen, just by lifting that little chin."

Her face showed no reaction. "Is that all you
brought me in here to say?" she demanded coolly.

"You know damned well it isn't." For a moment
he had the grace to look uncomfortable, and a dull
flush stained the brutal cheekbones. "Jessica, what
you saw . . . it wasn't serious."

"That really doesn't matter to me," she thrust
scornfully, "because our relationship isn't serious,
either. You don't have to explain yourself to me,
Nikolas; I have no hold on you. Conduct your little
affairs as you please; I don't care."

His entire body jerked under the force of her
words and the flush died away to a white, strained
look. His eyes grew murderous and an instant before
he moved she realized that she had gone too far,
pushed him beyond control. She had time only to
suck in her breath to cry out in alarm before he was
across the room with a lithe, savage movement, his
hands on her shoulders. He shook her violently, so
violently that her hair tumbled down about her
shoulders and tears were jerked from her eyes before
his mouth closed on hers and his savage kiss took her
breath away. When she thought that she would faint
under his onslaught, he lifted her slumping body in
his arms and carried her to the soft, worn sofa where
their host had obviously spent many comfortable
hours. Fiercely he placed her on it and covered her
body with his, holding her down with his heavy
shoulders and muscular thighs. "Damn you!" he
whispered raggedly, jerking her head back with
cruel fingers tangled in her hair. "You have me tied

in knots; I can't even sleep without dreaming about you, and you say you don't care what I do? I'll make you care, I'll break down that wall of yours—"

He kissed her brutally, his lips bruising hers and forcing a moan of protest from her throat, but he paid no attention to her distress. With his free hand he slid down the zipper of her dress and pulled the cloth from her shoulders, and only then did his mouth leave hers to press his sensual attack on the soft mounds of her breasts.

Jessica moaned in fright when her mouth was free, but as his hot lips moved hungrily down her body, a wanton need surged through her. She fought it fiercely, determined not to surrender to him after what had passed between them tonight, knowing that he thought her little better than a whore. And then he had gone straight into Diana's arms! The memory of the smugly victorious smile the woman had given her sent tears streaming down her face as she struggled against his overpowering strength. He ignored her efforts to free herself and moved to press completely over her, his hands curving her against his powerful, surging contours. He was feverish with desire and she was helpless against him; he would have taken her, but when he raised his head from her throbbing breasts, he saw her tear-drenched face and stopped cold.

"Jessica," he said huskily. "Don't cry. I won't hurt you."

Didn't he understand? He had already hurt her; he'd torn her heart out. She turned her head away from him with a jerky movement and bit her bruised lip, unable to say anything.

He eased his weight from her and pulled his handkerchief from his pocket to wipe her face. "It's just as well," he said grimly. "I don't want to make love to you for the first time on a sofa in someone else's house. I want you in a bed, *ma chère,* with hours in which I can show you how it should be between a man and a woman."

"Any woman," she said bitterly, remembering Diana.

"No!" he refuted fiercely. "Don't think of her, she means less than nothing to me. I was foolish—I'm sorry, darling. I wanted to ease myself with her, to relieve the tension that you arouse and won't satisfy, and instead I found that she leaves me cold."

"Really?" Jessica taunted, glaring at him. "You didn't look so cold to me."

He tossed the tear-wet handkerchief aside and captured her chin with one hand. "You think not? Did I act as if I was carried away by passion?" he demanded, forcing her to look at him. "Did I kiss her as I kiss you? Did I say sweet things to her?"

"Yes! You called her— No," she interrupted herself, becoming confused. "You said she was lovely, but you didn't—"

"I didn't call her darling, as I call you, did I? One kiss, Jessica! One kiss and I knew that she couldn't even begin to damp down the fires you've lit. Won't you forgive me for one kiss?"

"Would you forgive me?" she snapped, trying to turn her head away, but he held her firmly. Against her will she was softening, letting him talk her out of her resolve. The heavy weight of his limbs against her was comforting as he wrapped her in the security of his strength, and she began to feel that she could forgive any transgression so long as she could still touch him.

"I would have snatched you away from any man foolish enough to touch you," he promised her grimly, "and broken his jaw. I don't think I could control myself if I saw someone kissing you, Jessica. But I'd never walk away from you; I'd take you with me."

She shuddered and closed her eyes, recalling those awful moments when she had watched their embrace. "Neither can I control *my*self, Nikolas," she admitted hoarsely. "I can't bear to watch you make love to another woman. It tears me apart."

"Jessica!"

It was the first admission she had made that she cared for him, even a little. Despite their closeness over the past weeks, she had still resisted him in that, had refused to tell him that she cared. Now she could no longer hide it.

"Jessica! Look at me. *Look at me!*" Fiercely he shook her and her eyes flew open to stare into his blazing, triumphant eyes. "Tell me," he insisted, bending closer to her, his mouth poised above hers. His hand went to her heart, felt the telltale pounding, and lingered to tenderly stroke the soft womanly curves he found.

"Tell me," he whispered, and brushed his lips against hers.

Her arms went about his shoulders, clinging tightly to his strength as her own was washed away in the floodtide of her emotion. "I love you," she moaned huskily. "I've tried not to—you're so . . . arrogant. But I can't help it."

He crushed her to him so tightly that she cried out, and he loosened his hold immediately. "Mine," he muttered, pressing hot kisses over her face. "You're mine, and I'll never let you go. I adore you, darling. For weeks I've been half-mad with frustration, wanting you but afraid of frightening you off. You'll have no more mercy from me, you'll be my woman now!" And he laughed exultantly before he sat up and helped her to pull her gown back up. He zipped it for her, then his hard hands closed about her waist.

"Let's leave now," he said, his voice rough. "I want you so badly!"

Jessica shivered at the raw demand in his voice, elated but also frightened. The time had come when he would no longer allow her to draw away from him, and though she could feel her heart blooming at his admission of love, she was still wary of this man and the control he had over her.

Nikolas sensed her hesitation and pulled her close to him with a possessive arm. "Don't be frightened," he murmured against her hair. "Forget whatever has happened to you; I'll never do anything to hurt you. You said that you aren't frightened of me, but you are, I can tell. That's why I've suffered through these weeks of hell, waiting for you to lose your fear. Trust me now, darling. I'll take every care with you."

She buried her face against his shoulder. Now was the time to tell him that she had never made love before, but when she gathered her courage enough to raise her head and open her mouth, he forestalled her by laying his fingers gently across her bruised lips. "No, don't say anything," he whispered. "Just come with me, let me take care of you."

Her hair was a tumbled mass about her shoulders and she lifted her hands to try to twist it up again. "Don't bother," Nikolas said, catching her hand. "You look adorable, if anyone should see you, but we'll leave by the back way. Wait here while I make our excuses to our host; I'll only be a moment."

Left by herself, Jessica sat down and tried to gather her dazed and scattered thoughts. Nikolas loved her, he had admitted it. Love was the same as "adore," wasn't it? Certainly she loved him, but she was also confused and uncertain. She had always thought that a mutual declaration of love led to sweet plans for the future, but instead Nikolas seemed to plan only on taking her to bed. She tried to tell herself that he was an extremely physical man, and that afterward he would want to talk about wedding plans. It was just that she had always dreamed, in her heart, of going to her husband in white, and of deserving the symbol of purity. For a moment she toyed with the idea of telling Nikolas she didn't want to leave, but then she shook her head. Perhaps she had to prove her love for Nikolas by trusting him as he had requested and giving him the full measure of her love.

Then it was too late to worry, because Nikolas came back, and she drowned in the possessive glow of his dark eyes. Her nervousness was swamped by her automatic response to his nearness and she leaned pliantly against him as he led her out of the house by the back way and to his car parked down the narrow, quiet street.

London was a golden city by night, gleaming like a crown on the banks of the Thames, and it had never seemed more golden to her than it did tonight, sitting quietly beside Nikolas as he drove through the city. She looked at the familiar landmarks as if she had never seen them before, caught by the unutterable loveliness of the world she shared with Nikolas.

He didn't drive her home, as she had expected, but instead they went to his penthouse. That alarmed her, though she wasn't sure why, and she hung back, but he pulled her into the elevator and held her close, muttering hot words of love to her. When the elevator doors slid open, he took her hand and led her down the quiet, dim hallway to his door. Unlocking it, he let her inside and followed, locking the door behind him with a final-sounding click. She had gone a few steps forward and now stood very still in the darkness, and with a flick of his finger he switched on two lamps. Then he went over to his telephone console to make sure his automatic answering service was on.

"No interruptions tonight," he said, turning to her now. His eyelids drooped sensuously over his gleaming eyes as he came to her and drew her against his hard body. "Do you want anything to drink?" he asked, his lips moving against her temples.

She closed her eyes in ecstasy, breathing in the heady male scent of him, basking in his warmth. "No, nothing," she replied huskily.

"Nor do I," he said. "I don't want alcohol dulling my senses tonight; I want to enjoy every moment. You've obsessed me from the first moment I saw you, so forgive me if I seem to . . ." He paused, trying to find the word, and she smiled tenderly.

"If you seem to gloat?" she murmured.

"Gloat is too strong a word, but I do admit to a sense of triumph." He grinned.

She watched with a pounding heart as he shed his dinner jacket and draped it over a chair. His tie followed, and his satin waistcoat, then he came to her and she shrank back at the look on his face. So would the Spartan warriors of long ago have looked, proud and savage and lawless. He frightened her, and she wanted to run, but then he had her in his arms and his mouth covered hers and all thoughts fled as her senses were filled with him.

He lifted her and carried her along the corridor to his bedroom, shouldering the door closed behind them, then crossing to the huge bed and standing her before it.

Sanity fought with desire and she choked, "No, Nikolas, wait! I have to tell you—"

"But I can't wait," he interrupted huskily, his

breathing ragged. "I have to have you, darling. Trust me, let me wipe out the touch of the others who have hurt you."

His mouth shut off anything else she might have said. He was far more gentle than she would ever have expected, his hands moving over her with exquisite tenderness, molding her to him as his lips drank greedily of hers. She gasped at the surge of pleasure that warmed her, and she curled her slender arms about his neck, arching herself against his powerful form and hearing his deep groan reverberating in her ears like music. With shaking hands he unzipped her gown and slid it down her hips to lie in a silky pool about her feet. He caught his breath at the slim, graceful delicacy of her body, then he snatched her close to him again and his mouth lost its gentleness as he kissed her hungrily. He muttered love words in French and Greek as his strong, lean fingers removed her underwear and dropped it carelessly to the floor, and she thrilled at the hoarse desire so evident in his voice. It was right, it had to be right, he loved her and she loved him. . . .

Feverishly she unbuttoned his silk shirt, her lips pressing hot little kisses to his flesh as she revealed it. She had never caressed him so freely before, but she did so now, discovering with delight the curling hair that roughened his chest and ran in a narrow line down his abdomen. Her fingers flexed mindlessly in that hair, pulling slightly, then her hands dropped to his belt and fumbled awkwardly with the fastening.

"Ah . . . darling," he cried, his fingers closing almost painfully on hers. Then he brushed her hands aside and helped her, for she was trembling so badly that she couldn't manage to undo the belt.

Rapidly he stripped, and she caught her breath at the sight of his strong, incredibly beautiful body. "I love you," she moaned, going into his arms. "Oh, Nikolas, my love!"

He shuddered and lifted her, placing her on the bed and following her down, his mouth and hands all over her, rousing her to wilder, sweeter heights, then slowing and letting her drift back to awareness before he intensified his efforts again and took her to the brink of madness before drawing away. He was seducing her carefully, making certain of her pleasure, though he was going wild with his own pleasure as he stroked her lovely curves and soft hollows.

At last, aching with the need for his complete possession, Jessica moved her body urgently against him. She didn't know how to demand what she needed; she could only moan and clutch at him with frantic fingers. Her head moved mindlessly from side to side, rolling on the tawny pillow of her hair. "Nikolas—ah, beloved," she moaned, scarcely knowing what she said as the words tripped over themselves coming from her tongue. She wanted only his touch, the taste of his mouth on hers. "I never knew—oh, darling, please! Being your wife will be heaven." Her hands moved over his muscled ribs, pulling at him, and she called out to him with surrender plain in her voice, "Nikolas . . . Nikolas!"

But he had gone stiff, pulling away from her, and he rose up on his elbow to look at her. After a moment she realized that she had been deserted and she turned her head to look at him questioningly. "Nikolas?" she murmured.

The silence lengthened and thickened, then he made an abrupt, savage movement with his hand. "I've never mentioned marriage to you, Jessica. Don't delude yourself; I'm not that big a fool."

Jessica felt the blood draining from her face and she was glad of the darkness, of the dim lights that left only black and white images and hid the colors away. Nausea roiled in her stomach as she stared up at him. No, he wasn't a fool, but *she* was. Fiercely she fought back the sickness that threatened to overwhelm her, and when she spoke, her tone was even, almost cool.

"That's odd. I thought marriage was a natural result of love. But then, you've never actually said that you love me, have you, Nikolas?"

His mouth twisted and he got out of bed, walking to the window to stand looking out, his splendid body revealed to her in its nudity. He wasn't concerned with his lack of dress, standing there as casually as if he wore a suit and tie. "I've never lied to you, Jessica," he said brutally. "I want you as I've never wanted another woman, but you're not the type of woman I would ever take as my wife."

Jessica ground her teeth together to keep from crying out in pain. Jerkily she sat up against the pillows and drew the covers up over her nakedness, for she couldn't be as casual about it as he could. "Oh?" she inquired, only a slight strain revealed in her voice, for, after all, hadn't she had years of experience in hiding her feelings? "What type of woman am I?"

He shrugged his broad shoulders. "My dear, that's rather obvious. Just because Robert Stanton married you doesn't make it any less an act of prostitution, but at least he married you. What about all the others? They didn't bother. You've had some unpleasant experiences that have turned you against men, and I was prepared to treat you with a great deal of consideration, but I've never considered making you my wife. I wouldn't insult my mother by taking a woman like you home to be introduced to her."

Pride had always been a strong part of Jessica's character and it came to her rescue now. Lifting her chin, she said, "What sort of woman would you take home to Mama? A nun?"

"Don't get vicious with me," he snarled softly in warning. "I can deal with you in a way that will make your previous experiences seem like heaven. But to answer your question, the woman I marry will be a virgin, as pure as the day she was born, a woman of both character *and* morals. I admit that you have the character, my dear; it's the morals that you lack."

"Where will you find this paragon?" she mocked, not at all afraid of him now. He had already hurt her as badly as she could ever be hurt; what else could he do?

He said abruptly, "I have already found her; I intend to marry the daughter of an old family friend. Elena is only nineteen, and she's been schooled in a convent. I wanted to wait until she's older before we became betrothed; she deserves a carefree youth."

"Do you love her, Nikolas?" The question was torn from her, for here, after all, was an even deeper pain, to think that he loved another woman. By contrast to this unknown, unseen Elena, Diana seemed a pitiful rival.

"I'm fond of her," he said. "Love will come later, as she matures. She'll be a loving, obedient wife, a wife I can be proud of, a good mother to my children."

"And you can take her home to Mama," Jessica mocked in pain.

He swung away from the window. "Don't mock my mother," he hissed between his teeth. "She's a wonderful, valiant woman; she knew your late husband—are you surprised? When she heard of his disastrous marriage, she was shocked and dismayed, as most people were. Her friends here in London who wrote to her about you didn't ease her worries for an old friend. Should I insult her now by showing up with you in tow and saying, 'Mother, do you remember the gold-digger who took Robert Stanton for all he was worth and ruined the last years of his life? I've just married her.' Were you really such a fool as to think that, Jessica?"

Jessica flung aside the covers and stood up, her bearing erect and proud, her head high. "You're right about one thing," she said in a clipped voice. "I'm not the woman for you."

He watched silently as she went over to her gown and picked it up from the floor, slipping quickly into it. As she slid her feet into her shoes, she said, "Good-bye, Nikolas. It's been an interesting experience."

"Don't be so hasty, my dear," he jeered cruelly. "Before you walk out that door, you should consider that you could gain even more by being my mistress than you did by marrying Robert Stanton. I'm prepared to pay well."

Bitter pride kept her from reacting to that jibe. "Thanks, but no, thanks," she said carelessly, opening the door. "I'll wait for a better offer from another man. Don't bother seeing me out, Nikolas. You aren't dressed for it."

He actually laughed, throwing back his arrogant head. "Call me if you change your mind," he said by way of good-bye, and she walked out without looking back.

She called Charles early the next morning and told him that she would be out of town for several weeks. She hadn't cried, her eyes had remained dry and burning, but she knew that she couldn't remain in London. She would return only when Nikolas had left, flown back to his island. "I'm going to the cottage," she told Charles. "And don't tell Nikolas where I am, though I doubt that he'll bother to ask.

If you let me down in this, Charles, I swear I won't ever speak to you again."

"Had a spat, did you?" he asked, amusement evident in his voice.

"No, it was really a rather quiet parting of the ways. He called me a whore and said I wasn't good enough to marry, and I walked out," she explained coolly.

"My God!" Charles said something under his breath, then said urgently, "Are you all right, Jessica? Are you certain you should go haring off to Cornwall by yourself? Give yourself time to calm down."

"I'm very calm," she said, and she was. "I need a holiday and I'm taking it. You know where I am if anything urgent comes up, but other than that, I don't expect to see you for several weeks."

"Very well. Jessica, dear, are you certain?"

"Of course. I'm perfectly all right. Don't worry, Charles. I'm taking Samantha and the pups with me; they'll enjoy romping around Cornwall."

After hanging up, she made certain everything in the house was turned off, picked up her purse and walked out, carefully locking the door behind her. Her luggage was already in the car, as were Samantha and her wiggling, energetic family, traveling in a large box.

The rest in Cornwall would do her good, help her to forget Nikolas Constantinos. She had had a close call and she was grateful that she had escaped with her self-respect intact. At least she had prevented him from realizing how shattered she was.

Turning it over and over in her mind as she made the long drive to Cornwall, she wondered if she hadn't known all along just what Nikolas thought of her. Why else had she mentioned marriage at such a moment, when he was on the brink of making love to her? Hadn't she subconsciously realized that he would not let her think he intended marriage in order to seduce her?

She was glad that she hadn't told him that she was a virgin; he would have laughed in her face. She could have proved it to him, he would no doubt have demanded proof, but she was too proud. Why should she prove anything to him? She had loved Robert and he had loved her, and she would not apologize for their marriage. Somehow she would forget Nikolas Constantinos, wipe him out of her thoughts. She would not let his memory destroy her life!

Chapter Seven

$\mathcal{F}$or six weeks Jessica pored over the newspapers, searching for any notice, however small, to indicate that Nikolas had returned to Greece. He was mentioned several times, but it was always to say that he was flying here or there for a conference, and a day or so later she would read that he had returned to London. Why was he staying in England? He had never before remained for so long, always returning to his island at the first opportunity. She had no contact with Charles, so she couldn't ask him for any information, not that she would have anyway. She didn't want to know about Nikolas, she told herself fiercely time and again, but that didn't ease the ache in her heart that kept her lying awake night after night and turned food to ashes in her mouth.

She lost weight, her already slim figure becoming fragile. Instead of recovering, she was in danger of going into a Victorian decline, she told herself mockingly, but no amount of willpower could make her swallow more than a bite or two of food at any meal.

Long walks with Samantha and the gamboling puppies for company tired her out but did not reduce her to the state of exhaustion that she needed in order to sleep. After a while she began to feel haunted. Everything reminded her of Nikolas, though nothing was the same as it had been in London. She heard his voice, she remembered his devouring kisses, his fierce possessiveness. Perhaps he hadn't loved her, but he had certainly wanted her; he had been quite blatant about his desire.

Had he expected her to return to him? Was that why he was still in London? The thought was heady, but she knew that nothing had changed. He would take her on his terms, or not at all.

Still she lingered at the cottage, walking every day down to the beach, where the vacationers romped and children went into ecstatic fits over the five fat, prancing puppies. They had been weaned now, and mindful of their increasing size she gave them away one by one to the adoring children. Then there was only Samantha left with her, and the days trickled slowly past.

Then, one morning, she looked at herself in the mirror as she was braiding her hair, really looked at herself, and was stunned at what she saw. Had she really allowed Nikolas Constantinos to turn her into this pale, fragile creature with huge, dark-circled eyes? What was wrong with her? She loved him, yes; in spite of everything he had said to her, she still loved him, but she wasn't so weak in spirit that she would let him destroy her!

She began to realize that it solved nothing to hide away here in Cornwall. She wasn't getting over him;

if anything, she was being eaten alive by the need to see him, to touch him.

Suddenly her chin lifted as an idea came to her. She still loved him, she could not rid herself of that, but it was no longer the pure, innocent love that she had offered him the first time. Bitter fires had scorched her heart. For the burned remains of that sweetness, physical love might be enough. Perhaps in his arms she might find that all of her love had been burned out and she would be free. And if not—if she found that in spite of everything she continued to love him—in the years to come, when he was married to his pure, chaste little Elena, she would have the memories and knowledge of his passion, passion such as Elena would never know.

Then she realized that when she became his mistress he would know that no other man had ever touched her. What would he think? Would he apologize, beg her forgiveness? The thought left her curiously unmoved, except for the bitterly humorous thought that the only way she could prove her virtue to him was by losing it. The situation was ironic, and she wondered if Nikolas would appreciate the humor of it when he knew.

Without consciously admitting it, her mind was made up. She would accept Nikolas on his terms, give up her respectability and chastity for the physical gratification that he could give her. But she would not let him support her; she would keep her independence and her pride, and when he married his pure little Greek girl, she would walk away and never see him again. She would be his mistress, but she would not be a party to adultery.

So she packed her clothing and closed up the cottage, put Samantha in the car and began the long drive back to London. The first thing she did was call

Charles and tell him that she had returned, assuring him that she was fine. He had to go out of town that afternoon or he would have come over, and she was glad that their meeting was postponed. If Charles saw her now, so thin and wan, he would know that something was dreadfully wrong.

That same problem worried her the next morning as she dressed. She couldn't get up the courage to call Nikolas; he might tell her that he was no longer interested, and she felt that she had to see him again even if he turned her down to her face. She would go to his office, be very calm and nonchalant about it—but could she carry it off when she looked so very fragile?

She used her makeup carefully, applying slightly more blusher than she normally used and taking extra care with her eyes. Her hair would have to be left down to hide the thin lines of her neck and soften the fleshless contours of her cheekbones. When she dressed, she chose a floaty dress in a soft peach color, and was satisfied when she looked in the mirror. Nothing could quite disguise how delicate she had become, but she looked far from haggard.

As she drove to ConTech, she remembered the first time she had made this drive to meet Nikolas. She had been rushed, irritable, and not at all pleased. Now she was going to offer him what she had never thought to offer any man, the use and enjoyment of her body without benefit of marriage, and the only comfort she could find was that her body was all he would have. She had offered him her heart once, and he had scorned it. Never again would she give him the chance to hurt her like that.

Everyone recognized her now as she went up in the elevator, for she had often met Nikolas for lunch. Surprised murmurs of "Good morning, Mrs. Stanton" followed her, and she wondered for the first time if Nikolas was pursuing someone else now, but it really made no difference if he was. He could only turn her down if he was no longer interested, and any other rival would eventually have to give way to the precious, innocent Elena.

The receptionist looked up as she entered, and smiled warmly. "Mrs. Stanton! How nice it is to see you again!"

The greeting seemed genuinely friendly, and Jessica smiled in return. "Hello, Irena. Is Nikolas in today?"

"Why, yes, he is, though I believe he's planning a trip this afternoon."

"Thank you. I'll go in, if I may. Andros is here?"

"On guard as usual," Irena said, and wrinkled her nose in a private little communication that actually made Jessica laugh aloud. Evidently Andros had not endeared himself to the rest of the staff.

Calmly she walked into the office, and immediately Andros rose from his seat. "Mrs. Stanton!" he exclaimed.

"Hello, Andros," she returned as he eyed her with frank dislike. "I'd like to see Nikolas, please."

"I'm sorry," he refused in coolly neutral tones, though his eyes sparkled with delight at being able to turn her down. "Mr. Constantinos has someone with him right now and will be unable to talk to you for some time."

"And he's leaving on a business trip this afternoon," said Jessica dryly.

"Yes, he is," Andros said, his lips quirking in triumph.

Jessica looked at him for a moment, anger building in her. She was sick and tired of being treated like dirt, and from this moment on she planned to fight back. "Very well," she said. "Give him a message for me, please, Andros. Tell him that I'm willing to agree to his terms, if he's still interested, and he can get in touch with me. That's all."

She turned on her heel and heard Andros strangle in alarm. "Mrs. Stanton!" he protested. "I can't—"

"You will have to," she cut in as she opened the door, and had a glimpse of the consternation in his black eyes as she left the office. He had damned himself either way now, for if he passed on the message Nikolas would know that Andros had refused her entrance, and he would not dare withhold the message, for if Nikolas ever found out—and Andros knew that Jessica would make certain he did—there would be hell to pay. Jessica smiled to herself as she walked back to the elevator. Andros had had that coming for a long time.

The elevator took its time arriving, but she wasn't impatient. The way she figured it, Nikolas would hear from Andros in about ten minutes, and he would try to reach her on the phone when he had decided that she had had enough time to get home. If she was late getting back, that was all to the good. Let Nikolas wait for a while.

Several other people were in the elevator when it finally did arrive, and it was necessary to stop at every floor before she finally reached the entrance level. She crossed to the glass doors, but as she reached out to push them open, a dark-clothed arm reached past her and opened it for her. She raised her head to thank the man for his courtesy, but the words stuck in her throat as she stared up into the leaping black eyes of Nikolas.

"You've terrified Andros out of ten years of his life," he said easily, taking her arm and ushering her through the door.

"Good. He deserved it," she replied, then eyed him curiously. He was carrying his briefcase, as if he had left for the day. "But how did you get down so fast?"

"The stairs," he admitted, and grinned down at her. "I wasn't taking a chance of letting you get away from me today and not being able to find you before I have to leave this afternoon. That's probably the only reason Andros found the courage to give me your message so promptly; he knew I'd break his neck if he waited until later. You *were* serious, Jessica?"

"Perfectly," she assured him.

He still held her arm, his fingers warm and caressing, but his grip was unbreakable nonetheless. A limousine had drawn up to the curb and he led her to it. The driver jumped out and opened the back door and Nikolas helped her into the spacious back seat, then got in beside her. He gave the driver her address and then closed the sliding window between them.

"My car is here," she told him.

"It'll be perfectly safe until we return," he said, carrying her fingers to his lips for a light kiss. "Or did you think I could calmly leave on a dull business trip after receiving a message like that? No, darling, it's impossible. I'm taking you with me." And he gave her a look of such burning, primitive hunger that she shivered in automatic reaction to his sexuality.

"But I can't just leave," she objected. "Samantha—"

"Don't be silly," he interrupted softly. "Do you think I can't arrange to have a small dog looked after, or that I'd allow such a small thing to stand in my way? Samantha can be taken to an excellent kennel. I'll handle all the details; all you have to do is pack."

"Where are we going?" she asked, turning her head to look at the passing city streets. Evidently his desire had not waned, for there was no hesitation in his manner.

"To Paris, just for a couple of days. A perfect city to begin a relationship," he commented. "Unfortunately I'll be busy during the day with meetings, but the nights will be ours completely. Or perhaps I'll simply cancel the meetings and keep you in bed the entire time."

"Not good business practice," she said lightly. "I won't nag at you if you have to go off to your meetings."

"That's not very good for my ego," he teased, rubbing her wrist with his strong fingers. "I'd like to think that you burn for my touch as I do for yours. I'd nearly reached the limit of my patience, darling; another week and I'd have gone to Cornwall after you."

Startled, she looked at him. "You knew where I was?"

"Of course. Did you think I'd let you simply walk out on me? If you hadn't come back to me, I was going to force the issue, make you mine even if you bit and clawed, but I don't think you'd have resisted for long, h'mmm?"

It was humiliating to think that she hadn't been out of his reach even in Cornwall; he had known where she was and been content to let her brood. She turned her head again to stare blindly out the window, vainly trying to find comfort in the fact that he was, after all, still attracted to her. He might not love her, not as she understood love, but she did have some power over him.

He lifted her hand again and gently placed his lips on her soft palm. "Don't pout, darling," he said softly. "I knew that you'd come back to me when you decided to be realistic. I can be a very generous man; you'll want for nothing. You'll be treated like a queen, I promise you."

Deliberately Jessica pulled her hand away. "There are several things I want to discuss with you, Nikolas," she said in a remote tone. "There are conditions I want met; otherwise, I'm not interested in any sort of a relationship with you."

"Of course," he agreed dryly, his strong mouth curving into a cynical smile. "How much, my dear? And do you want it in cash, stocks or jewels?"

Ignoring him, she said, "First, I want to keep my own house. I don't want to live with you. You can visit me, or I'll visit you if you prefer that, but I want a life apart from yours."

"That's not necessary," he snapped, his straight brows pulling together over suddenly thunderous eyes.

"It's very necessary," she insisted evenly. "I don't delude myself that any relationship with you will be permanent, and I don't want to find myself forced to live in a hotel because I've given up my own home. And as I said, I'm not interested in living with you."

"Don't be so certain of that," he mocked. "Very well, I agree to that condition. You're always free to move in with me when you change your mind."

"Thank you. Second, Nikolas"—here she turned to him and fixed him with an even stare, her green eyes clear and determined, her soft voice nevertheless threaded with steel so that he knew she meant every word—"I will never, under any circumstances, accept any money or expensive gifts from you. As you told Amanda Waring, I don't need your money. I'll be your lover, but I'll never be your kept woman. And finally, on the day you become engaged to your

Elena, I'll walk away from you and never see you again. If you're an unfaithful husband, it won't be with me."

A dark blush of anger had swept over his features as she spoke, then he became motionless. "Do you think my marriage would change the way you feel about me?" he demanded harshly. "You might feel now that you could walk away from me, but once you've known my touch, once we've lain together, do you truly think that you could forget me?"

"I didn't say I would forget you," she said, her throat becoming thick with anguish. "I said I'd never see you again, and I mean it. I believe very strongly in the marriage vows; I never looked at another man when I was married to Robert."

He shoved a hand roughly through his hair, disturbing the tidy wave and making it fall down over his forehead. "And if I don't agree to these last two conditions?" he wanted to know. He was obviously angry, his jaw tight, his lips compressed to a grim line, but he was controlling it. His eyes were narrowed to piercing slits as he watched her.

"Then I won't go with you," she replied softly. "I want your word that you'll abide by those conditions, Nikolas."

"I can make you go with me," he threatened almost soundlessly, his lips scarcely moving. "With one word from me, you can be taken away from England without anyone knowing where you are or how you left. You can be secluded, forced to live as I say you will live."

"Don't threaten me, Nikolas," she said, refusing to be frightened. "Yes, I know you can do all of those things, but you'll be defeating your own purpose if you ever resort to such tactics, for I won't be bullied. You *do* want a willing woman in your arms, don't you?"

"You damned little witch," he breathed, pulling her to him across the seat with an iron grip on her wrist. "Very well, I agree to your conditions—if you think you have the willpower to enforce them. You can probably refuse any gifts from me without being bothered by it, but when it comes to leaving me— we'll see. You're in my blood, and I'm in yours, and my marriage to Elena won't diminish the need I have to sate myself with your soft body, my dear. Nor do I think you could leave me as easily as you've planned, for haven't you come back to me now? Haven't you just offered yourself to me?"

"Only my body," she made clear. *"You* set those terms, Nikolas. You get only my body. The rest of me stays free."

"You've already admitted that you love me," he said roughly. "Or was that just a ploy to try to trap me into marriage."

Despite the pain in her wrist where he held her so tightly, she managed a nonchalant shrug. "What do you know of love, Nikolas? Why talk about it? I'm willing to sleep with you; what more do you want?"

Abruptly he tossed her wrist back into her lap. "Don't make me lose my temper," he warned. "I might hurt you, Jessica. I'm aching with the need to possess you, and my patience is thin. Until tomorrow, my dear, walk softly."

From the look on his face, it was a warning to be taken seriously. She sat quietly beside him until the chauffeur stopped the limousine outside her house, then she allowed him to help her out. He leaned down and gave instructions to the chauffeur to pick up his luggage and return, then he and Jessica went up the walk. He took the key from her and unlocked the door, then opened it for her. "Can you be ready in an hour?" he asked, glancing at his watch. "Our flight leaves at noon."

"Yes, of course, but don't I need a booking?"

"You're taking Andros's seat," he replied. "Andros will be taking a later flight."

"Oh, dear, now he certainly will be cross with me," she mocked as she crossed to the stairway.

"He'll have to control his irritation," said Nikolas. "Go on; I'll arrange for Samantha and the pups."

"Just Samantha," she corrected. "I gave the pups away while we were in Cornwall."

"That should certainly make things easier," he said, grinning.

Jessica went up to her room and pulled her suitcases out again. All of this packing was becoming monotonous. Carefully she folded clothing and essentials into her leather cases, matching her outfits with shoes and accessories. Nikolas sauntered in when she was only half-finished and stretched out on the bed as if he had every right to be there, surveying her through half-closed eyes.

"You've lost weight," he said quietly. "I don't like it. What have you been doing to yourself?"

"I've been on a diet," she replied flippantly.

"Diet, hell!" He came off the bed and caught her arm, his other hand cupping her chin and turning her face up to his. Black eyes went sharply over her features, noting the shadows under her eyes, the defenseless quiver of her soft mouth. His hand quested boldly down her body, cupping her breasts and stroking her belly and hips. "You little fool!" he breathed sharply. "You're nothing but a shadow. You've nearly made yourself ill! Why haven't you been eating?"

"I wasn't hungry," she explained. "It's nothing to act up about."

"No? You're on the verge of collapse, Jessica." He put his arms about her and pulled her tightly to him, lowering his head to kiss her temples. "But I'll take care of you now and make certain that you eat enough. You'll need your strength, darling, for I'm a man with strong needs. If I were a gentleman, I would allow you a few days to regain your strength, but I'm afraid that I'm too selfish and too hungry for you to allow you that."

"I wouldn't want you to," she whispered against his chest, her arms moving slowly about him, feeling with growing desire his strong, hard body pressing to her. She had missed him so badly! "I need you, too, Nikolas!"

"I would take you now," he murmured, "but the car will be back soon and I really need more time than that to satisfy these weeks of frustration. But tonight—just wait until tonight!"

For a long moment she simply rested her head on his broad chest; she was tired and depressed, and glad to have his strength to rest upon. Though she had made her decision, it was against her basic nature to go against the morals of a lifetime, and sadly she realized that her love for Nikolas had not diminished despite her bitter pride. She would have to come to terms with that, just as she had accepted that, while he wanted her physically, he did not love her and probably never would. Nikolas had planned his life and he was not a man to allow anyone to upset his plans.

Only a few hours later, Jessica sat alone in the luxurious suite that Nikolas had reserved, staring about as if dazed. After their flight had landed at Orly, Nikolas had bundled her through customs at top speed and into a taxi; after a mad ride through the Paris traffic, he had deposited her in this hotel and left immediately for his meeting. She felt abandoned and desolate, and her nerves were beginning to quiver as feeling returned to them. For weeks she had been numbed, not feeling anything except the agony of rejection, but now, as she looked about her, she began to wonder just what she was doing here.

Vaguely she studied her surroundings, noting how exactly the pale green carpet picked out the green threads in the blue-green brocade of the sofa she sat upon and the heavy swag of the curtains. A lovely suite . . . even the flowers were color-coordinated. A perfect setting for a seduction, when the lights were low and Nikolas turned his smoldering dark eyes on her.

Her mind shied away from the image of Nikolas, not wanting to think of the coming hours. She had agreed to be his lover, but now that the time was here, she felt rebellious. She thought of what he would say if she refused to go through with it and decided that he would be furious. She pushed the idea away, but as the minutes ticked away, the thought returned again and again, stronger each time, until at last she got up and paced the room in agitation as pain crawled along her nerves.

Had the pain of rejection unhinged her mind? Whatever had she been thinking of? She wouldn't be Nikolas Constantinos's mistress; she wouldn't be any man's mistress! Hadn't Robert instilled more self-respect into her than that? Nikolas didn't love her; he would never love her. His sole motivation was lust, and giving her virginity to him to prove her innocence would be her loss and mean nothing to him. Virginity wouldn't make him love her.

She remembered the tales from her teenage years, tales of girls whose boyfriends pressured them to "prove their love." Then, in a few weeks, the boyfriends were running after some other girl. She had been too withdrawn herself to get into such a situation; she had never really even dated, but she had thought at the time that the girls were such fools. Anyone could see that the boys were just after sex, any way they could get it. Wasn't it the same situation now? Oh, Nikolas was a far cry from a fumbling teenage boy, but all he wanted was sex. He might pretty it up with words like "want" and "need," and call her darling now and then and tell her that he adored her, but basically it was the same urge.

It was simply that she was a challenge to him, that was why he was so determined to make love to her. He couldn't accept defeat; he was far too fiery and arrogant. Everything about her challenged him, her coolness, her resistance to his lovemaking.

She had been standing at the window, looking out at the twinkling Parisian lights as they blinked on in the darkness, for some time when Nikolas returned. She didn't turn as he entered the room and he said softly, "Jessica? What's wrong, darling?"

"Nothing," she said flatly. "I'm just looking."

She heard the muffled thud as he dropped his briefcase and then he came to stand behind her, his warm hands sliding over her arms and crossing in front of her, pulling her back against his body. His head bent and his lips burned on the side of her neck. For a moment she went limp as a spark of desire arced across her nerve endings, then she twisted away from him in a rush of panic.

He frowned at her and took a step toward her; as he did, she retreated, holding her hands out to ward him off.

"Jessica?" he questioned, baffled.

"Don't come near me!"

"What do you mean?" he demanded, his brows snapping together. "What kind of game are you playing now?"

"I—I've changed my mind," she blurted. "I can't do it, Nikolas. I'm sorry, but I just can't go through with it."

"Oh, no, you don't!" he exploded, closing the distance between them with two long strides and catching her arm as she tried to whirl away from him. "Oh, no, you don't," he breathed savagely, jerking her to him. "No more waiting, no more putting me off. Now, Jessica. *Now.*"

She read his intent in his glittering black eyes as he bent down to lift her in his arms. Terror bloomed in her mind and she twisted madly in an effort to evade his lips, trying to throw herself out of his grasp. Tears poured out of her eyes and she began sobbing wildly, begging him not to touch her. Hysteria began to build in her as she realized she could not escape his brutal hold and her breath strangled in her chest.

Suddenly he seemed to realize that she was terrified; startled, he put her on her feet and stared down into her twisted, bloodless face.

Chapter Eight

"All right," he said in a strained voice, backing away from her, his hands held up as if to show he was unarmed. "I won't touch you, I promise. See? I'll even sit down." He suited his actions to his words and stared at her, his black eyes somber. "But God in heaven, Jessica, *why?*"

She stood there on trembling legs, trying to control her sobs and find her voice to explain, but no words would come and she only returned his gaze dumbly. With a groan he brought his hands up and rubbed his eyes as if he was tired, and he probably was. When he dropped his hands loosely onto his knees, his expression was grim and determined. "You win," he said tonelessly. "I don't know what your hang-up about sex is, but I accept that you're too frightened to come to me without some assurance about the future. Damn it, if marriage is what it takes to get you, then you'll have your marriage. We can be married on the island next week."

Shock made her grope weakly for the nearest chair, and when she was safely sitting down, she said in a quavering voice, "No, you don't understand—"

"I understand that you have your price," he muttered angrily. "And I've been pushed as far as I can be pushed, Jessica, so don't start an argument now. You *will* sleep with a husband, won't you? Or do you have another nasty little surprise saved up for me after you have the ring on your finger?"

Anger saved her—clean, strength-giving anger spurting into her veins. It stiffened her spine and dried her tears. He was too arrogant and bullheaded to listen to her, and she was tempted for a minute to throw his offer back in his face, but her heart stopped her. Maybe he was proposing for all the wrong reasons, but it was still a proposal of marriage. And however angry he was now, at both her and himself, he would calm down and she would be able to tell him the truth. He would have to listen; she would make him. He was frustrated now and in no mood to be reasoned with; the best thing to do was not make him angry.

"Yes," she said almost inaudibly, lowering her head. "I'll sleep with you when we're married, no matter how frightened I get."

He heaved a sigh and leaned forward to rest his elbows on his knees in a posture of utter weariness. "Only that saved you tonight," he admitted curtly. "You really were frightened, you weren't faking it. You've really been treated roughly down the line, haven't you, Jessica? But I don't want to hear about it, I can't take it now."

"All right," she whispered.

"And stop looking like a whipped kitten!" he shouted, getting to his feet and pacing angrily to the window. He shoved his hands deeply into his pockets and stood staring out at the brightly lit streets. "I'll telephone Maman tomorrow," he said, reining in his temper. "And I'll try to get out of my meeting fairly early so we can shop for your wedding gown. Since we'll have to get married on the island, all of the trimmings will be expected," he explained bitterly.

"Why does it have to be on the island?" she questioned hesitantly.

"Because I grew up there," he growled. "The island belongs to me, and I belong to the island. The villagers would never forgive me if I got married anywhere but there, with all the traditional celebrations. The women will want to fuss over my bride; the men will want to congratulate me and give me advice on handling a wife."

"And your mother?"

He turned to face her and his eyes were hard. "She'll be hurt, but she won't question me. And let me warn you now, Jessica, that if you ever do anything to hurt or insult my mother, I'll make you wish you'd never been born. Whatever you've been through before will seem like heaven compared to the hell I'll put you through."

She gasped at the hatred in his eyes. Desperately she tried to defend herself and she cried out, "You know I'm not like that! Don't try to make me a villain because things haven't gone as you'd have liked them! I didn't want it to be this way between us."

"I can see that," he said grimly. "You'd have preferred it if I'd been as gullible as Robert Stanton, seeing only your angelic face and willing to give you anything you wanted. But I know you for what you are, and you won't take me to the cleaners like you did that old man. You had a choice, Jessica. As my mistress, you'd have been spoiled rotten and treated like a queen. As my wife, you'll have my name and very little else, but you made your choice and you'll live with it. Just don't expect any more generous settlements like I gave you for those stocks, and above all, remember that I'm Greek, and after the wedding you'll belong to me body and soul. Think about that, darling." He gave the endearment a sarcastic bite and she winced away from the savagery of his tone.

"You're wrong," she said in a trembling voice. "I'm not like that, Nikolas; you know I'm not. Why are you saying such awful things? Please, let me tell you how it was—"

"I'm not interested in how it was," he shouted suddenly, his face filled with the rage he could no longer control. "Don't you know when to shut up? Don't push me!"

Shaking, she turned away from him and crossed to the bedroom. No, she couldn't do it. No matter how much she loved him, it was plain that he'd never love her, and if she made the mistake of marrying him, he would make her life a misery. He'd never forgive her for bringing him to the point where he'd agreed to marriage. He was proud and angry, and as he had said, he was Greek. A Greek never forgot a grievance; a Greek went after vengeance.

It would be better to make a clean break, never to see him again. It would be impossible to forget him, of course, but she knew that any sort of marriage between them was impossible. She had lived with scorn and suspicion from strangers, but she couldn't take it from her husband. It was time she left England completely, returned to the States, where she could live in quiet seclusion.

"Put that suitcase back," he said in a deadly voice from the doorway as she lifted her case from the closet.

Paling, she cast him a startled glance. "It's the only way," she pleaded. "Surely you see that marriage between us wouldn't work. Let me go, Nikolas, before we tear each other to pieces.''

His mouth twisted cynically. ''Backing out, now that you know you won't be able to twist me around your little finger? It won't work, Jessica. We'll be married next week—unless you want to pay the price for walking out of this hotel without me?''

She knew what he meant and her chin went up. Without a word, she shoved her suitcase back onto the shelf and closed the door.

''I thought so,'' he murmured. ''Don't get any more ideas about running out on me, or you'll regret it. Now come back in here and sit down. I'll order dinner sent up and we'll work out the details of our arrangement.''

He was so cold-blooded about it that the last thing she wanted to do was talk to him, but she went ahead of him and took a seat on the sofa, not looking at him.

He ordered dinner without asking her preference, then he called Andros, who was on the floor below them, and told him to come to the suite in an hour, he wanted him to take some notes. Then he replaced the receiver and came to take a seat on the sofa beside her. Uneasily Jessica edged away from him and he gave a short bark of laughter.

''That's odd behavior for a prospective bride,'' he mocked. ''So standoffish. I won't let you get away with that, you know. I'm paying for the right to touch you when I please and however I please, and I don't want any more playacting.''

''I'm not playacting,'' she denied shakily. ''You know I'm not.''

He eyed her thoughtfully. ''No, I suppose you're not. You're afraid of me, aren't you? But you'll do what I want, if I marry you first. Too bad that kills any sense of mercy I might have possessed.''

There was no convincing him. Jessica fell silent and tried to draw together the shreds of her dignity and composure. He was furious, and her attempts to establish her innocence were only making him that much angrier, so she decided to go along with him. If nothing else, she could salvage her pride.

"Nothing else to say?" he jeered.

She managed a cool shrug. "Why waste my time? You'll do what you want anyway, so I might as well go along for the ride."

"Does that mean you've agreed to marry me?" The tone was mocking, but she sensed the seriousness underlying the mockery and she realized that he wasn't certain that she'd stay.

"Yes, I'll marry you," she replied. "On the same conditions that I agreed to be your mistress."

"You backed out of that," he pointed out unkindly.

"I won't back out of this."

"You won't get a chance to. The same conditions, eh? I seem to remember that you didn't want to live with me; needless to say, that condition doesn't stand."

"The part about the money does," she said, turning her green eyes on him, opaque and mysterious with the intensity of her thoughts. "I don't want your money. Anything that I want, I'll pay for myself."

"That's interesting, even if it isn't convincing," he drawled, putting one strong brown hand on her throat and lightly stroking her skin. "If you're not marrying me for my money, why are you marrying me? For myself?"

"That's right," she admitted, meeting his gaze squarely.

"Good, because that's all you're getting," he

muttered, leaning toward her as if drawn irresistibly by her mouth.

His lips fastened angrily on hers; his hands were hard and punishing and he pulled her close to him, but she didn't struggle. She rested pliantly against him and let him ravage her mouth until the anger began to fade and the hungry desire in him became stronger. Then she kissed him back, tentatively, and the pressure of his hard mouth lessened.

The long kiss provided an outlet for his black anger and she could sense him growing calmer even as his passion flared. He was prepared to wait now; he knew that she would be his within a week. He drew back and stared down into her pale face with its soft, trembling lips, then he kissed her again, hard.

The arrival of their dinner interrupted them and he released her to get to his feet and open the door. He seemed in a calmer frame of mind now, and as they ate, he even made small talk, telling her about his meeting and the problems that had been discussed. She relaxed, sensing that the worst of his temper had passed.

Andros arrived right on cue just as they were finishing the meal, and his dark eyes flashed at her in silent hostility before he gave his attention to Nikolas.

"Jessica and I are going to be married," Nikolas announced casually. "Next week, on the island. Tuesday. Make all the arrangements and notify the press that an engagement has been announced, but give them no details about when the wedding will take place. I'll call Maman myself, early tomorrow morning."

Andros's astonishment was plain, and though he didn't look at Jessica again, she sensed his dismay.

No doubt his nose was more than a little out of joint to learn that the woman he actively disliked was going to marry his employer!

"We'll also have a prenuptial agreement drawn up," Nikolas continued. "Take all of this down, Andros, and have it on Leo's desk tomorrow morning. Tell him I want it back the day after tomorrow at the latest. It will be signed before we go to the island."

Andros sat down and opened his pad, his pen at the ready. Nikolas gave Jessica a considering stare before he started speaking again.

"Jessica renounces in advance all monetary claims against my estate," he drawled, sitting down and stretching his long legs out before him. "Should we be divorced, she will be entitled to no alimony and no property except such gifts as I have made to her, which will be her personal property."

Andros flashed Jessica a startled look, as if expecting her to disagree, but she sat quietly, watching Nikolas's dark, brooding face. She felt calm now, though she knew that her entire future was at stake. Nikolas had agreed to marriage when she had thought that he never would, so it was a start.

"While we're married," Nikolas continued, leaning his black head back against the sofa, "Jessica will conduct herself with strict propriety. She's not to leave the island without my personal escort, or with my permission and a substitute escort that I've chosen. She will also turn over the handling of all her income from her first husband to me." Now he, too, looked at Jessica, but still she made no protest. Her business affairs would be in marvelously competent hands with Nikolas, and she had no fears of him cheating her.

Then a thought occurred to her, and before she could halt herself, she said evenly, "I suppose that's one way of getting back the money you paid for my stocks."

Nikolas's jaw went rigid and she wished that she'd held her tongue rather than make him even angrier. She wasn't even protesting letting him have control of the money; she hadn't wanted it anyway. He wanted to have her completely under his power and she was willing to go along with him. It was a chance she was taking, but she had to hope that when he found out how wrong he was, he would soften his stand.

After a tense moment Nikolas delivered his final condition. "Last of all, I shall have final authority over any children that we should have. In case of divorce, I'll retain custody, though of course Jessica will be permitted visitation rights if she wants to come to the island. Under no circumstances will she be permitted to take the child or children away from the island or to see them without my permission."

Pain twisted her heart at that last and she hastily turned her head away so they couldn't see the welling of tears in her eyes. He seemed so hard! Perhaps she was being a fool; perhaps he'd never come to love her. Only the thought that he would know beyond a doubt that she came to him an innocent gave her the courage to agree to his conditions. He would at least realize that she wasn't going to corrupt their children.

If only there would be children! Nikolas seemed to take it for granted that their marriage wouldn't last, but already she knew that for her it was forever. No matter what he did, she would always be married to him in her heart. She wanted to have his children, several children, miniature replicas of him with black hair and black, flashing eyes.

"No comments, Jessica?" Nikolas asked softly, the jeering tone plain in his voice.

Jerking her thoughts back from a delightful vision of herself holding a tiny black-eyed baby in her arms, she stared at him for a moment as if she didn't recognize him, then she gathered herself and replied almost inaudibly, "No. I agree to everything you want, Nikolas."

"That's all," he said to Andros, and when they were alone again, he snapped, "You won't even make a token protest to keep any children, will you? Or are you hoping that I'll pay you to stay away from them? If so, disillusion yourself. You won't get a penny from me under any circumstances!"

"I agreed to your conditions," she cried shakily, her control broken by a heavy pain in her chest. "What more do you want? I've learned that I can't fight you, so I won't waste my breath. As for any children we might have, I want children—I want *your* children—and the only way I'll ever leave them will be if you physically throw me off the island. And don't insult me by insinuating that I won't be a good mother."

He stared down at her, a muscle in his jaw jerking out of control. "You say you can't fight me," he muttered hoarsely, "but you still deny me."

"No, no," she moaned, despairing of ever making him understand. "I'm not refusing you. Can't you see, Nikolas? I'm asking more from you than you're offering, and I'm not talking about money. I'm talking about yourself. So far you've offered me only the same part of yourself that you gave Diana, and I want more than that."

"And what about you?" he growled, getting to his feet and pacing restlessly about the room. "You won't even give me that much; you hold yourself away and demand that I give in to you in every respect."

"You don't have to marry me," she pointed out sharply, abruptly weary of their bickering. "You can let me walk out that door, and I promise you that you'll never see me again, if that's what you want."

His mouth twisted savagely. "You know I can't do that. No, you've got me so twisted inside that I've got to have you; I'll never be worth a damn if I can't satisfy this ache. It's not a wedding, Jessica, it's an exorcism."

His words still rang in her ears the next day as she paced the suite, waiting for him to return from his meeting. Andros was there; he had been there all morning, watching her, not talking, and his silent vigilance rasped painfully on her nerves. It had been a hellish night, sleeping alone in the big bed that Nikolas had intended to share with her, listening to him turn restlessly on the sofa. She had offered to take the sofa and let him have the bed, but he had glared at her so fiercely that she hadn't insisted. They had both slept very little.

Earlier, he had phoned his mother and Jessica had shut herself in the bathroom, determined not to listen to the conversation. When she came out of the bathroom, Nikolas had gone and Andros was there.

Just when she thought she couldn't stand the silence any longer, Andros spoke, and she nearly jumped out of her skin. "Why did you agree to all of Niko's conditions, Mrs. Stanton?"

She looked at him wildly. "Why?" she demanded. "Do you think he was in any mood to be reasonable? He was like a keg of dynamite waiting for some fool to set him off."

"You're not afraid of him, though," Andros observed. "At least, you're not afraid of his temper. Most people are, but you've always dared him to do his worst. I've been turning it over and over in my head, and I can think of only one reason why you'd let him make those insulting conditions."

"Oh? What have you decided?" she asked, pushing her heavy hair away from her eyes. She had been too upset that morning to put it up and now it tumbled untidily over her shoulders.

"I think you love him," Andros said quietly. "I think you're willing to marry him under any conditions because you love him."

She gulped at hearing it put into words. Andros was watching her with a different light in his dark eyes, a certain acceptance and the beginnings of understanding. "Of course I love him," she admitted in a tight whisper. "The only problem is making him believe it."

Suddenly Andros smiled. "You don't have a problem, Mrs. Stanton. Niko is besotted with you. When he calms down, he'll realize, as I did, that under the conditions he set, the only reason you had for marrying him is love. It's only because he's so angry now that it hasn't already occurred to him."

Andros didn't know the whole of it, but still his words gave her hope. He said that Nikolas was besotted with her. That was a little hard to believe; Nikolas was always so much in control, but it was true that he was willing to marry her if he couldn't have her any other way.

Nikolas arrived then, preventing her from talking with Andros any longer, but she felt better. The two men conferred over a sheaf of papers that Nikolas took out of his briefcase, then Andros took the papers to return to his room and Nikolas turned to Jessica.

"Are you ready?" he asked remotely.

"Ready?" She didn't understand.

He sighed impatiently. "I told you that we'd shop for your wedding dress. And you'll have to have rings, Jessica, they'll be expected."

"I'll have to put up my hair," she said, turning to the bedroom, and he followed her.

"Just brush it and leave it down," he ordered. "I like it better down."

Wordlessly she obeyed him and took out her lipstick. "Wait," he said, catching her wrist and pulling her around to him. She knew what he wanted and her heart lightened as she leaned against him and lifted her mouth for his kiss. His lips pressed on hers and his hot breath filled her mouth, making her dizzy. He wanted more; he wasn't content with kisses, but with a quiver of his body he pulled away from her and once again the look in his eyes bordered on the murderous.

"Now you can put on your lipstick," he muttered, and slammed out of the bedroom.

With a shaking hand she applied the lipstick. His temper hadn't improved, and she was afraid that to deny him even her kisses would make him that much worse. No, nothing would satisfy Nikolas but her full surrender, and she wished fervently that the next week would fly past.

But how could an entire week fly by when even the afternoon dragged? She could feel the tension building up in her as they sat at the quiet, exclusive jewelers and examined the trays of rings that he set out. Nikolas was no help at all; he merely sat back and told her to pick out what she liked, he didn't care. Nothing he could have said would have been better calculated to demolish any joy Jessica might have felt in the proceedings. On the other hand, the jeweler was so nice and tried to be so helpful that she hated to disappoint him with her disinterest, so she forced herself to carefully examine each and every ring that he thought she might like. But try as she might, she couldn't choose one. The brightly winking diamonds might have been glass for all she cared; she wanted only to find a quiet corner and weep her eyes out. At last, with tension cracking in her voice, she said, "No—no! I don't like any of them!" and made as if to get to her feet.

Nikolas stopped her with an iron grip on her wrist and he forced her back into her chair. "Don't get upset, darling," he said in a gentler tone than he had used all day. "Calm down; you mustn't weep or it will upset Monsieur. Shall I pick one out for you?"

"Yes, please," she said in a stifled voice, turning her face away so he couldn't see her eyes brimming with the tears he had said she mustn't shed.

"I don't care for the diamonds either, Monsieur," Nikolas was saying. "Her coloring needs something warmer . . . yes, emeralds to match her eyes, in a gold setting."

"Of course—I have just the thing!" Monsieur said excitely, taking the trays of diamonds away.

"Jessica?"

"What?" she asked, still not turning around to face him.

She should have known that he'd never allow her to keep her head turned away from him. One long forefinger stroked along her jaw, then gently forced her face to turn to him. Black eyes took in her pallor, her tense expression, noted the wetness that threatened to overflow from her eyes.

Without a word, he took out his handkerchief and wiped her eyes as if she was a child. "You know I can't bear for you to cry," he whispered. "If I promise not to be such a beast, will you smile for me?"

It wasn't in her to deny him anything when he was being so sweet, even if he had been as cold as ice only a moment before. Her lips parted in a gentle smile and Nikolas touched her mouth with his finger, tracing her lip line. "That's better," he murmured. "You understand why I won't kiss you here, but I want to, very much."

She kissed his fingers in answer, then he saw the jeweler returning and he straightened up, taking his hand away, but his brief attentions had put color in her cheeks and she was smiling hazily.

"Ah, this is more like it," Nikolas said, pouncing on a ring as soon as the jeweler set the tray down before them. He took Jessica's slender hand and slid the ring onto it; it was too big, but she caught her breath at the sight of it. "What a lovely color," she breathed on a sigh.

"Yes, this is what I want," Nikolas decided. The square-cut emerald was not so big that it looked awkward on her graceful hand, and the rich, dark green looked better on her than a thousand diamonds would have. Her golden skin and tawny hair were a perfect setting for her mysterious Egyptian green eyes, and the emerald ring was only an echo of her own coloring. Brilliant diamonds surrounded the emerald, but they were small enough that they didn't detract from the deep color of the gem. He removed it gently from her finger and gave it to the jeweler, who carefully put it aside and measured Jessica's finger. "And a wedding ring," Nikolas added.

"Two," inserted Jessica bravely, meeting his eyes. After a moment he gave in, nodding his permission.

"I don't like wearing rings," he said as they left the jewelers, his arm hard about her waist.

"We're going to be married, Nikolas," she said, turning to face him and putting both hands on his chest. "Shouldn't we try as hard as we can to make a success of our marriage? Or are you going into it with divorce already on your mind?" Her voice quivered at that thought, but she met his dark gaze squarely.

"I don't have anything on my mind except having you," he said bluntly. "Rings aren't important to me. If you want me to wear a wedding ring, then I'll wear one. A ring won't stop me if I want to be free of you."

She nearly choked on the pain that welled up in her chest and she turned abruptly away, fighting for composure. By the time he caught up with her she had managed to pull her cool mask in place again and she revealed nothing of her inner hurt.

When they were in the taxi, she heard him give the address of a well-known couturier and she said quietly, "I don't know what you have in mind, Nikolas, but there isn't time to have a gown made. A ready-to-wear gown will be fine with me."

He didn't even glance at her, and after his gentleness in the jewelry shop, the chill was that much colder. "You're forgetting who I am," he snapped. "If I want a gown ready for you by tomorrow afternoon, the gown will be ready."

There was nothing to say to that, because it was true, but she thought of the people who would be sitting up all night to do the delicate stitchery that had to be done by hand and she knew that it wasn't worth it. But Nikolas had a set to his jaw that dissuaded her from arguing with him, and she sat back in miserable silence.

So far as Jessica knew, Nikolas was not inclined to personally select clothing for his women, but he was recognized the instant he stepped into the cool foyer of the salon. Immediately a tall, slender woman with severely styled ash-blond hair was gliding across the dove-gray carpet toward them, welcoming them to the salon, and if Monsieur Constantinos wished to see anything in particular . . .

Nikolas was all charm, raising the woman's fingers to his lips, his wolfish black eyes bringing a wave of color to her cheeks that owed nothing to artificiality. Nikolas introduced Jessica, then said smoothly, "We're to be married next week in Greece. I managed to convince her only yesterday, and I want to have the wedding immediately, before she can change her mind. But this leaves very little time for the gown, you understand, as we are leaving for Greece the day after tomorrow."

The woman snapped to attention and assured him that a gown could indeed be ready, if they would like to see some models. . . .

A parade of models appeared, some wearing white, but the majority in pastel colors, delicately flattering colors that were nevertheless not virginal white. Nikolas looked them all over carefully and finally chose a gown with classically simple lines and requested it in a shade of pale peach. Jessica suddenly frowned. This was her wedding gown, and she was entitled to wear the traditional white.

"I don't like peach," she said firmly. "In white, please, Madame."

Nikolas glared at her and the woman looked startled, but Jessica stood her ground. It was to be white or nothing. At last Nikolas gave in, for he didn't want to make a scene in front of extremely interested witnesses, and Jessica was taken into the dressing room to be measured.

"You made a fool of yourself, insisting on white," Nikolas said curtly on the way back to the hotel. "Your name is recognized even in France, Jessica."

"It's my wedding, too," she said stubbornly.

"You've already been married, my sweet; it should be old hat to you by now."

Her lower lip trembled at that cut and she quickly firmed it. "Robert and I were married in a civil ceremony, not a religious one. I'm entitled to a white gown, Nikolas!"

If he caught her meaning, he ignored it. Or perhaps he simply didn't believe it. He said grimly, "After your history, you should count yourself lucky I'm marrying you at all. I have to be the world's biggest fool, but I'll worry about that afterward. One thing is for certain, as my wife you'll be the most well-behaved woman in Europe."

She turned her head in frustration, staring out the window at the chic Parisian shoppers, the elegant cafés. She had seen nothing of Paris except fleeting glimpses through the window of the taxi and the gay, mocking lights of the night winking up into her hotel window.

It was too late to back out now, but she was aware of the awful, creeping knowledge that she had made a mistake in agreeing to the marriage. Nikolas was not a man to forgive easily, and not even the knowledge that she was not promiscuous would make him forget that, to his way of seeing it, she had sold herself to him for a price—marriage.

Chapter Nine

here!" Andros shouted to Jessica above the roar of the helicopter blades. "That is Zenas."

She leaned forward to watch eagerly as the small dot in the blue of the Aegean began to grow bigger, then it was rushing toward them and they were no longer over the sea but over the stark, barren hills with the shadow of the helicopter flitting along below them like a giant mosquito. Jessica glanced at Nikolas, who was at the controls, but he didn't acknowledge her presence by so much as the flicker of an eyelash. She wanted him to smile at her, to point out the landmarks on his island, but it was only Andros who touched her arm and directed her attention to the house they were approaching.

It was a vast, sprawling house, built on the cliffside with a flagstone terrace enclosing three sides of the house. The roof was of red tile; the house itself was white and cool amid the shade of orange and lemon

159

trees. Looking down, she could see small figures leaving the house and walking up to the helipad, which was built off to the right of the house on the crest of a small hill. A paved drive connected the house to the helipad, but Andros had told her that there was only one vehicle on the island, an old army jeep owned by the mayor of the village.

Nikolas set the helicopter down so lightly that she didn't even feel a bump, then he killed the engine and pulled off his headset. He turned a grim, unsmiling face to Jessica. "Come," he said in French. "I will introduce you to Maman—and remember, Jessica, you're not to upset her."

He slid open the door and got out, ducking his head against the wind whipped up by the still-whirling rotors. Jessica drew a deep breath to steady her pounding heart and Andros said quietly, "Not to worry. My aunt is a gentle woman; Nikolas is not at all like her. He is the image of his father, and like his father before him he is protective of my aunt."

She gave him a grateful smile, then Nikolas beckoned impatiently and she clambered out of the helicopter, holding desperately to the hand Nikolas had extended to help her. He frowned a little at the coldness of her fingers, then he drew her forward to the group that had gathered at the edge of the helipad.

A small woman with the erect bearing of a queen stepped forward. She was still beautiful despite her white hair, which she wore in an elegant Gibson Girl style, and her soft, clear blue eyes were as direct as a child's. She gave Jessica a piercing look straight into her eyes, then she looked swiftly at her son.

Nikolas bent down and pressed a loving kiss on the delicately pink cheek, then another on her lips. "Maman, I've missed you," he said, hugging her to him.

"And I've missed you," she replied in a sweet voice. "I'm so glad you're back."

With his arm still about his mother, Nikolas beckoned to Jessica, and the look he gave her as she stepped closer warned her to behave. "Maman, I'd like you to meet my fiancée, Jessica Stanton. Jessica, my mother, Madelon Constantinos."

"I'm happy to meet you at last," Jessica murmured, meeting that clear gaze as bravely as possible, and she discovered to her astonishment that she and Madame Constantinos were nearly the same size. The older woman looked so fragile that Jessica had felt like an Amazon, but now she found their eyes on the same level and it was a distinct shock.

"And I'm happy to meet you," Madame Constantinos said, moving out of Nikolas's embrace to put her own arms around Jessica and kiss her on the cheek. "I was certainly surprised to receive Niko's phone call announcing his intentions! It was . . . unexpected."

"Yes, it was a sudden decision," Jessica agreed, but her heart sank at the coolness of the old woman's tone. It was obvious that she was less than happy over her son's choice of a bride. Nevertheless, Jessica managed a tremulous smile, and Madame Constantinos's manners were too good to permit her to exhibit her displeasure any more openly. She had spoken in English, very good English with a slight drawl that she could only have picked up from Nikolas, but as she turned to introduce Jessica to the other people she switched to French and Greek. Jessica didn't understand any Greek, but all of the people spoke some French.

There was Petra, a tall, heavyset woman with black hair and eyes and the classic Greek nose, and laughter shining in her face. She was the housekeeper and her employer's personal companion, for they had been together since Madame Constantinos had come to the island. There was a natural grace and pride about the big woman that made her beautiful despite her almost manly proportions, and a motherly light gleamed in her eyes at the barely concealed fear and nervousness on Jessica's face.

The other woman was short and plump, her round face as gentle as any Jessica could remember. She was Sophia, the cook, and she patted Jessica's arm with open affection, ready to accept immediately any woman that Kyrios Nikolas brought home to be his bride.

Sophia's husband, Jason Kavakis, was a short, slender man with solemn dark eyes, and he was the groundskeeper. He and Sophia lived in their own cottage in the village, but Petra was a widow and she had her own room in the villa. These three were the only staff at the villa, though the women from the village were all helping with the preparations for the wedding.

The open, unrestrained welcome that she received from the staff helped Jessica to relax and she smiled more naturally as Madame Constantinos linked arms with Nikolas and began organizing the transfer of their luggage to the villa. "Andros, please help Jason carry the bags down." Then she removed her arm and gave Nikolas a little push. "And you, too! Why should you not help? I will take Mrs. Stanton to her room; she is probably half-dead with fatigue. You've never learned to take a trip in easy stages."

"Yes, Maman," he called to her retreating back, but his dark eyes looked a warning at Jessica.

Despite the coolness of her welcome from Madame Constantinos, Jessica felt better. The old lady was not an autocratic matriarch, and Jessica sensed that beneath her restraint she was a pert, gentle old woman who treated her son as if he was simply her son, rather than a billionaire. And Nikolas himself had immediately softened, becoming the Niko who had grown up here and who had known these people since babyhood. She couldn't imagine him intimidating Petra, who had probably diapered him and watched his first toddling steps, hard as it was for Jessica to picture Nikolas as an infant or a toddler. Surely he had always been tall and strong, with that fierce light in his dark eyes.

The villa was cool, with the thickness of its white walls keeping out most of the brutal Greek sun, but the quiet hum of central air-conditioning told her that Nikolas made certain his home was always at a comfortable temperature.

She had already realized that Nikolas's tastes were Greek, and the villa bore that out. The furnishings were sparse, with vast amounts of open floor space, but everything was of the highest quality and built to last for years. The colors were of the earth, soft brick tones for the tiles of the floor, over which were scattered priceless Persian rugs, muted greens and natural linen for the furniture upholstery. Small statues in different shades of marble were set in niches, and here and there were vases of incredible delicacy, sitting comfortably in the same room with pottery that had surely been produced by the villagers.

"Your bedroom," said Madame Constantinos, opening the door of a square white room with graceful arched windows and furnishings done in shades of rose and gold. "It has its own bath attached," she continued, crossing the room to open a door and indicate a tiled bath. "Ah, Niko, you must show Jessica about the villa while Petra unpacks for her," she said without pause when Nikolas appeared with Jessica's luggage and set it in the middle of the floor.

Nikolas smiled, his eyes twinkling. "Jessica would probably like a bath instead; I know I would! Well, darling?" he asked, turning to Jessica with the smile still lingering in his eyes. "You have your choice, shall it be a guided tour or a bath?"

"Both," she said promptly. "Bath first, though."

He nodded and left the room with a careless "I'll be along in half an hour, then," thrown over his shoulder. Madame Constantinos took her leave soon after, leaving Jessica standing in the middle of the floor looking about the charming room and feeling deserted. She pulled off her travel-worn clothing and took a leisurely bath, returning to the room to find that Petra had efficiently unpacked for her in the meantime. She dressed in a cool sun dress and waited for Nikolas, but the time passed and after a while she realized that he didn't mean to return for her. He had simply offered to give her a tour to please his mother; he had no intention of spending that much time in her company. She sat quietly on the bed and wondered if she had a prayer of ever winning his love.

It was much later, after a light dinner of fish and *soupa avgolemono*, which was a lemon-flavored chicken soup Jessica found delicious, that Nikolas approached her as she stood on the terrace watching the waves roll onto the beach so far below. She would have liked to avoid him, but that would have looked odd, so she remained at the wall of the terrace. His hard fingers clasped her shoulders and drew her back against him; his head bent down to hers and it must have looked as though he was whispering sweet nothings in her ear, but what he said was, "Have you said anything to Maman to upset her?"

"Of course not," she whispered vehemently, giving in to the force of those fingers and leaning against his chest. "I haven't seen her at all from the time she took me to my room until dinner. She doesn't like me, of course. Isn't that what you wanted?"

"No," he said, his mouth curving bitterly. "I didn't want you here at all, Jessica."

Her chin rose proudly. "Then send me away," she dared him.

"You know I can't do that either," he snapped. "I'm living in torment, and I'll either crawl out of it or I'll pull you down with me." Then he released her and walked away, and she was left with the bitter knowledge of his hatred.

The day of her wedding dawned clear and bright with the remarkable clarity that only Greece had. She stood in the window and looked out at the barren hills, every detail as sharp and clear as if she had only to reach out her hand to touch them. The crystalline sunlight made her feel that if she could only open her eyes wide enough she would be able to see forever. She felt at home here, on this rocky island with its bare hills and the silent company of thousands of years of history, the warm and unquestioning welcome of the dark-eyed people who embraced her as one of their own. And today she would marry the man who owned all this.

Though Nikolas's hostility was still a barrier between them, she felt more optimistic today, for today the terrible waiting was over. The traditional ceremony and the exuberant celebrations that followed would soften him; he would have to listen to her tonight, when they were alone in his bedroom, and he would know the final truth when she gave him the unrivaled gift of her chastity. Smiling, she turned away from the window to begin the pleasant ritual of bathing and dressing her hair.

In the few days that she had been on the island she had already become steeped in the traditions of the people. She had imagined that they would be married in the small white church with its arched windows and domed roof, the sunlight pouring through the stained glass, but Petra had set her right about that. The religious ceremony was seldom performed in the church, but rather in the house of the groom's godfather, or *koumbaros,* who also provided the wedding entertainment. Nikolas's godfather was Angelos Palamas, a rotund man of immense, gentle dignity, his hair and eyebrows white above eyes as black as coal. An improvised altar had been set in the middle of the largest room of Kyrios Palamas's house, and she and Nikolas would stand before the altar with the priest, Father Ambrose. She and Nikolas would wear wreaths of orange blossoms on their heads, the wreaths blessed by the priest and linked by a ribbon, as their lives would be blessed and linked.

With measured, dreamy movements, she braided her hair in a fat single braid and coiled it on her head in the hairstyle that signified maidenhood. In a little while Madame Constantinos and Petra would come in to help her dress, and she went to the closet and took down the zippered white plastic bag that held her wedding gown. She hadn't looked at it before, exercising a childish delight in saving the best for last, and now her hands were tender as she laid the bag on the bed and unzipped it, being careful not to catch any of the material in the zipper.

But when she drew the delicate, lovely dress out, her heart and breathing stopped, and she dropped it as if it had turned into a serpent, turning blindly away with hot tears pouring down her cheeks. He had done it! He had countermanded her instructions while she was in the dressing room being measured, and instead of the white dress she had dreamed of, the creation that lay crumpled on the bed was a pale peach in color. She knew that the salon hadn't made a mistake; she had been too positive in her request for white for that. No, it was Nikolas's doing, and she felt as if he had torn out her heart.

Wildly she wanted to destroy the dress, and she would have if she had had anything else suitable, but she hadn't. Neither could she bring herself to pick it up; she sat in the window with the scalding tears blinding her and sticking in her throat, and that was how Petra found her.

Strong, gentle arms went about her and she was drawn against the woman's bosom and rocked tenderly. "Ah, it is always so," Petra crooned in her deep voice. "You weep, when you should laugh."

"No," Jessica managed in a strangled voice, pointing in the direction of the bed. "It's my gown."

"The wedding gown? It is torn, soiled?" Petra went over to the bed and picked up the gown, inspecting it.

"It was supposed to be *white*," Jessica whispered, turning her small, drowned face back to the window.

"Ah!" Petra exclaimed, and left the room. She returned in only a moment with Madame Constantinos, who went at once to Jessica and put her arm about her shoulders in the first warm gesture she'd made.

"I know you're upset, my dear, but it's still a lovely gown and you shouldn't let a mistake ruin your wedding day. You'll be beautiful in it—"

"Nikolas changed the color," Jessica explained tautly, having conquered the rush of tears. "I insisted on white—I was trying to make him understand, but he wouldn't listen. He let me think the dress would be white, but while I was in the dressing room, he changed the color."

Madame Constantinos caught her breath. "You insisted—what are you saying?"

Wearily Jessica rubbed her forehead, seeing that now she would have to explain. Perhaps it was just as well for Madame Constantinos to know the whole story. She searched for a way to begin and finally blurted out, "I want you to know, Madame—none of the things you've heard about me are true."

Slowly Madame Constantinos nodded, her blue eyes sad. "I think I had already realized that," she said softly. "A woman who had traveled as many roads and known as many lovers as have been attributed to you would have had some of that knowledge in her face, and your face is innocent of any such knowledge. I had forgotten how gossip can spread like a cancer and feed on itself, but you have reminded me and I promise I won't forget again."

Encouraged, Jessica said hesitantly, "Nikolas told me that you were a friend of Robert's."

"Yes," Madame Constantinos acknowledged. "I had known Robert Stanton for most of my life; he was a dear friend of my father's, and beloved of the entire family. I should have remembered that he saw things far more clearly than the rest of us. I've thought many harsh things about you in the past, my dear, and I'm deeply ashamed of myself. Please, can you possibly forgive me?"

"Oh, of course," Jessica cried, jumping to her feet to hug the older woman and wipe at the tears that welled anew. "But I want to tell you how it was, how I came to marry Robert. After all, you have a right to know, since I'm going to marry your son."

"If you'd like to tell me, please do so, but don't feel that you owe an explanation to me," Madame Constantinos replied. "If Niko is satisfied, then so am I."

Jessica's face fell. "But he isn't satisfied," she said

bitterly. "He believes all of the tales he's heard, and he hates me almost as much as he wants me."

"Impossible," the older woman gasped. "Niko couldn't be that much of a fool; it's so plain that you're not a scheming adventuress!"

"Oh, he believes it, all right! It's partly my fault," she admitted miserably. "At first, when I wanted to hold him off, I let him think that I—I was frightened because I'd been mistreated. I've tried since then to explain to him, but he simply won't listen; he refuses to talk about my 'past affairs' and he's furious because I won't go to bed with him—" She stopped, aghast at what she had blurted out to his mother, but Madame Constantinos gave her a startled look, then burst into a peal of laughter.

"Yes, I can imagine that would make him wild, because he has his father's temperament." She chuckled. "So, you must convince my blind, stubborn son that your experience is wholly fictional. Do you have any idea how you might accomplish such a thing?"

"He'll know," Jessica said quietly. "Tonight. When he realizes that I have a right to a white wedding dress."

Madame Constantinos gasped as at last she realized the significance of the dress. "My dear! But Robert—no, of course not. Robert was not a man to wed a young girl for physical gratification. Yes, I think I must hear how this came about, after all!"

Quietly Jessica told her of how she had been young and alone and Robert had wanted to protect her, and of the vicious gossip she had endured. She left out nothing, not even how Nikolas had come to propose to her, and Madame Constantinos was deeply troubled when the tale ended.

"There are times," she said slowly, "when I would like to smash a vase over Niko's head, even if he is my son!" She looked at the wedding gown. "Have you nothing else to wear? Nothing white?"

Jessica shook her head. "No, nothing. I'll have to wear it."

Petra brought crushed ice and folded it in hand towels to make compresses for her eyes, and after half an hour all traces of her tears had gone, but she was unnaturally pale. She moved slowly, all vitality gone from her, all sparkle killed. Gently Madame Constantinos and Petra dressed her in the peach gown and set the matching veil on her head, then they led her from the room.

Nikolas wasn't there; he was already at the home of his godfather, but the villa was filled with relatives, aunts and uncles and cousins who smiled and chattered and patted her as she passed. None of her friends were there, she realized with a start, but then, there were only two: Charles and Sallie. That made her feel more alone, chilled as if she would never again be warm.

Andros was to escort her down the path that led to the village, and he waited for her now, tall and dark in a tuxedo, and momentarily looking so much like Nikolas that she gasped. Andros smiled and gave her his arm; his manner had warmed over the past few days and now he was frankly solicitous as he discovered how she trembled, how cold her hands were.

Nikolas's female relatives rushed outside to form an aisle from the top of the hill down to the village, standing on both sides of the path. As she and Andros reached them, they began to toss orange blossoms down on the path before her, and the village women were there in traditional dress, tossing small, fragrant white and pink blossoms. They began to sing, and she walked on flowers down the path to join the man she would marry, but still she felt frozen inside.

At the door of Kyrios Palamas's house Andros gave her over to the arm of Nikolas's godfather, who led her to the altar, where Nikolas and Father Ambrose waited. The altar, the entire room, danced with candles, and the sweet smell of incense made her feel as if she was having a dream. Father Ambrose blessed the wreaths of orange blossoms that were set on their heads as they knelt before the altar, and from that moment on it was all a blur. She had been coached on what to say and she must have made the proper responses; when Nikolas made his vows, his deep, dark voice reverberated inside her head and she looked around a little wildly. Then it was over, and Father Ambrose joined hands with them and they walked around the alter three times while little Kostis, one of Nikolas's innumerable cousins, walked before them waving a censer, so they progressed through clouds of incense.

Almost immediately the crowded room burst into celebration, everyone laughing and kissing each other, while cries of "The glass! The glass!" went up. The newly married couple was laughingly shoved to the hearth, where a wineglass was turned upside down. Jessica remembered what she should do but her reactions were dulled by her misery and Nikolas easily beat her, his foot smashing the wineglass while the villagers cheered that Kyrios Constantinos would be the master in his house. As if it could ever be any other way, Jessica thought numbly, turning away from the devilish gleam in Nikolas's black eyes.

But he caught her back to him, his hands hard on her waist and his eyes glittering as he forced her head up. "Now you're legally mine," he muttered as he bent his head and captured her lips.

She didn't fight him, but the response that he had always known was lacking. He raised his head, frowning when he saw the tears that clung to her lashes. "Jessica?" he asked questioningly, taking her hand, his frown deepening when he felt its iciness, though the day was hot and sunny.

Somehow, though afterward she wondered at her stamina, she made it through the long day of feasting and dancing. She had help in Madame Constantinos and Petra and Sophia, who gently made it clear that the new Kyria was weak with nerves and not able to dance. Nikolas threw himself into the celebration with an enthusiasm that surprised her until she remembered that he was Greek to the bone, but even with all the laughing and dancing and the glasses of ouzo he consumed, he returned often to his bride and tried to entice her appetite with some delicacy he had brought. Jessica tried to respond, tried to act normally, but the truth was that she couldn't make herself look at her husband. No matter how she argued with herself, she couldn't escape the fact that she was a woman, and her woman's heart was easily bruised. Nikolas had destroyed all of her joy in her wedding day with the peach gown and she didn't think she would ever be able to forgive him.

It was late; the stars were already out and the candles were the only illumination in the house when Nikolas approached her and gently swung her up into his arms. No one said anything; no jokes were made as the broad-shouldered man left the house of his godfather and carried his bride up the hill to his own villa, and after he had disappeared from view, the celebration began again, for this was no ordinary wedding. No, the Kyrios had finally taken a bride, and now they could look forward to an heir.

As Nikolas carried her up the path with no visible effort, Jessica tried to gather her scattered wits and push her unhappiness aside, but still the cold misery lay like a lump in her chest. She clung to him with her arms around his neck and wished that it was miles and miles to the villa and perhaps then she would be more in control of herself by the time they arrived. The cool night air soothed her face and she could hear the rhythmic thunder of the waves as they pounded against the rocks, and those seemed more real to her than the flesh-and-blood man who carried her in his arms.

Then they were at the villa and he carried her around the side of the terrace until he reached the double sliding glass doors of his bedroom. They opened silently at his touch and he stepped inside, letting her slide gently to the floor.

"Your clothes have been brought in here," he told her softly, kissing the hair at her temple. "I know you're frightened, darling; you've been acting strange all day. Just relax; I'll fix myself a drink while you're changing into your nightgown. Not that you'll need a nightgown, but you do need some time to calm down," he said, grinning, and suddenly she wondered just how many glasses of ouzo he'd had.

He left her and she stared wildly around the room. She couldn't do it; she couldn't share that big bed with him when she felt as she did. She wanted to scream and cry and scratch his eyes out, and in a sudden burst of tears and sheer temper she tore the peach gown off and looked around for scissors to destroy it. There were no scissors to be found in the bedroom, however, so she tore at the seams until they ripped apart, then she threw the gown on the floor and kicked it.

She drew a deep, shuddering breath into her lungs and wiped the furious tears off her cheeks. The gesture had been childish, she knew, but she felt better for it. She hated that gown, and she hated Nikolas for ruining her wedding day!

He would be returning soon, and she didn't want

to face him while wearing nothing but her underwear, but neither did she have any intention of putting on a seductive nightgown for his benefit. She threw open the closet door and grabbed the one pair of slacks she had with her and a pullover top. Hastily she snatched the top over her head just as the door opened.

Thick silence reigned as Nikolas took in the tableau of her standing there clutching a pair of slacks and staring at him with anger and fear plain in her wide eyes. His black gaze wandered to the tattered wedding gown on the floor, then back to her.

"Settle down," he said softly, almost in a whisper. "I'm not going to hurt you, darling, I promise—"

"You can keep your promises," she cried hoarsely, dropping the slacks to the floor and pressing her hands to her cheeks as the tears began to slide from her eyes. "I hate you, do you hear? You—you *ruined* my wedding day! I wanted a white gown, Nikolas, and you had them use that horrible peach! I'll never forgive you for that! I was so happy this morning, then I opened the bag and saw that ugly peach thing and I—I— Oh, damn you, I've cried enough over you; I'll never let you make me cry again, do you hear? I hate you!"

Swiftly he crossed the room to her and put his hands on her shoulders, holding her in a grip that didn't hurt but nevertheless held her firmly. "Was it so important to you?" he murmured. "Is that why you haven't looked at me all day, all over a silly gown?"

"You don't understand," she insisted through her tears. "I wanted a white one, and I wanted to keep it and give it to our daughter for *her* wedding—" Her voice broke and she began to sob, trying to turn her head away from him.

With a muttered curse he pulled her to him and

held her tightly in his arms, his dark head bent to rest atop her tawny one. "I'm sorry," he whispered into her hair. "I didn't understand. Don't cry, darling; please don't cry."

His apology, so unexpected, had the effect of startling her out of her tears, and with a caught breath she raised her tear-wet eyes to stare at him. For a moment, their eyes held; then his midnight gaze slipped to her mouth, and as quickly as that he was kissing her, pulling her even closer to his powerful frame as if he could make her a part of himself, his mouth hungrier and more devouring than it had ever been before. She tasted the ouzo he had been drinking, and it made her drunk, too, so that she had to cling to him even to stand upright.

Impatiently he scooped her up in his arms and carried her to the bed, and for a moment she stiffened in alarm as she remembered that she still hadn't told him the truth. "Nikolas . . . wait!" she cried breathlessly.

"I've been waiting," he said thickly, his restless mouth raining kisses across her face, her throat. "I've waited for you until I thought I would go mad. Don't push me away tonight, darling—not tonight."

Before she could say anything else, his mouth closed over hers again. In the sweet intoxication sweeping over her at the touch of his lips, she momentarily forgot her fears, and then it was too late. He was beyond listening to her, beyond the reach of any plea as he responded only to the force of his passion.

Still she tried to reach him. "No, wait!" she said, but he ignored her as he pulled her top over her head, momentarily smothering her in the folds of material before he freed her from it and tossed the garment aside. His eyes were glittering feverishly as he stripped her underwear away, and her pleas for patience stuck in her throat as he dropped his robe and covered her with his powerful body. Panic bloomed in her, and she tried to control it, forcing herself to think of other things until she regained some small measure of self-control, but it was useless. A thin sob tore out of her throat as Nikolas drew her down into the fathomless well of his desire, and blindly she clung to him as the only tower of strength in a wildly shaking world.

Chapter Ten

Jessica lay in the darkness listening to Nikolas's even breathing as he slept, and her flesh shrank when he moved in his sleep and his hand touched her breast. Slowly, terrified of waking him, she inched away from his hand and off the bed. She couldn't just lie there beside him when every nerve in her body screamed for release; she'd go for a walk, try to calm herself down and sort out her tangled emotions.

Silently she pulled on the discarded slacks and top and let herself out through the sliding doors onto the terrace. Her bare feet made no sound as she walked slowly around the terrace, staring at the faint glow of the breakers as they crashed onto the rocks. The beach drew her; she could walk down there without taking the risk of waking anyone, though she doubted that anyone would still be up now. It had to be nearing dawn; or perhaps it wasn't, but it seemed as though she had spent hours in that bedroom with Nikolas.

Depression weighed on her shoulders like a rock. How silly and stupid she had been to think she would be able to control Nikolas even for a moment. If he had loved her, it might have been possible, but the raw truth of the matter was that Nikolas felt nothing for her except lust, and now she had to live with that knowledge.

She walked slowly along the rim of the cliff, hunting for the narrow, rocky path that led down to the beach, and when she found it, she began a careful descent, well aware of the treacherously loose rocks along the path. She gained the beach and found that only a thin strip of sand was above the tide and that the incoming waves washed about her ankles as she walked. The tide must be coming in, she thought absently; she'd have to keep watch on it and climb up before the water got too deep.

For just a moment she had managed to push away thoughts of Nikolas, but now they returned, swooping down on her tired mind like birds of prey. She had wagered her happiness in the battle with him and she had lost. She had given her innocence to a man who didn't love her, all for nothing. Nothing! In the dark, savage hours of the night it had been forced into her consciousness that she had gained nothing, and he had gained everything. He had wanted only the release he could find with her flesh, not her virginity or her love. She felt used, degraded, and the bitterest knowledge of all was that she had to see it through. He'd never allow her to leave him. She had learned to her cost that mercy was not a part of Nikolas's character.

She almost choked on her misery. It hadn't been at all as she had imagined. Perhaps if Nikolas had been tender, adoring, easy with her, she wouldn't feel so shocked and shattered now. Or perhaps if he hadn't been so frustrated, if he hadn't drunk so much ouzo, he would have been more patient, better able to cope with her fright. If, if! She tried to excuse him by telling herself that he had been pushed past control; she told herself over and over that it was her own fault; she should have made him listen before. But after a day of unbroken pain and unhappiness, it was too much for her to handle just now.

A wave suddenly splashed above her knees and with a start she looked about. The tide was still coming in, and the path was a long way down the beach. Deciding that it would be easier to climb over the rocks than to resist the tide, she clambered up on the jagged rocks that lined the beach and began picking her way over them. She had to watch every step, for the moonlight was treacherous, making her misjudge distances. Several times she wrenched her ankles, despite taking all the care in the world, but she persisted and at last, when she looked up, she saw that she was only a few feet from the path.

In relief she straightened and stepped onto a flat rock; but the rock was loose and she dislodged it, sending it skittering down, to splash into the water. For a moment she teetered, trying to regain her balance, but another rock slipped under her foot and with a cry she fell sideways. Her head banged against a rock and instant nausea boiled in her stomach; only instinct kept her clawing at the rocks, trying to catch herself before she fell the entire distance. Her hands tore other rocks loose and she fell painfully, the loose rocks bouncing down onto her and knocking others loose in their turn. She had started a small avalanche and they piled up against her.

When the hail of rocks had stopped, she raised her

head and gasped painfully for breath, not certain what had happened. Her head throbbed alarmingly, and when she put her hand up, she felt the rapidly swelling knot under her hair. At least she wasn't bleeding, as far as she could tell, and she hadn't fallen into the water. She sat for a moment trying to still the alarming sway of her vision and the nausea that threatened. The nausea won, and she retched helplessly, but afterward she didn't feel any better. Slowly she realized that she must have hit her head harder than she had first thought, and her exploring fingers told her that the swelling now extended over almost the entire side of her head. She began to shiver uncontrollably.

She wasn't going to get any better sitting here; she needed to get to the villa and wake someone to call a doctor. She tried to stand and groaned aloud at the pain in her head. Her legs were like dead weights; they didn't want to move. She tried again to stand, and it wasn't until another rock was dislodged by her struggles that she saw the rocks lying across her legs.

Well, no wonder she couldn't stand, she told herself fuzzily, pushing at the rocks. She could move some of them, despite the dizziness that made her want to lay her head down and rest, and she pushed those into the sea where it boiled only a few feet below her.

But some of the rocks were too heavy, and her lower legs were securely pinned. She had made a mess of her midnight walk, just as she had made a mess of her marriage; it seemed she couldn't do anything right! Helplessly she began to laugh, but that hurt her head and she stopped.

She tried shouting, knowing that no one would hear her above the booming of the tide, especially as far away as she was from the villa, and shouting hurt her head even worse than laughing had. She fell silent and tilted her head back to stare at the two moons that swung crazily in the sky. Two moons. Two of everything.

A wave hit her in the face and it cleared her senses for a moment. The tide was still coming in. How high did the tide get here? She couldn't remember noticing. Was it nearly high tide now? Would the water soon start dropping? Smiling wearily, she leaned over and rested her throbbing head on her curled-up arm.

A long time later she was roused by the sound of someone shouting her name. Oddly, she couldn't raise her head, but she opened her eyes and stared through the dim gray light of dawn, trying to see who had called her. She was cold, so cold, and it hurt to keep her eyes open. With a sigh, she closed them again. The shout came again, and now the voice was strangled. Perhaps someone was hurt and needed help. Gathering her strength, she tried to sit up, and the explosion of pain in her head sent her reeling into a tunnel of darkness.

Nightmares tormented her. A black-eyed devil kept bending over her, hurting her, and she screamed and tried to push him away from her, but he kept coming back when she least expected it. She wanted Nikolas, he would keep the devil from hurting her, but then she would remember that Nikolas didn't love her and she knew she had to fight alone. And there was the pain in her head, her legs, that stabbed at her whenever she tried to push the devil away. Sometimes she cried weakly to herself, wondering when it would end and someone would help her.

Gradually she realized that she was in a hospital.

She knew the smells, the sounds, the starchy white uniforms that moved around. What had happened? Oh, yes, she had fallen on the rocks. But even when she knew where she was, she still cried out in fear when that big, black-eyed man leaned over her. Part of her knew now that he wasn't a devil; he must be a doctor, but there was something about him . . . he reminded her of someone. . . .

Then at last she opened her eyes and her vision was clear. She lay very still in the high hospital bed, mentally taking stock of herself and discovering what parts worked, what parts didn't work. Her arms and hands generally obeyed commands, though a needle was taped to the inside of her left arm and a clear plastic line attached it to an upside-down bottle that hung over her head. She frowned at the apparatus until that became clear in her mind and she knew it for what it was. Her legs worked also, though every movement was painful and she was stiff and sore in every muscle.

Her head. She had banged her head. Slowly she raised her right arm and touched the side of her head. It was still swollen and tender, but her hair was still there, so she knew that the injury hadn't been serious enough to warrant surgery. All in all, she was extremely lucky, because she hadn't drowned, either.

She turned her head and discovered immediately that it wasn't a smart move; she closed her eyes against the bursting pain, and when it had subsided to a tolerable ache, she opened her eyes again, but this time she didn't move her head. Instead, she looked about the hospital room carefully, moving nothing but her eyes. It was a pleasant room, with curtains at the windows, and the curtains were drawn back to let in the golden crystal of the sunshine. Comfortable-looking chairs were set about the room, one right beside her bed and several others against the far wall. An icon was set in the corner, a gentle little statue of the Virgin Mary in colors of blue and gold, and even from across the room Jessica could make out the gentle, glowing patience on her face. She sighed softly, comforted by the delicate Little Mother.

A sweet fragrance filled the room, noticeable even above the hospital smells of medicine and disinfectant. Great vases of flowers were set about the room, not roses as she would have expected, but pure white French lillies, and she smiled as she looked at them. She liked lillies; they were such tall, graceful flowers.

The door opened slowly, almost hesitantly, and from the corner of her eye Jessica recognized the white of Madame Constantinos's hair. She wasn't foolish enough to turn her head again but she said, "Maman," and was surprised at the weakness of her own voice.

"Jessica, love, you're awake again," Madame Constantinos said joyously, coming into the room and closing the door behind her. "I should tell the doctor, I know, but first I want to kiss you, if I may. We've all been so worried."

"I fell on the rocks," Jessica said by way of explanation.

"Yes, we know," Madame Constantinos said, brushing Jessica's cheek with her soft lips. "That was three days ago. To complicate the concussion you had, you developed an inflammation in your lungs from the soaking you received, all on top of shock. Niko has been frantic; we haven't been able to make him leave the hospital even to sleep."

Nikolas. She didn't want to think about Nikolas. She thrust all thoughts of him out of her tired mind.

"I'm still so tired," she murmured, her eyelashes fluttering closed again.

"Yes, of course," Madame Constantinos said gently, patting her hand. "I must tell the nurses now that you're awake; the doctor will want to see you."

She left the room and Jessica dozed, to be awakened some unknown time later by cool fingers closing around her wrist. She opened her eyes to drowsily study the dark, slightly built doctor who was taking her pulse. "Hello," she said when he let her wrist down onto the bed.

"Hello, yourself," he said in perfect English, smiling. "I am your doctor, Alexander Theotokas. Just relax and let me look into your eyes for a moment, h'mmm?"

He shone his little pencil flashlight into her eyes and seemed satisfied with what he found. Then he listened intently to her heart and lungs, and at last put away his chart to smile at her.

"So, you've decided at last to wake up. You sustained a rather severe concussion, but you were in shock, so we postponed surgery until you had stabilized, and then you confounded us by getting better on your own," he teased.

"I'm glad," she said, managing a weak smile. "I don't fancy myself bald-headed."

"Yes, that would have been a pity," he said, touching a thick tawny strand. "Until you consider how adorable you would have been with short baby curls all over your head! Nevertheless, you've been steadily improving. Your lungs are almost clear now and the swelling is nearly gone from your ankles. Both legs were badly bruised, but no bones were broken, though both ankles are sprained."

"The wonder is that I didn't drown," she told him. "The tide was coming in."

"You were soaking wet anyway; the water reached at least to your legs," he told her. "But you've improved remarkably; I think that perhaps in another week or ten days you may go home."

"So long?" she questioned sleepily.

"You must wait until your head is much better," he said, gently insistent. "Now, you have a visitor outside who is pacing a trench in the corridor. I will light a candle tonight in thanks that you have recovered consciousness, for Niko has been a wild man and I was at my wits' end trying to control him. Perhaps after he has talked to you he will get some sleep, eh, and eat a decent meal?"

"Nikolas?" she asked, her brow puckering with anxiety. She didn't feel up to seeing Nikolas now; she was so confused. So many things had gone wrong between them. . . .

"No!" she gasped, reaching out to clutch the doctor's sleeve with weakly desperate fingers. "Not yet—I can't see him yet. Tell him I've gone back to sleep—"

"Calm down, calm down," Dr. Theotokas murmured, looking at her sharply. "If you don't want to see him, you don't have to. It's simply that he has been so worried, I thought perhaps you might tell him at least to go to a hotel and get a good night's sleep. He has been here for three days, and he's scarcely closed his eyes."

Madame Constantinos had said much the same thing, so it must be true. Taking a deep breath, she steadied her wildly tingling nerves and breathed out an assenting murmur.

The doctor and his retinue of nurses left the room, and immediately the door was pushed open again as Nikolas shouldered his way past the last nurse to leave. After one shocked glance, Jessica looked away. He needed to shave and his eyes were hollow and red with exhaustion. He was pale, his expression strained. "Jessica," he said hoarsely.

She swallowed convulsively. After that one swift glance, she knew that the devil who had tormented her in her nightmares was Nikolas; the devil had had those same dark, leanly powerful features. She remembered him bending over her that night, her wedding night, and she shuddered.

"You—you look terrible," she managed to whisper. "You need to sleep. Maman and the doctor said you haven't slept—"

"Look at me," he said, and his voice sounded as though he was tearing it out of his throat.

She couldn't. She didn't want to see him; his face was the face of the devil in her nightmares, and she still lingered halfway between reality and that dream world.

"Jessica, my God, look at me!"

"I can't," she choked. "Go away, Nikolas. Get some sleep; I'll be all right. I just—I just can't talk to you yet."

She sensed him standing there by her side, willing her to look at him, but she closed her eyes again on an acid burning of tears, and with a smothered exclamation he left the room.

It was two days before he visited her again and she was grateful for the respite. Madame Constantinos had carefully explained that Nikolas was asleep, and Jessica believed it. He had looked totally exhausted. According to his mother, he slept for thirty-six hours, and when she reported with satisfaction in her voice that Niko had finally woken up, Jessica began to brace herself. She knew that he would be back, and she knew that this time she wouldn't be able to put him off. He had given in to her the last time only because she was still so groggy and he had been tired; she wouldn't have that protection now. But at least now she could think clearly, though she still had no idea what she would do. She only knew her emotions; she only knew that she bitterly resented him for ruining her wedding day, childish though she knew she was being about that. She was also angry, with him and with herself, because of the fiasco of their wedding night. Anger, humiliation, resentment and outraged pride all warred within her, and she didn't know if she could ever forgive him.

She had improved enough that she had been allowed out of bed, even though she went no farther than the nearest chair. Her head still ached sickeningly if she tried to move rapidly, and in any case her painful ankles did not yet permit much walking. She found the chair to be marvelously comfortable after lying down for so long, and she talked the nurses into leaving here there until she tired; she was still sitting up when Nikolas came.

The afternoon sun streamed in through the windows and caught his face, illuminating starkly the strong bone structure, the grim expression. He looked at her silently for a long moment, and just as silently she stared back, unable to think of anything to say. Then he turned and hung the Do Not Disturb sign on the door, or at least she thought that was what it said, as she couldn't read Greek.

He closed the door securely behind him and came around the foot of the bed to stand before her chair, looking down at her. "I won't let you run me out this time," he said grimly.

"No," she agreed, looking at her entwined fingers.

"We have a lot to talk about."

"I don't see why," she said flatly. "There's nothing to say. What happened, happened. Talking about it won't change anything."

His skin tightened over his cheekbones and suddenly he squatted down before her so he could look into her face. His chiseled lips were pulled into a thin line and his black eyes burned over her face. She almost flinched from him; fury and desire warred in his eyes, and she feared both. But she controlled herself and gave him back look for look.

"I want to know about your marriage," he demanded curtly. "I want to know how you came to me still a virgin, and damn it, Jessica, I want to know why in hell you didn't tell me!"

"I tried," she replied just as curtly. "Though I don't know why. I don't have to explain anything to you," she continued, unable to give in to his anger. She had endured too much from Nikolas; she couldn't take any more.

A vein throbbed dangerously in his temple. "I have to know," he muttered in a low tone, his voice becoming strained. "God in heaven, Jessica— please!"

She trembled to hear that word from him, to hear Nikolas Constantinos saying please to anyone. He, too, was under a great deal of tension; it was revealed in the rigid set of his shoulders, the uncompromising lines of his mouth and jaw. She let out her breath on a shuddering sigh.

"I married Robert because I loved him," she finally muttered, her fingers picking unconsciously at the robe she wore. "I still do. He was the kindest man I've ever known. And he loved me!" she asserted with a trace of wildness, lifting up her tangled tawny head to glare at him. "No matter how much filth you and people like you throw at me, you can't change the fact that we loved each other. Maybe—maybe it was a different kind of love, because we didn't sleep together, didn't try to have sex, but I would have given my life for that man, and he knew it."

His hand lifted, and even though she shrank back in the chair, he put his hand on her throat, caressing her soft skin and letting his fingers slide warmly to her shoulder, then downward to cup a breast where it thrust against her robe. Despite the tingle of alarm that ran along her skin, she didn't object to his touch, because she had learned to her cost that he could be dangerous when he was thwarted. Instead, she watched the raw hunger that leaped into his eyes.

His gaze lifted from where his thumb teased and aroused her flesh to probe her face. "And this, Jessica?" he asked hoarsely. "Did he ever do this to you? Was he incapable? Did he try to make love to you and fail?"

"No! No to all of it!" Her voice wobbled out of control and she took a deep breath, fighting for poise, but it was hard to act calm when the mere touch of his thumb on her breast was searing her flesh. "He never tried. He said once that love was much sweeter when it wasn't confused by basic urges."

"He was old," Nikolas muttered, suddenly losing patience with the robe and tugging it open, exposing the silky nightgown underneath. His fingers slid inside the low neckline to cup and stroke the naked curves under the silk, making her shudder with mingled response and rejection. "Too old," he continued, staring at her bosom. "He'd forgotten the fires that can burn away a man's sanity. Look at my hand, Jessica. Look at it on your body. It drove me mad to think of an old man's spotted, shriveled hand touching you like this. It was even worse than thinking of you with other men."

Involuntarily she looked down and a wild quiver ran through her at the contrast of his strong, dark fingers on her apricot-tinted flesh. "Don't talk about him like that," she defended shakily. "I loved him! And one day you, too, will be old, Nikolas."

"Yes, but it will still be *my* hand doing the touching." He looked up again and now two spots of color were spreading across his cheekbones as he became more aroused. "It wouldn't have made any difference how old he was," he admitted raggedly. "I couldn't bear the thought of any other man touching you, and when you wouldn't let me make love to you, I thought I'd go mad with frustration."

She couldn't think of anything to say and she drew back so that his hand was dislodged from her breast. Temper flared in his eyes and she realized that Nikolas would never be able to accept her will over his, even in the matter of her own body. The thought killed the tiny heat of response in her and she threw out coolly, "None of that matters now; it's over with. I think it would be best if I returned to London—"

"No!" he snapped savagely, rising to his feet and pacing about the small room with the restless stride of a panther. "I won't let you run away from me again. You ran away the other night and look what happened to you. Why, Jessica?" he asked, his voice suddenly husky. "Were you so frightened of me that you couldn't stay in my bed? I know that I— My God, why didn't you tell me? Why didn't you make me listen? By the time I realized, it was impossible for me to stop. It won't be like that again, sweet, I promise. I felt so guilty; then, when I saw you lying across those rocks, I thought that you'd—" He stopped, his face grim, and suddenly Jessica remembered the voice she thought had been pure imagination, calling out her name. So it had been Nikolas who had found her.

But his words froze her emotions in her breast. He felt *guilty*. She could think of a lot of reasons he could have given her for wanting her to stay, but few of them would have so insulted her sense of pride. She'd *swim* back to England before she'd stay with him merely to let him assuage his sense of guilt! She wanted to rage at him in her hurt and humiliation, but instead she pulled a mantle of deceptive calm about her and strove instinctively for her mask of cool disdain, so carefully cultivated over the years. "Why should I have told you?" she asked in a remote little voice, ignoring the fact that she had tried to do that very thing for weeks. "Would you have believed me?"

He made a slashing movement with his hand, as if that wasn't important. "You could have had a doctor examine you, given me proof," he growled. "You could have let me find out for myself, but in a manner much less brutal than what you endured. If you'd told me, if you hadn't fought . . ."

For a moment she merely stared at him, astonished at his unbelievable arrogance. Regardless of his billions and his surface sophistication, underneath he was Greek to the core of him and a woman's pride counted for nothing.

"Why should I prove anything to you?" she jeered out of the depths of her misery. "Were you a virgin? Who set you up to judge my character?"

Dark anger washed into his face and he took one long stride toward her, reaching out as if he longed to shake her, but then he remembered her injuries and he let his arms fall. She glared at him stonily as he drew a deep breath, obviously trying to control his temper. "You brought it on yourself," he finally snapped, "if that is your attitude."

"Is it my fault you're a bully and a tyrant?" she challenged, hearing her voice rise with temper. "I tried to tell you from the day we met that you were wrong about me, but you categorically refused to listen, so don't try to throw it all back on me! I should never have come back from Cornwall."

He stood looking down at her, his hard face unreadable, then his mouth twisted bitterly. "I'd have come after you," he said.

She pushed away the disturbing words and sought for control over her temper. When she could speak without any heat, she said distantly, "It's all over, anyway; it's no use crying about what might have been. I suggest a quiet, quick divorce—"

"No!" he gritted murderously. "You're my wife, and you'll stay my wife. I'm a possessive man, and I don't let my possessions go. You're mine, Jessica, in fact as well as in name, and you'll stay on the island even if I have to make you a prisoner."

"What a charming picture!" she cried in sudden desperation. "Let me go, Nikolas. I won't stay with you."

"You'll have to," he told her, his black eyes gleaming. "The island is mine, and no one leaves without my permission. The people are loyal to me; they won't help you to escape no matter how you charm them."

Impotently she glared at him. "I'll make you a laughingstock," she warned.

"Try it, my dear, and you'll find out the extent of a Greek husband's authority over his wife," he warned. "I won't look such a laughingstock when you're sitting on pillows."

"You'd better not lay a hand on me!" she said furiously. "You may be Greek, but I'm not, and I won't be punished by you."

"I doubt if it will be necessary," he said, drawling now, and she knew that he was once more in command of the situation and aware of what he was going to do. "You'll be more cautious now about pushing me, won't you, love?"

"Get out!" she shouted, rising to her feet in a temper that made her forget her tender head, and she was forcefully reminded of her injuries as nauseating pain crashed into her skull and she wobbled on her unsteady feet. Instantly he was beside her, lifting her in his arms and placing her on the bed, easing her down onto the pillows. Through a haze of pain she said again, "Go away!"

"I'll go, until you've calmed down," he told her, leaning over her like the devil in her dreams. "But I'll be back, and I'll take you back to the island with me. Like it or not, you're my wife now and you'll stay my wife." On those final words he left her, and she stared through a mist of tears at the ceiling, wondering how she could endure such open warfare in the place of marriage.

Chapter Eleven

$\mathcal{B}$ut it wasn't open warfare. Nikolas wouldn't allow that, and she was helpless to fight him. The only weapon she had was her coldness, and she used that relentlessly, not giving an inch to him when he came to visit her. He ignored her lack of response and talked to her pleasantly, telling her of the day-to-day happenings on the island and the people who asked about her. Everyone sent their love and wanted to know when she would be out of the hospital, and she found it extraordinarily difficult to keep from responding to that. In the few short days she had been on the island she had been made so welcome that she missed the people there, especially Petra and Sophia.

It was on the morning that she was released from the hospital that Nikolas shredded her self-possession, and he did it so easily that afterward she realized he had only been waiting until she was stronger to take action. When he sauntered into her room and found her already dressed and ready to leave, he kissed her casually before she could draw back, then released her before she could react to that, either.

"I'm glad you're ready," he commented, picking up the small suitcase containing the few clothes he had brought for her stay in the hospital. "Maman and Petra gave me strict orders to bring you back as soon as possible, and Sophia has cooked a special dinner for you. Would you like to have *soupa avgolemono,* eh? You liked that, didn't you?"

"Why don't you save yourself the trouble of taking me back and just put me on a plane for London?" she asked coolly.

"And what if you did go to London?" he returned, looking down at her with exasperation in his eyes. "You'd be alone, the butt of more cruelty than you can imagine, especially if you're pregnant."

Stunned, she looked up at him and he said mockingly, "Unless *you* took precautions? No? I didn't think so, and I confess that the thought never entered my mind."

Impotently she glared at him. She wanted to hit him, and at the same time she melted oddly inside at the thought of having his baby. Damn him, in spite of everything, she knew with a bitter sense of resignation that she still loved him. It wasn't something she would recover from, yet she wanted to hurt him because he had hurt her. She was shocked at the violence of her feelings and she tore her gaze away from him, looking down at her hands.

It took every ounce of her willpower to keep the tears from falling and she said defeatedly, "All right. I'll stay until I know if I'm going to have a baby or not."

"That could take a while," he told her, smiling smugly. "After your fall, your entire system could be out of balance. And I intend to do everything I can to make you pregnant if that's what it takes to keep you on the island."

"Oh!" she cried, drawing away from him, shattered at the thought. Her panic was plain in her eyes as she stared at him. "Nikolas, no. I can't take that again."

"It won't be like that again," he assured her, reaching out to catch her arm.

"I won't let you touch me!"

"That's another right husbands have over wives." He grinned, pulling her to him. "Make up your mind to it now, pet; I'm going to be exercising my marital rights. That's why I married you."

She was so upset that she went without protest to the taxi he had waiting, and she didn't talk to him at all on the drive through Athens to the airport. At any other time she would have been enchanted with the city, but now she was frightened by his words and her head had begun to ache.

Nikolas's own helicopter was at the airport, fueled up and ready for flight, and through a haze of pain Jessica realized that he must have brought her to the hospital in the helicopter. She had no memory of anything after the last time she fainted on the rocks, and suddenly she wanted to know what had happened.

"Nikolas, you found me, didn't you? When I fell?"

"Yes," he said, frowning. He slanted a look down at her and his gaze halted, surveying her pale, strained face.

"What happened then? After you found me, I mean."

He took her arm and led her across the tarmac to the helicopter, walking slowly and letting her lean on him. "At first I thought you were dead," he said remotely, but the harsh breath he drew told her that the memory wasn't something he could handle easily, even now. "When I got down to you, I found that you were still alive and I dug you out from under those rocks, then carried you back up to the villa. Sophia was already up; she was beginning to cook when she saw me coming up the path with you, and she ran to help me."

They had reached the helicopter and he opened the door, then lifted her onto the seat and closed the door securely. He walked around and slid his long frame onto the seat in front of the controls and reached for the headset. He looked at it in his hand, frowning absently. "You were soaked, and shivering," he continued. "While Andros contacted the hospital and made arrangements for transportation from the airport to the hospital, Maman and I stripped you and wrapped you in blankets, then we flew here. You were in deep shock and surgery was postponed, though the doctors were concerned, but Alex told me that you almost certainly wouldn't survive major surgery at that time; your condition had to stabilize before he could even consider it."

"Then I got better," she finished for him, smiling wanly.

He didn't smile in return. "Your responses were better," he muttered. "But you developed a fever, and your lungs were inflamed. Sometimes you were unconscious; sometimes you were delirious and screamed whenever I or any of the doctors came near you." He turned his head to look at her, his eyes flat and bitter. "At least it wasn't just me; you screamed at every man."

She couldn't tell him that it had been him she had feared, and after a moment of silence he put the headset on and reached for the radio controls. Jessica leaned her head back and closed her eyes, willing the throb in her temples to go away, but when the rotors began turning, it increased the pain and she winced. A hand on her knee brought her eye-lids fluttering open and at Nikolas's concerned, questioning gaze she put her hands over her ears to let him know what was wrong. He nodded and patted her leg sympathetically, which made her want to cry. She closed her eyes again, shutting out the vision of him.

Unbelievably, she slept on the flight back to the island. Perhaps there was something in the medication she was still taking that made her drowsy, but Nikolas had to wake her when the flight was over and she sat up in confusion to see what seemed like the entire population of the island turned out for her arrival. Everyone was smiling and waving and she waved back, touched to tears by the warmth she felt from the islanders. Nikolas jumped from the helicopter, yelling something that made everyone laugh, then he reached her side as she released her seat belt and he slid the door open.

With an ease that both frightened and elated her, he reached in and lifted her against his chest. "I can walk," she protested.

"Not down the hill," he said. "You're still too wobbly. Put your arms around me, love; let everyone see what they want to see."

It was true that when she slid her arms around his muscular neck it seemed to please everyone, and several jocular-sounding remarks were made to him, to which he responded with grins and several remarks of his own. Jessica promised herself that she would learn Greek without delay; she wanted to know what he was saying about her.

He carried her down to the villa and straight to his bedroom, for she couldn't think of it as theirs. As he placed her on the bed, she looked around wildly, and before she could choke the words back, she cried out, "I can't sleep here, Nikolas!"

With a sigh he sat down on the edge of the bed. "I'm sorry you feel that way, darling, because you'll have to sleep here. Rather, you'll have to sleep with me, and that's what has you worried, isn't it?"

"Can you blame me?" she questioned fiercely.

"Yes, I can," he returned calmly, his black eyes implacable. "You're an intelligent, adult woman, and you should be capable of realizing that future lovemaking between us will be nothing like our wedding night. I was half-drunk, frustrated, and I lost control. You were frightened and angry and you fought me. The result was predictable and you got hurt. It won't be like that again, Jessica. The next time I take you, you'll enjoy it as much as I will."

"Can't you understand that I don't want you?" she flashed, unreasonably angry that he should so calmly plan on making love to her when she had said he couldn't. "Really, Nikolas, your conceit must be colossal if you imagine that I'd want to sleep with you after that night."

Temper flamed in his eyes. "You can thank God that I know you so well, Jessica, or I'd make you regret those words!" he snapped. "But I *do* know you, and I know that when you're hurt and frightened you strike back like a spitting, clawing kitten, and you have years of practice in putting on that cold mask of yours. Oh, no, darling, you don't fool me. No matter how your pride tells you to resist me, I remember a night in London when you came to me and whispered that you loved me. You were sweet and shy that night; you weren't acting. Do you remember it, too?"

Jessica's eyes closed in horror. That night! How could she forget? And how like Nikolas to remember the secret she had said aloud, thinking that he'd return the sweet words and admit to loving her. But he hadn't, not then and not since. Words of passion had come from his lips, but never words of love. Shaking, she cried out, "Remember? How can I forget? Like a fool I let you get too close to me, and the words were barely out of my mouth when you slapped me in the face with your true opinion of me. At least you opened my eyes, jerked me out of my silly dream. Love isn't immortal, Nikolas. It can die."

"Yours didn't die," he murmured confidently, a smile curving his hard, chiseled lips. "You married me, and you wanted your white gown for the wedding. You wore your hair in the style of a virgin; yes, I noticed. Everything you did shouted that you were marrying me forever, and that's how it will be. I've hurt you, darling, and I've made you unhappy, but I'll make it up to you. By the time our first baby is born, you'll have forgotten that I ever made you shed a tear."

That remark almost made her leap off the bed, and to prove him wrong she promptly burst into tears, which played havoc with her headache. With a comforting murmur Nikolas took her in his arms and lay down on the bed with her to hold her close and whisper soothingly to her, and perversely his nearness did calm her. At last she hiccuped into silence and nestled closer against him, her face buried in his shirt. Out of that doubtful sanctuary she said hesitantly, "Nikolas?"

"Yes, darling?" he muttered, his deep voice rumbling under her ear.

"Will—will you give me a little time, please?" she asked, raising her tear-stained face to him.

"I'll only give you time to recover completely," he replied, brushing her hair back from her temples with gentle fingers. "Beyond that, I won't wait. I can't. I still want you like mad, Mrs. Constantinos. Our wedding night was a mere appetizer."

She quivered in his arms at the sudden vision she had of being devoured by him, as if he were a hungry animal. She felt torn by indecision, loving him but unable to give in to him, to trust him or know what he was about. "Please don't rush me," she whispered. "I'll try; I really will. But I—I don't know if I'll ever be able to forgive you."

One corner of his mouth jerked before he firmed his lips together and said, "Forgive me or not, you're still mine, and I'll never let you go. I'll repeat it as many times as I have to to make you believe me."

"We've made a mess of it, Niko," she whispered painfully, tears filling her eyes again as she used the shortened, affectionate version of his name for the first time.

"Yes, I know," he muttered, his eyes going bleak. "We'll just have to try to salvage something and make our marriage work."

After he had gone, Jessica lay on the bed trying to quiet her confused emotions; she felt so many things at once that she was helpless to sort them out. With part of herself she wanted to melt into his arms and give in to the love which she still felt for him in spite of everything that had happened; the other part of her was bitterly angry and resentful and wanted to get as far away from him as possible. For years, she had suppressed pain and loneliness, but Nikolas had ripped away the barrier of her self-control and she could no longer push away or ignore the aches. Her long-controlled emotions were boiling out of her in a bitter release, and she resented the way he had torn away her defenses.

What a mockery of a marriage, she thought tiredly. A woman shouldn't require defenses against her husband; a marriage should be based on mutual trust and respect, and even now Nikolas felt neither of those things for her. She had thought that when he realized how wrong his assumptions concerning her had been, his entire attitude would change, but she'd been wrong. Perhaps he no longer resented her so bitterly, but he still would not allow her any authority concerning her own life. He wanted to control her, make her every movement subject to his whim, and Jessica didn't think she could tolerate a life like that.

After a time she dozed, and woke to the long shadows of late afternoon. Her headache had eased; in fact, it was gone, and she felt better than she had since the accident. Getting out of bed, she walked carefully to the bathroom, fearing an onset of her headache, but it didn't return and gratefully she stripped off her wrinkled clothing and ran water in the huge, red-tiled sunken tub. Petra had supplied the bathroom with an assortment of toiletries that surely Nikolas had never used, unless he had a hidden passion for perfumed bubble bath, and she poured the liquid liberally into the tub until it had mountains of foam in it.

After pinning her hair up, she stepped into the tub and sank down until the bubbles tickled her chin. She reached for the soap, then gave a frightened squeal as the door opened without warning. Nikolas stepped through, a worried frown creasing his brow, but the frown turned into a grin as he surveyed her where she lay, all but submerged in the bubbles. "Sorry, didn't mean to startle you," he said.

"I'm taking a bath," she said indignantly, and his grin spread wider.

"So I see," he agreed, dropping his tall frame onto the floor by the tub and sprawling out to lean on his elbow. "I'll keep you company, since this is the first time I've been privileged to witness your bath and wild horses couldn't drag me away."

"Nikolas!" she wailed, her cheeks flushing red.

"Now, calm down," he soothed, reaching out to run a finger over her nose. "I promised you that I wouldn't make a pass at you, and I won't, but I didn't promise that I wouldn't get to know my wife and let her become accustomed to me."

He was lying. Suddenly she knew that he was lying and she jerked away from his hand, tears springing to her eyes. "Get away from me!" she cried hoarsely. "I don't believe you, Nikolas! I can't stand it. Please, please go away!" If he stayed, he would take her to bed and make love to her, regardless of his promise. He had only told her that to catch her off guard, and she couldn't submit to him again. Shuddering sobs began to quake through her body, and with a muffled curse he got to his feet, his face darkening with fury.

"All right," he said through gritted teeth. "I'll leave you alone. God, how I'll leave you alone! A man can take only so much, Jessica, and I've had it! Keep your empty bed; I'll sleep elsewhere." He stormed out of the bathroom, slamming the door behind him with a force that jarred it on its hinges, and a second later she heard the bedroom door slam, too.

She winced and drew a shuddering breath, trying to control herself again. Oh, it was useless; this marriage would never work. Somehow she'd have to convince Nikolas to set her free, and after tonight that shouldn't be too difficult.

Nikolas, however, proved himself unyielding in his refusal to let her leave the island. She was aware that he looked at the situation as a battle he had every intention of winning, despite her constant maneuvering to keep a comfortable distance between them. She also saw that his anger at her in the bathroom had been largely staged, for what reason she didn't know. He was irritated that she didn't fall into his arms whenever he touched her, the way she had prior to their marriage, but he had no intention of denying himself the pleasures of her body if he could find the slightest weakness in her resistance. He was simply waiting, watching her carefully, ready to pounce.

The strain of keeping up a front of calmness and serenity before everyone else was telling on her, but she didn't want to distress Nikolas's mother, or even Petra or Sophia. Everyone had been so kind to her—after her release from the hospital she had been coddled shamelessly by the entire household— that the last thing she wanted was to worry them with a warlike atmosphere. By silent, mutual consent, she and Nikolas let it be assumed that he slept in another room because her head still ached and his restlessness interfered with her sleep. As she was still plagued by headaches if she tried to exert herself in any way, the explanation was accepted without question.

Without making a big production out of it, she pretended that she was not recovering as rapidly as she really was, using her physical condition as a weapon against Nikolas. She rested frequently and would sometimes slip away without comment to lie down with a cold, damp cloth over her eyes and forehead. Someone would usually check on her before too long, and in that manner she made certain the entire household was aware of her delicacy. She hated to trick them like that, but she had to protect herself, and she was aware that she would have to take whatever chance presented itself if she was to escape from the island. If everyone thought her weaker than she actually was, she had a better chance of succeeding.

The opportunity presented itself the next week when Nikolas informed them at the dinner table that he and Andros were flying to Athens the following morning; they would spend the night and return to the island the next day. Jessica was careful not to look up, certain that her expression would give her away. This was it! All she had to do was to hide on board the helicopter, and once they had landed in Athens and Nikolas and Andros had left to attend their meeting, she could slip out of the craft, walk into the terminal building, and purchase a ticket for a flight out of Athens.

She spent the evening making her plans; she retired early and packed the essentials she would take with her in the smallest suitcase she had, then replaced the case in the closet. She checked her purse to make certain that the money she had brought was still in her wallet; it was, as Nikolas no doubt felt certain that no one on the island was susceptible to a bribe, and in that he was probably correct. But she hadn't even thought of that, and now she was glad that she hadn't, as he would probably have taken the money away from her if she had tried something like that.

She counted the money carefully; when she had left England to travel to Paris with Nikolas, she had provided herself with enough cash to buy anything she might want, or to cover any emergency she was likely to encounter. Every penny was still there. She wasn't certain that it was enough to purchase a ticket to London, but she could certainly get out of Greece. Even if she could only get as far as Paris, she could telephone Charles and have him wire extra funds to her. Nikolas had control of her business concerns, but she hadn't emptied her bank account, and those funds were still available to her.

Later, when everyone had retired, she would take the suitcase and hide it in the helicopter. From her previous trips in it, she knew that there was a small space behind the rear seats, and she thought that there was enough room for both herself and the suitcase. To be certain, she would take a dark blanket and huddle under it on the floor if she couldn't get behind the seats. Remembering the construction of the helicopter, she thought it would be possible for someone to hide in that manner. The helicopter was built to carry six passengers, and the seats were broad and comfortable. Nikolas would pilot the craft himself, and Andros would be in the seat next to him; there would be no reason for them to look behind the rear seats.

As a plan, it had a lot of drawbacks, relying too heavily on chance and happenstance, but it was the only plan she had and probably the only chance she would have, as well, so she had to take the risk. It wasn't in her mind to disappear forever, but only until she'd had the chance to become certain within herself how she felt about Nikolas, and whether or not she wanted to continue with their marriage. All she asked was a little time and a little distance, but Nikolas wouldn't willingly give her what she needed. Jessica felt that she had been pushed and pulled more than she could stand. From the moment she had met Nikolas, he had maneuvered and manipulated her until she felt more like a doll than a woman, and it had become essential to her that she regain control of her own life.

Once, naïvely, she had thought that love could solve any problem, but that was another dream that had been shattered. Love didn't solve anything; it merely complicated matters. Loving Nikolas had brought her a great deal of pain and very little in the way of happiness. Some women could have been content with the physical gratification that he offered and accepted that he didn't love them in return, but Jessica wasn't certain that she possessed the sort of strength that required. That was what she had to discover about herself: whether she loved Nikolas enough to live with him regardless of the circumstances, whether she could make herself accept the fact that she had his desire but not his love. A lot of marriages were based on less than love, but she had to be certain before she let herself be maneuvered once again into a corner with nowhere to turn.

She knew her husband; his plan was to get her pregnant, thereby tying her irrevocably to the island and to him. She also knew that she had very little time left before he began putting his plan into action. He'd left her alone thus far, but she was nearly fully recovered now, and she sensed with sharpened instincts that he was now entirely unconvinced by her charade and would come to her bed at any time. She knew that she had to escape now if she was to have that time by herself to decide on a calm, reasonable level whether she could continue living with him.

After putting her purse away, she prepared for bed and turned out the lights, not wanting to do anything suspicious. She lay quietly in bed, her body relaxed but her mind alert to every sound in the villa.

The bedroom door opened, and a tall, broad-shouldered form threw a long shadow over her. "Are you awake?" Nikolas asked quietly.

For answer, Jessica reached out and switched on the lamp. "Is something wrong?" She struggled up to prop herself on her elbow, her eyes wide and wary as she watched him enter the room and close the door behind him.

"I need a few things from the closet," he informed her, and her heart stopped as she watched, paralyzed, while he crossed to the closet and slid the doors open. What if he should take the suitcase that contained the clothing she had packed? Why hadn't she insisted that he take his things out of the closet? But that would have looked odd to his mother, and in all honesty he hadn't taken advantage of the situation. What clothing he needed, he took from the closet sometime during the day, and never at times when he might find her undressed.

He took down one of his own suitcases made of dark brown leather, and she drew a shuddering breath of relief. He looked at her sharply. "Are you feeling all right? You look ill."

"Just the usual headache." She forced herself to answer calmly, and before she could stop herself she blurted out, "Do you want me to pack for you?"

A grin slashed the darkness of his face. "Do you think I'll make an unholy mess of folding my shirts? I manage well enough, but thank you for the offer. When I return," he added thoughtfully, "I think I'll take you back to Dr. Theotokas for another examination."

She didn't want that, but as she planned to be gone before then she made no protest. "Because of the headaches? Didn't he say that it would take time for them to go away?"

He took a shirt from the clothes hanger and folded the garment neatly before placing it in the opened suitcase. "Yes, but I think you should be making a better recovery than you are. I want to make certain there aren't any other complications."

Like a pregnancy? The thought sprang without

warning into her mind, and she began to tremble. It was possible, of course, but surely too early to tell. She didn't have any idea herself as yet. But wouldn't it be ironic if she managed to escape Nikolas's clutches and found that she was already pregnant? She wasn't certain what she would do if those circumstances arose, so she pushed the thought from her mind.

Conversation lapsed, and she propped herself higher on the pillow and watched as he completed his packing. When he closed the case and set it aside, he came to sit beside her on the bed. Uneasy at his nearness, she didn't say anything, her eyes unwavering as she watched him. A crooked little smile twitched at his lips. "I'll be leaving at dawn," he murmured, "so I won't wake you up. Will you give me a good-bye kiss tonight?"

She wanted to refuse; yet part of her yielded, held her motionless as he bent down and lightly pressed his mouth to hers. It wasn't a demanding kiss, and he straightened away from her almost immediately. "Good night, darling," he said softly, and putting his hands on her ribcage he eased her down beneath the light covers and began to tuck them in around her. She raised her eyes to meet his and gave him a small, timid smile, but it was enough to still his hands in their occupation.

He caught his breath, and his dark eyes began to gleam as the muted glow of the lamp caught their expression. "Good night," he said again, and leaned over her.

This time his mouth lingered, moving over her lips and molding them to meet the pressure of his. The pressure wasn't intense, but still the contact remained, warm and enticing, his breath sweet and heady with the wine they had had with dinner. Unconsciously she put her hand on his arm and stroked her fingers upward to clasp his shoulder, then on to curve about his neck. He deepened the kiss, his tongue meeting hers and exploring, making exciting forays against the sensitive places he found, and Jessica felt herself drifting into the red haze of sensual pleasure, not yet alarmed by his touch.

With a slow movement he folded the covers down far enough to let the soft curves of her breasts become visible to his avid gaze. He lifted his head from hers and watched as his long fingers slid beneath the thin silk of her nightgown and curved over the rich flesh, then moved up again to catch the strap and draw it down her arm. Jessica made a small gesture of fear, but he was being so slow and gentle that she didn't struggle; instead her lips sought his flesh eagerly, tasting the slightly salty taste of the skin along his cheekbone, the curve of his jaw. He turned his head and their mouths met again, and her eyelashes fluttered closed. The leisurely movement of his hand urged the pink silk slowly lower, baring the upper curve of one breast. Then the delicate rosy nipple was free and his hand left the strap to capture her exposed beauty.

"Now I'll kiss you good night," he whispered and he shifted so that his mouth slid down the arched curve of her throat. He paused, and his tongue explored the sensitive hollow between her neck and shoulder blade, making her shiver with a delight which was rapidly growing beyond her control. She didn't care. If he had only been this slow and tender on their wedding night, perhaps none of their problems would still exist. She lay quietly under his wandering touch, enjoying the delicate sensations and the spreading heat in her body.

Then his lips continued their journey and moved down the satin slope to close hotly over the throbbing bud. She moaned aloud and arched her back, her hand clenched in the rich thickness of his hair as she held his head to her. The gently pulling motions of his mouth set sharp twinges of pure physical desire shooting along her nerve endings. Her trembling intensified, and she started to reach for him; then he released her flesh and lifted his head, drawing back from her.

He was smiling, but the smile was sharp with triumph. "Good night, darling," he murmured, drawing the strap onto her shoulder again. "I'll see you in two days." Then he was gone, taking the suitcase and closing the door silently behind him, and Jessica lay on the bed, biting her lips to keep from screaming in both fury and frustration. He'd done that deliberately, seducing her with his gentleness until she forgot her fear, then not taking her to fulfillment. Were his actions motivated by revenge for the way she'd refused his advances before, or was it all a calculated maneuver to bring her to heel? She rather thought it was the latter, but she was more determined than ever not to give in to him. She would *not* be his sexual slave!

The thought of her escape gave her grim pleasure. He was so certain of his victory; let him wonder what had gone wrong when he found that his wife had fled rather than sleep with him. Nikolas was far too selfish and self-confident; it would do him a world of good to have someone stand up to him every so often.

She set the alarm on the clock for two A.M., then settled down in the bed, hoping she could sleep. She did, eventually, but had had only a few hours of rest when the alarm went off. She silenced it quickly and got out of bed, then used the flashlight that was always in the drawer of the table by the bed to find her jeans, shirt, and a pair of crepe-soled shoes. She inched the closet door open and removed the small suitcase, then went over to the sliding glass doors that led to the terrace. She released the lock with only a faint click, her hands steady as she slid the door open just enough to allow her to slip through the opening. Hastily she switched off the flashlight, hoping no one was up at this hour to see the betraying light.

There was no moon, but the faint starlight was enough to guide her as she avoided the furniture set about the terrace and made her way silently around to the front of the house. She left the terrace and followed the flagstone path which led up the hill to the helicopter pad. She had gone only a short distance when her legs began to ache and tremble with fatigue, an unwelcome reminder that she truly wasn't completely recovered. Her heart was hammering in her chest when she finally reached the helicopter, and she paused for a moment, breathing rapidly.

The door of the aircraft opened easily, and she crawled inside, banging her hip painfully with the suitcase and muttering an imprecation at the unwieldy luggage. She switched the flashlight on again to pick her way between the seats to the rear. The space behind the rear seats was a mere two feet deep, and she found immediately, by trying to curl up inside it, that it could not accommodate both herself and the suitcase. She placed the suitcase on the floor between the last two sets of seats, but decided that it could be seen too easily in that location.

She studied the interior of the helicopter for a minute, then folded herself once again into the hiding place and stood the suitcase between herself and the back of the seat; the seat was tilted forward a little, but not enough to be noticeable, she hoped. The position was cramped, and she wouldn't be able to move at all until they had landed in Athens and Nikolas and Andros had left, but it was the best she could manage. She left the suitcase in position and crawled out, her legs and arms already stiff from the short time she had been crouching there. She had intended to bring a blanket but had forgotten it, and now she promised herself that when she hid herself prior to takeoff she would have a blanket to cushion the hardness of the cold metal.

Elated, she carefully crept down the hill and into her bedroom and closed the sliding door behind her. She could have waited in the helicopter, but she had a cautious hunch that Nikolas might look in on her before he left, and she intended to be snug in her bed; underneath the nightgown, though, she would still have on her clothes.

Then she saw that she would have to remove her shirt if she didn't want it to be visible above the nightgown, and she wouldn't have a chance to put it on again. She would have very little time in which to reach the helicopter ahead of the two men, and she didn't want to waste any of it in dressing. She would keep the shirt on, and pull the covers up under her chin.

She kicked her shoes off and stood them beside the bed on the side away from the door, then lay down to rest. She wasn't even tempted to nap; her blood was racing through her veins in excitement, and she waited impatiently for the faint sounds in the silent house that would indicate that someone was moving around.

The sky was just beginning to lighten when she caught the sound of water running and knew that she hadn't long to wait now. She turned on her side to face the door and pulled the covers up snugly under her chin. Forcing herself to breathe deeply and steadily, she waited.

She didn't hear his footsteps; he moved as silently as a big cat, and the first indication she had of his presence was when the door opened almost without a sound and a thin sliver of light fell across the bed. Jessica concentrated on her breathing and peeped through her lashes at him as he stood in the doorway watching her. The seconds ticked away and panic began to coil in her stomach; why was he waiting? Did he sense that something was out of the ordinary?

Then he closed the door with a slow movement, and she drew a deep, shuddering breath of relief. She threw back the covers and slid her feet into the waiting shoes, then snatched up the dark brown blanket that she had gotten out earlier but forgotten to take with her, and let herself out the sliding doors.

Her heart was in her throat, interfering with her breathing as she ran as silently as she could around the house and up the hill. How long did she have? Seconds? If they left the house before she was inside the helicopter, they would see her. Had Nikolas been dressed? She couldn't remember. Panting, she gained the crest of the hill and threw herself at the helicopter, wrenching at the door. It had opened so easily before, but now it was stubborn, and she fumbled at it for several agonizing seconds before the handle turned and the door opened. She scrambled in and closed the door, throwing a hasty look at the house to see if they were coming. No one was in sight yet, and she slumped in the front seat, limp with relief. She hadn't known that escaping would be so nerve-racking, she thought tiredly. Her entire body ached from the unaccustomed exertion, and her head had begun to throb.

Her movements were slower as she crawled to the

back of the helicopter and tilted the seat forward to allow her into her hiding place. She spread the blanket and curled up in the small space, her head pillowed on her arm. She was so tired that, despite the uncomfortable position, she felt herself begin to drift into sleep, and it wasn't until Nikolas and Andros boarded the helicopter that she jerked herself back to awareness. They had noticed nothing unusual, it seemed, but she held her breath.

They exchanged a few words in Greek, and she gnawed her lip in frustration that she couldn't understand them. Madame Constantinos and Petra had taught her a few words, but she hadn't made much progress.

Then she heard the whine of the rotor as it began turning, and she knew that her plan had worked.

The vibration of the metal made her feel as if her skin were crawling, and already she had a cramp in her left calf. She cautiously moved her arm to rub the painful cramp, glad that the beating roar of the blades drowned out all sound. The noise reached a peculiar whine, and they lifted off, the aircraft tilting forward as Nikolas turned it away from the house and toward the sea that lay between the island and Athens.

Jessica had no idea how long the flight lasted, for her head was aching so badly that she closed her eyes and tried to lose herself in sleep. She didn't quite succeed, but she must have dozed because it was the cessation of noise as the blades slowed that alerted her to the fact that they had landed. Nikolas and Andros were talking, and after a moment they both left the helicopter. Jessica lay there listening to the dying whir of the blades. She was afraid to get out immediately in case they were still in the area, so she counted slowly to one thousand before she left her hiding place.

She was so stiff that she had to sit in a seat and rub her protesting legs before they would obey her, and her feet tingled as the circulation was restored. Retrieving the suitcase from behind the seat, she peered out, but could see no one who resembled her husband; so she took a deep breath, opened the door, and climbed out of the helicopter.

It surprised her that no one paid any attention to her as she walked casually across the tarmac and entered the terminal building. She knew from her own experiences that comings and goings at air terminals were carefully watched, and the very fact that no one stopped her to ask her business made her uneasy. It was still early, and though there were a good many people in the building it lacked the crush of the later hours; the women's rest room was almost empty, and none of the women there noticed her as she slipped into one of the stalls and locked the door, then opened her suitcase and took out her purse and the dress she was going to wear. Marveling at the modern fabrics which didn't wrinkle, she stripped off her jeans and shirt and folded them into the open case, then struggled into panty hose and pulled the dress over her head. The smooth, silky fabric felt good against her skin, and she settled the ice blue garment into place, then contorted her arms behind her back to do up the zipper. Comfortable, classic pumps completed the outfit. She placed her other shoes in the suitcase, then fastened it and picked it up in one hand, together with her purse, and left the cubicle.

She did a quick job on her hair, twisting it up and securing it loosely with a few pins, and added glossy coral color to her mouth. Her eyes stared back at her from the mirror, wide and filled with alarm, and she wished that she had sunglasses to hide behind.

Leaving the security of the rest room, she approached the ticket counter and asked the cost of a tourist class ticket to London. Luckily the fare was well within her means, and she purchased a ticket for the next available flight, but there she was stalled. The next flight wasn't until after lunch, and Jessica quailed at the thought of waiting that long. She would be missed on the island long before that; probably even now it had been noticed that she wasn't to be found. Would they search the island first, or notify Nikolas that his wife had disappeared? If only she'd thought to leave a note telling them that she'd gone with Nikolas! That way, no one would have known that she was missing, until Nikolas returned without her.

Her stomach protested its emptiness; so she went to the restaurant and ordered a light breakfast, then sat at the small table trying to force the food down her tight throat. The thought of something going wrong at this late stage was horrifying.

Leaving most of her meal on the plate, she purchased a fashion magazine and tried to ignore her anxiety as she flipped through the glossy pages, noting the newest styles. A glance at her watch increased her anxiety; surely Nikolas had been notified by now. What would he do? He had endless resources; he could tighten security to make certain that she didn't leave the country. She had to be on that jet before he discovered that she had left the island.

The clock ticked slowly, laboriously on. She forced herself to sit quietly, not wanting to draw attention to herself by pacing or in any way betraying her nervousness. The terminal was crowded now as tourists poured into Athens, and she tried to concentrate on the stream of people. How much longer? It was almost noon now. An hour and a half and she would be on her way, provided that there were no delays in takeoff.

When she felt someone at her elbow, she didn't respond immediately, hoping that it was a stranger, but the utter stillness told her that this was a forlorn hope. Fatalistically, Jessica turned her head and gazed calmly into the stony black eyes of her husband.

Though his face was expressionless, she could feel the force of his anger, and she knew that he was livid. Never before had she seen him this angry, and it took more courage than she had known she possessed to stand before him and give him back look for look, but she did it, lifting her chin defiantly. A savage glitter lit his eyes for a brief second, then he disciplined himself and leaned down to pick up her suitcase. "Come with me," he uttered between clenched teeth, and his long fingers wrapped around her arm to ensure that she did as he had ordered.

Chapter Twelve

*H*e took her out to the parking area, where a dark blue limousine waited; to her embarrassment, Andros sat in the back. He moved to the opposite end of the seat, and Nikolas helped Jessica in, then climbed in beside her. He spoke sharply to the driver, and the vehicle was set in motion.

It was an utterly silent drive. Nikolas was grim, unspeaking, and she had no intention of unleashing his temper if she could avoid it. In a way, she decided that she was grateful for Andros's presence, as it forced her husband to restrain himself. She couldn't even think about later, when they would be alone.

The limousine stopped at the front entrance of a hotel so modern it would have fit in in the middle of Los Angeles more than in a city which had existed for thousands of years. Dragged along like a child in tow, she was forced to match Nikolas's long strides as they entered the hotel and took the elevator up to the penthouse. He probably owned the hotel, she thought wryly.

She was braced for the worst, and it was an anticlimax when he opened the door and ushered her inside the luxurious apartment, said tersely to Andros, "Don't let her out of your sight," and then left without even glancing at her.

When the door had closed behind him, Andros whistled soundlessly between his teeth. He looked at Jessica ruefully. "I've never seen him so angry before," he told her.

"I know," she said, letting out her breath in a long sigh. "I'm sorry you had to be involved."

He shrugged. "He won't be angry with me unless I let you escape from me, and I don't intend to do that. I'm attached to my neck, and prefer to remain so. How did you leave the island?"

"I hid on the helicopter," she explained, sitting down in one of the extremely comfortable chairs and running her fingers over the royal blue upholstery. "I had it all planned, and it worked like a charm— except that the flight to London wasn't until after lunch."

He shook his head. "It wouldn't have made any difference. Don't you know that Niko would have traced you long before your flight landed, and you would have been met as you left the plane? Met and detained?"

She hadn't thought of that, and she sighed. If only she had left that note! "I wasn't leaving him for good," she explained, her voice troubled. "But I need some time by myself to think. . . ." She halted, unwilling to discuss her marriage with Andros. He was much friendlier than he had been before he discovered that she loved Nikolas, but some basic reserve made it difficult for her to be so open.

Andros sat down across from her, his lean, dark face anxious. "Jessica, please remember that Niko isn't a man of compromises; yet he has constantly compromised his own rules since he met you. I don't know what has gone wrong between you. I thought that after the wedding things would be better. Would it make you feel more confident to know that Nikolas must care for you, or he wouldn't act as he does?"

No, that didn't help. Sometimes she thought that Nikolas was capable of feeling nothing but lust for her, and guilt that their wedding night had been such a fiasco for her. Their relationship was so tangled that she wondered if anything could save it now.

"Where did he go?" she asked, her spirit draining from her as she remembered how he had refused to look at her. She had insulted him, deceived him, and he wouldn't easily forgive her.

"Back to the meeting he was attending," answered Andros. "It was urgent, or he wouldn't have returned."

Another black mark against her. He had left an important meeting to collect her, and he would be furious that others knew his wife was attempting to leave him.

"No one else knew," said Andros, guessing her thoughts. "He told me only when we were on the way to the airport."

Thank heaven for small favors, she thought, though she doubted that it would make much difference to Nikolas's temper.

There was nothing to do but wait for him to return; though there were books aplenty in the apartment, she couldn't settle down to read. Andros ordered lunch for both of them, and again she had to force herself to eat. After that, time dragged. She put records on the stereo and tried to relax, a useless effort; instead she paced the room, rubbing her arms as if she were chilled.

The magnificent sun was setting when the door finally opened and Nikolas entered, his dark face still a mask which revealed nothing. He didn't say a word to Jessica but conversed with Andros in rapid Greek. Finally Andros nodded and left the apartment, and she was alone with Nikolas.

Her stomach tightened in anticipation, but still he didn't look at her. Pulling his tie loose from his neck, he muttered, "Order dinner while I shower. And don't even try to leave; the staff will stop you before you reach the street."

She believed him and bit her lip in consternation as he disappeared into one of the rooms that opened off the lounge area. She hadn't explored the apartment, having been too nervous to have any interest in her surroundings, so she had no idea of what the different rooms were. Obediently she lifted the telephone and ordered dinner from someone who spoke excellent English, subconsciously choosing those foods that she had noticed Nikolas particularly liked. Was it a feminine instinct, to soothe away male ire by an offering of food? she wondered. When she realized what she had done, she smiled wryly at herself, feeling a strange kinship with cavewomen from thousands and thousands of years ago.

The food arrived as Nikolas reentered the lounge, his black hair still damp from his shower. He was simply dressed in black pants and a white silk shirt which clung to his body in patches where his skin was wet, leaving his dark skin visible beneath the thin fabric. She watched his face, trying to gauge the extent of his anger, but it was like trying to read a blank wall.

"Sit down," he said remotely. "You've had a busy day; you need to replenish your strength."

The lamb chops and artichoke hearts were the best she had ever tasted, and she was able to eat with an improved appetite despite his hostile presence across from her. She was nearly finished before he spoke again, and she realized that he had waited until then to keep from upsetting her and ruining her appetite.

"I called Maman," he said, "and told her that you were with me. She was frantic, of course; they all were. You'll apologize for your thoughtlessness when we return home, though I managed to gloss over it by telling Maman that you had smuggled yourself to Athens in order to be with me. She was glad that you felt well enough to pursue me so romantically," he finished sarcastically, and Jessica flushed.

"I didn't think of leaving a note until it was too late," she confessed.

He shrugged. "No matter. You'll be forgiven."

She placed her fork carefully beside the plate and gathered her courage. "I wasn't leaving you," she offered in explanation. "At least—"

"It damned well looked as though you were!" he snapped.

"Not permanently," she persisted.

"You're right about that. I would have had you back within two days at the most." He appeared to be on the verge of saying something else, but he bit back the words and said instead, "If you've finished, it would probably be wise if you took your bath now. I'll probably break your neck if I have to listen to your excuses right now!"

For a moment, Jessica sat there defiantly; then she pressed her lips together and did as he had directed. He was in no mood to be reasonable right now, and if she listened to very much more of his sarcasm she was likely to lose her own temper, and she didn't want that to happen. Scenes between herself and Nikolas could quickly become violent and always ended in the same manner, with him making love to her.

She locked herself in the giant bathroom and took a shower, not being in the mood for a long, relaxing bath in the tub. As she toweled herself dry, she noticed a dark blue robe hanging on a hook on the door, and as she hadn't brought a nightgown with her she borrowed the robe and tied it about her. It was enormous, and she had to roll the sleeves up before her hands peeped out. She had to lift the hem in order to walk, and she held the gathered material in her hand as she left the bathroom.

"Very fetching," Nikolas drawled from his reclining position on the bed.

Jessica stopped cold, glaring at him. He had turned off all the lights except for the bedside lamp, and the covers on the bed were turned back. He had also undressed.

She didn't pretend to misunderstand his intentions. Nervously she pushed her hair back from her face. "I don't want to sleep with you."

"That's good, because I have no intention of sleeping."

Her face flamed with temper. "Don't play word games with me! You know very well what I mean."

His black eyes were narrowed as he surveyed her from her bare feet to her disheveled hair. "Yes, I know very well that you have an aversion to sharing a bed with me, but I'm your husband, and I'm tired of my empty bed. It's obvious that if you're well enough to smuggle yourself to Athens, you're well enough to fulfill your wifely obligations."

"You're strong enough that I can't fight you off," she said fiercely. "But you know that I'm not willing.

Why can't you listen to me? Why do you refuse to let me decide for myself how I feel?"

He merely shook his head. "Don't try to throw up a smoke screen of words; it won't work. Take off the robe and come here."

Defiantly she crossed her arms and glared at him. "I wasn't leaving you!" she insisted. "I just wanted some time by myself to—to think and get myself on an even keel again, and I knew you'd never loosen the chains and let me go if I asked you."

"I'm sorry you feel that way about our marriage," he replied in a silky voice, his expression dangerous. "Jessica, darling, are you going to come here, or am I going to have to fetch you?"

"I expect you'll have to fetch me," she stated, not giving in an inch. She tensed all over at the thought of a repeat of his earlier lovemaking, and her face must have revealed the fear she felt because some of the sternness left his expression.

"You don't have to be afraid," he said, uncoiling his length from the bed with a wild grace. Her breath caught in her throat at the untamed beauty of his naked male body, but at the same time she stepped back in alarm.

"No. I don't want to," she said childishly, putting up a hand to ward him off. He merely caught it and used it to pull her close to him, the male scent of him enveloping her and making her feel surrounded by him.

"Don't fight me," he whispered, opening the robe with his free hand and pushing it away from her shoulders to let it drop about her feet in a blue pool. "I promise you won't be hurt, darling. It's time you learned about being my wife, and it's a lesson you'll enjoy."

Jessica shivered, rigid with anxiety, and goose

bumps roughened her skin as he leaned down to press his hot mouth into the tender hollow of her shoulder. She remembered the night before, when he had roused her gently into desire, then left her unfulfilled, a calculated move that had left her feeling both insulted and frustrated. His physical desires were hot and demanding, but his brain always remained alert and cool, unaffected by the wildly shifting emotions that kept her so unsettled. Was this merely another calculated maneuver as he tried to break her spirit, tame her into accepting his authority?

She wrenched away from him, shaking her head in denial. "No," she said again, though she had no hope that he would accept her refusal.

He moved swiftly, lifting her into his arms and carrying her the few steps to the bed. He placed her on the cool sheet and followed her down, his arms and legs securing hers and holding her motionless. "Just relax," he crooned, trailing soft kisses over her shoulder and neck, then up to her trembling lips. "I'll take care of you, darling; there's nothing to be afraid of this time."

Violently Jessica turned her head away from him, and he pressed his lips instead to the line of her jaw, the sensitive shell of her ear. She made a strangled sound of protest, and he murmured soothingly to her, continuing the light kisses as he trailed his fingers over her body, learning the soft slopes and curves and reassuring her that this time he wasn't going to be impatient with her.

She tried to hold herself away from the seductive quality of those light, elusive touches on her skin, but she wasn't cold by nature, and eventually her sense of awareness began to dim and grow hazy. Imperceptibly she began to relax in his arms, and her skin warmed, taking on the flushed glow of a woman who was awakening to desire. Still he lingered over her, stroking and petting her almost as if she were a cat, and finally she let her breath out in a tremulous sigh and turned her head to seek his mouth with hers.

His kiss was slow and deep, passionate without being demanding, and he continued until at last her control broke and she moved eagerly against him, her arms winding around his neck. Excitement coursed through her veins and she felt on fire, her skin burning, and only the touch of his hands and body gave her any relief.

Finally she could stand it no longer and clutched at him with desperate hands, and he moved over her and possessed her soft body with the urgent masculinity of his. Jessica caught her breath on a sob and arched herself beneath him, glorying in the sensation of oneness with him, intent on nothing but the growing, pulsing need of her body that he gently satisfied.

But he wasn't that easily satisfied; she had wounded his arrogant Greek pride in trying to leave him, and he spent the long hours of the night making her admit time and again that he was her physical master. He wasn't brutal; at no time did he lose control. But he aroused her with his insistent, prolonged caresses and forced her to plead with him for release. At the time, she was so submerged in sensuality that nothing mattered to her except being in his arms and accepting his lovemaking. It wasn't until she woke the next morning and looked over at her sleeping husband that a chill ran over her, and she wondered at his motivation.

Had the night been only a demonstration of his mastery of her? Not once, even in the depths of his own passion, had he uttered a word of love. She began to feel that his lovemaking had been as calculated as before, designed only to make her accept his domination; there was also his stated intention of making her pregnant.

She turned her head restlessly on the pillow, aware of a cold knot of misery in her stomach. She didn't want to believe any of that; she wanted him to love her as she loved him; yet what else could she think? Tears slipped down her cheeks as she stared at the ceiling. Charles had warned her from the beginning not to challenge Nikolas Constantinos. His instinct was to conquer; it was part of his nature, and yet she had thrown her own will into opposition to his at every turn. Was it any wonder that he was so determined to subdue her?

Since she had met him, she had been on an emotional seesaw, but suddenly the never-ending strain had become too much. She was crying, soundlessly, endlessly, and she couldn't stop, the pillow beneath her head becoming wet with the slow rain of her tears.

"Jessica?" she heard Nikolas ask sleepily, lifting himself onto his elbow beside her. She turned her head and looked at him, her lips trembling, her eyes desolate. A concerned frown puckered his brow as he touched his fingers to her wet cheek. "What's wrong?"

She couldn't answer; she didn't know what was wrong. All she knew was that she was so miserable she wanted to die, and she wept softly.

Some time later, a stern Dr. Theotokas gave her an injection and patted her arm. "It's only a mild sedative; you won't even go to sleep," he assured her. "Though it's my opinion that rest and time are all that are required to make you well again. A severe concussion isn't something one recovers from in a matter of days. You've overexerted yourself, both physically and emotionally, and now you're paying the price."

"I know," she managed to say, giving him a weak smile. Her tears had slowed, and already the sedative was making itself felt in the form of a creeping relaxation. Was her weeping a form of hysteria? Probably so, and the doctor wasn't a fool. She was nude in her husband's bed; he'd have had to be blind not to know how they had spent the night—therefore the discreet warning about overexerting herself.

Nikolas was talking to Dr. Theotokas in Greek, his voice hard, rough, and the doctor was being very positive in his replies. Then the doctor was gone, and Nikolas sat down on the bed beside her, putting one arm on the other side of her and propping himself up on it. "Are you feeling better?" he asked gently, his dark eyes examining her closely.

"Yes. I'm sorry," she sighed.

"Shhh," he murmured. "It's I who should be apologizing. Alexander has just cursed me for being seven kinds of fool and not taking better care of you. I won't tell you what he said, but Alexander knows how to make a point," he finished wryly.

"And . . . now?" she asked.

"Now we return to the island, and you're to spend your time doing nothing more tiring than lying on the beach." His gaze met hers squarely. "I've been forbidden to share your bed until you've completely recovered, but we both know the concussion isn't the only problem. You win, Jessica. I won't bother you again until it's what you want, too. I give you my word on that."

Seven weeks later, Jessica stood on the terrace and stared absently at the gleaming white yacht anchored out in the bay; unconsciously her hand went to her stomach, her fingers drifting over the flatness. His promise had been scrupulously kept, but it had been given too late. It would still be some time yet before her condition began to show, but already she had seen the little smiles that Petra and Sophia exchanged whenever she was unable to eat any breakfast yet raided the kitchen later with a ravenous appetite. In a thousand ways, she had betrayed herself to the women, from her increased sleepiness to the way she had learned to move slowly to prevent the dizziness which swept over her if she stood abruptly.

A baby! She wavered between a glowing contentment that she was actually carrying Nikolas's child, and a deep depression that the relationship between them hadn't improved at all since they had returned to the island. He was still restrained, cool. She knew that it distressed Madame Constantinos, but she couldn't bring herself to make up to Nikolas, and he wasn't doing any making up, either. He'd made it plain that she would have to take the next step, and she had backed off. If anything, she was more confused than before, with the knowledge of her pregnancy weighing on her. The yo-yo effect the pregnancy had on her emotions kept her unsettled, unable to decide on any course of action. But right now, she was just recovering from a bout of nausea and feeling resentful that Nikolas should have made her pregnant so easily, and she glared at the yacht below.

Andros had brought the yacht in yesterday. Nikolas had worked like a demon these past weeks, both to catch up on his work and to divert himself, but he had decided that a cruise would be a welcome change, and he had sent Andros to the marina where the yacht was berthed to bring it to the island. Nikolas had planned to leave in two days, with

Jessica and his mother along, and Jessica was beginning to suspect that he meant to settle things between them whether she liked it or not once he had her on the yacht. He had given his word that he wouldn't bother her, but he had probably never thought that the situation would last this long.

She resentfully turned away from the sight of the graceful ship and met Sophia's smiling dark eyes as she held out a glass of cool fruit juice. Jessica took the glass without protest, though she wondered how Sophia always knew just when her stomach was upset. A tray with dry toast and weak tea was also brought to her every morning now, and she knew that the coddling would intensify as her pregnancy advanced. The women hadn't said anything yet, knowing that she hadn't informed Nikolas of his impending fatherhood, but she would have to tell him soon.

"I'm going for a walk," she told Sophia, giving the empty glass back to her, and their ability to communicate had improved to the extent that Sophia understood her the first time and beamed at her.

Walking slowly, careful to avoid the sun whenever she could, Jessica picked her way cautiously down the steep path that led to the beach. She was joined by a leaping, prancing Samantha. Nikolas had even had the small dog brought over, and Samantha was having the time of her life, romping with unlimited freedom. The village children spoiled her terribly, but she had attached herself to Nikolas, and now Jessica made a face at her. "Traitor!" she told the dog, but Samantha barked so happily that she had to smile.

She found a piece of driftwood and amused herself by throwing it for Samantha to retrieve, but halted the game when the dog showed signs of tiring. She suspected that Samantha had managed to get in the family way again; Nikolas had reported, laughingly, that he'd seen her being very friendly with a native dog. She sat down on the sand and stroked the dog's silky head. "Both of us, my girl," she said ruefully, and Samantha whined in pleasure.

At length, she began retracing her steps up the path, concentrating on her footing to make certain she didn't fall. She was taken totally by surprise when a gruff voice behind her barked playfully, "What are you doing?" She shrieked in alarm, whirling about, and the sudden movement was too much. She had a glimpse of Nikolas's dark, laughing face before it swam sickeningly away from her, and she flung out both hands in an effort to catch herself as she pitched forward. She didn't know if she hit the ground or not.

When she woke, she was in her bedroom, lying on the bed. Nikolas was sitting on the edge of the mattress, washing her face with a cold wet cloth, his dark face set in stern lines.

"I—I'm sorry," she apologized weakly. "I can't think why I fainted."

He gave her a brooding glance. "Can't you?" he asked. "Maman has a very good idea, as do Petra and Sophia. Why haven't you told me, Jessica? Everyone else knows."

"Told you what?" She delayed, pouting sulkily, trying to put off the moment when she actually had to tell him.

His jaw tightened. "Don't play games with me," he said harshly, leaning over her with determination. "Are you having my baby?"

In spite of everything, a certain sweetness pierced her. There were only the two of them in the room, and this moment would never happen again. A slow smile, mysterious in its contentment, curved her lips as she reached for his hand. With a timeless gesture she placed his palm over her still-flat abdomen, as if he could feel his tiny child growing there. "Yes," she admitted in perfect serenity, lifting her glowing eyes to him. "We've made a baby, Nikolas."

His entire body quivered, and his black eyes softened incredibly, then he stretched out on the bed beside her and gathered her into his arms. His hand stroked her tawny mane of hair, the strong fingers trembling. "A baby," he murmured. "You impossible woman, why haven't you told me before? Didn't you know how happy you would make me? Why, Jessica?"

The heady sensation of his warm body lying against her so dazed her mind that she forgot to think of anything else. She had to gather her thoughts before she could answer. "I thought you'd gloat," she said huskily, running the tip of her tongue over her dry lips. "I knew you'd never let me go if you knew about the baby. . . ."

His gaze went to her mouth as if drawn by a magnet. "Do you still want to go?" he muttered. "You can't, you know; you're right in thinking that I'll never let you go. Never." His tone thickened as he said, "Give me a kiss, darling. It's been so long, and I need your touch."

It had been a long time. Nikolas had been strict about not touching her, perhaps doubting his control if he allowed himself to kiss and caress her. And once Jessica had recovered from her shock, she had missed his touch and his hungry kisses. Trembling slightly at the memory, she turned to him and lifted her face.

His mouth touched hers lightly, sweetly; this was not the type of kiss she had received from Nikolas before. She melted under the petal-soft contact, nestling closer to him and lifting her hand to his neck. Automatically her lips opened and her tongue darted out to touch his lips and move within to seek the caress of his own tongue. Nikolas groaned aloud and abruptly the kiss changed; his mouth became ravenous as the pressure increased. Instantly heat rose in Jessica's middle, the same mindless desire he had roused in her before pride and anger had forced them apart. She ached for him; she felt as if she would die without his touch. Her body arched to him, seeking relief that only he could give.

With a deep moan, Nikolas lost control. Every muscle in his big body was shaking as he opened her dress and removed it. The wild light in his eyes told her that he might hurt her if she resisted, reminding her for a stricken moment of their wedding night, but then that frightening vision faded and she moved against him. Her own shaking fingers unbuttoned his shirt, her lips searching across his hairy chest and making his breath catch. By the time she reached for his belt, his hand was there to help her and impatiently he shed his pants and moved over her.

His mouth was drink to a woman dying of thirst; his hands created ecstasy wherever they touched. Jessica gave herself to him simply, sweetly, pliant to his every whim, and he rewarded her tenfold with his care of her, his hungry enjoyment of her. She loved this man, loved him with all her heart, and suddenly that was all that mattered.

When she floated back to earth, she was lying in his arms, her head pillowed on his shoulder while he lazily stroked her body as one would a cat. Smiling, Jessica lifted her head to look at him and found that he was smiling, too, a triumphant, contented smile. His black eyes were sleepy with satiation as he met her gaze. "I had no idea pregnant women were so erotic," he drawled, and a fiery blush burned her face.

"Don't you dare tease me now!" she protested,

not wanting anything to spoil the golden glow that still enveloped her.

"But I'm not teasing. You were desirable before, God knows, but now that I know you have my child inside you, I don't want to turn you loose for even a moment." His deep voice went even deeper, became thick. "I don't think I can stay away from you, Jess."

Silently she played with the curls of hair on his chest. This afternoon had changed everything, not least of all her own attitude toward him. She loved him, and she was helpless before that fact. She had to put away her resentment and concentrate on that love, or she wouldn't have a life worth living, because she was bound mind and body to this man. Perhaps he didn't love her, but he was certainly not indifferent toward her. She would give him her love, wrap him about so tightly with the tender bonds of her heart that someday he would come to love her, too. And she had a powerful weapon in the child she carried; Nikolas would adore the baby.

A gnawing worry had been lifted from her mind. Since their return to the island, she had been terrified that he would make love to her, haunted by her contradictory but still bitter memories of their wedding night and the one other night she had spent with him. This afternoon, in the golden sunlight, he had proved to her that lovemaking could be sweet, too, and he had satisfied her with all the skill of an experienced lover. She knew now that with time those bitter memories would fade, lost in the newer memories of nights in his arms.

"No more empty nights," he growled, echoing her thoughts. He leaned over her, and his dark face was hard, almost brutal with a resurgence of his desire; unfortunately she was still thinking of their wedding night, and she gasped in alarm when she saw his face looking so much as he had looked then. Before she could stop herself, her hands were pushing at his shoulders, and she had cried out, "Don't touch me!"

He jerked back as if he had been slapped, his face going pale.

"Don't worry about that," he said tightly, swinging off the bed and grabbing up his pants. "I've done everything I can think of to make it up to you, and you've thrown it all back in my face. I have no more arguments, Jessica, no more persuasions. I'm tired, damn it, tired of—" He broke off and jerked his pants on, and Jessica came out of her frozen horror at what she had done.

"Nikolas, wait—it isn't—"

"I don't give a damn what it isn't!" he ripped out savagely, his jaw set like granite. "I won't bother you again." He slammed out of the bedroom without looking at her again and Jessica lay on the bed, stunned by the violence of his reaction and by the raw emotion that had been in his voice. She had hurt him, something she hadn't thought possible. Nikolas had always seemed so tough, so impervious to anything she said or did, except to be angry when she defied him. But he had his pride, too; perhaps he had finally tired of a woman who resisted him at every turn. The thought made her shrink inside, thinking of being without his absorbing interest in everything she did, his open appreciation of her body.

She left the bed, too, and pulled on her robe. Restlessly, miserably, she paced the room. How *could* she have done that to him? Just when she had admitted that she needed him, she had let her silly fears drive him away and she was totally lost without him. What would she do without his arrogant strength to bolster her when she was depressed or upset? From the day they had met he had supported her, protected her.

Her head had begun to throb and she rubbed her temples abstractedly. At last she gathered up her courage and pulled on her clothing with trembling hands. She had to find Nikolas and make him listen, explain why she had pushed him away.

When she entered the living room, Madame Constantinos was there and she looked up from her book as Jessica entered. "Are you all right, my dear?" she asked in her soft French, her sweet face worried.

"Yes," Jessica muttered. "I— Do you know where Nikolas is, Maman?"

"Yes, he and Andros have locked themselves in the study with strict orders not to be disturbed. Andros is flying to New York tomorrow and they are finalizing a merger."

Andros was handling that? Jessica passed a shaking hand over her eyes. Nikolas should have been handling that merger, she knew, but he was delegating the responsibility to Andros so he could take time to be with her on the yacht. How could she have been so blind?

"Is anything wrong?" Madame Constantinos asked worriedly.

"Yes—no. Yes, there is. We've had a quarrel," Jessica confessed. "I need to see him. He misunderstood something that I said."

"M'mmmm, I see," said his mother. She looked at Jessica with those clear blue eyes. "You told him of the child, then?"

Evidently her condition was well-known to all the women of the household, she reflected. She sat down and sighed wearily. "Yes. But that isn't why he's angry."

"No, of course not. Nikolas would never be angry at the thought of becoming a father," mused Madame Constantinos, smiling a little. "He is undoubtedly as proud as a peacock."

"Yes," Jessica admitted huskily, remembering the look on his face when she had told him of the baby.

Madame Constantinos was looking out the glass doors of the terrace, smiling a little. "So Niko is angry and upset, is he? Let him alone for tonight, my dear. He probably wouldn't listen to you anyway, right now, so let him stew in his own misery for a little while. That is a small-enough punishment for the misery he has caused you. You've never said why you were on the beach so early in the morning, my dear, and I haven't liked to ask, but I do have a fairly accurate picture of what happened that night. Yes, let Niko worry for tonight."

Tears welled in Jessica's eyes. "It wasn't all his fault, Maman," she defended Nikolas. She felt as if she would die. She loved him, and she had driven him away.

"Don't fret," Madame Constantinos advised serenely. "You cannot think clearly now. Tomorrow everything will be better, you'll see."

Yes, thought Jessica, gulping back her tears. Tomorrow she would try to make up to Nikolas for her past coldness, and she didn't dare think what she would do if he turned away from her.

Chapter Thirteen

$\mathscr{B}$y the time morning came, Jessica was pale with her own unhappy thoughts. She wanted only to heal the breach between her and Nikolas, and she was unsure how to go about it or if he even wanted to mend things between them. She was in agony from the need to see him and explain, to touch him; more than anything she needed to feel his arms about her and hear his deep voice muttering love words to her. She loved him! Perhaps there was no rhyme or reason to it, but what did that matter? She'd known from the first that he was the only man who could conquer the defenses she'd built about herself and she was tired of denying her love.

She dressed hurriedly, without regard for how she looked, and merely brushed her hair, then left it hanging down her back. As she rushed into the living room she saw Madame Constantinos sitting on the terrace and she went through the glass door to greet her. "Where is Niko, Maman?" she asked in a trembling voice.

"He's on board the yacht," the older woman answered. "Sit down, child; have your breakfast with me. Sophia will bring something light. Have you been ill this morning?"

Surprisingly she hadn't. That was the only good thing about this morning that she could see. "But I must see Nikolas as soon as possible," she insisted.

"All in good time. You cannot talk to him now, so you might as well have your breakfast. You must take care of the baby, dear."

Reluctantly Jessica sat down, and in just a moment Sophia appeared with a tray. Smiling, she set out a light breakfast for Jessica. In the halting Greek that Jessica had acquired in the weeks she'd been on the island she thanked Sophia and was rewarded by a motherly pat of approval.

Gulping, Jessica chewed at a roll, trying to force it past the lump in her throat. Far below them she could see the white gleam of the yacht; Nikolas was there, but he might as well be a thousand miles away. There was no way she could get out to him unless one of the fishermen would take her, and for that she would have to walk to the village. It wasn't such a long walk, and before, she would have done it without a second thought, but her pregnancy had badly undermined her stamina and she was hesitant about making it that far in the fierce heat. As Madame Constantinos had said, she had to take care of the precious life inside her. Nikolas would hate her if she did anything that could harm his child.

After she'd eaten enough to satisfy both her mother-in-law and Sophia, and had pushed the tray away, Madame Constantinos said quietly, "Tell me, dear, do you love Niko?"

How could she ask? wondered Jessica miserably.

It must be evident in every word she'd said since Nikolas had stormed out of her bedroom the day before. But Madame Constantinos's soft blue eyes were on her and she admitted in a strained whisper, "Yes! But I've ruined it—he'll never forgive me for what I said to him! If he loved me, it might be different—"

"How do you know that he doesn't love you?" demanded the older woman.

"Because all he's been concerned with since we met was going to bed," Jessica confessed in deep depression. "He says he wants me—but he's never said that he loves me."

"Ah, I see," said Madame Constantinos, nodding her white head knowingly. "Because he's never told you the sky is blue, you know that it can't possibly be that color! Jessica, my dear, open your eyes! Do you truly think Niko is so weak in character that he would be a slave to his lust? He wants you, yes— physical desire is a part of love."

Jessica didn't dare hope that it could be true that Nikolas loved her; on too many occasions he had totally ignored her feelings and she said as much to Madame Constantinos.

"I never said he is an amiable man," the other woman retorted. "I'm speaking from personal experience. Niko is the image of his father; they could be one and the same man. It wasn't always comfortable, being Damon's wife. I had to do everything his way or he would fly into a rage, and Niko is the same. He is so strong that sometimes he fails to understand that most people do not have that same strength, that he needs to soften his approach."

"But your husband loved you," Jessica pointed out softly, her eyes trained on the remote gleam of the yacht on the crystalline sea.

"So he did. But we had been married for six years

241

before he told me so, and then only because I was
suffering from the loss of our second child, a still-
birth. When I asked him how long he had loved me,
he looked at me in amazement and said, 'From the
first. How can a woman be so blind? Never doubt
that I love you, even when the words aren't said.'
And so it is with Niko.'' Quietly, her clear blue eyes
on Jessica, Madame Constantinos said again, "Yes,
Niko loves you.''

Jessica went even paler, shaken at the wild surge
of hope that shot through her. Did he love her?
Could he *still* love her, after yesterday?

"He loves you,'' reassured his mother. "I know
my son, as I knew my husband. Niko lost his head
over you; I have seen him look at you with such
yearning in his eyes that it took my breath away, for
he is a strong man and he doesn't love lightly.''

"But—but the things he's said,'' protested Jessica
shakily, still not daring to let herself hope.

"Yes, I know. He's a proud man, and he was
angry with himself that he couldn't control his need
for you. It is partly my fault, this trouble between
you and Niko. He loves me, and I was upset when I
thought my dear friend Robert had married a gold-
digger. Niko wanted to protect me, but he couldn't
make himself leave you alone. And you, Jessica,
were too proud to tell him the truth.''

"I know,'' said Jessica softly, and tears welled in
her eyes. "And I treated him so badly yesterday! I've
ruined it, Maman; he'll never forgive me now.'' The
tears dripped from her lashes as she remembered the
look that had been in Nikolas's eyes as he'd left her
bedroom. She wanted to die. She felt as if she'd
smashed paradise with her own hands.

"Don't fret. If you can forgive him for his pride,
my dear, he'll forgive you for yours.''

Jessica gasped at the thrust, then admitted to

herself the truth of it. She had used her pride to hold Nikolas away, and now she was paying for it.

Madame Constantinos placed her hand on Jessica's arm. "Niko is leaving the yacht now," she said gently. "Why don't you go to meet him?"

"I—yes," gulped Jessica, getting to her feet.

"Be careful," called Madame Constantinos after her. "Remember my grandchild!".

Her eyes on the small rowboat steadily narrowing the gap between it and the beach, Jessica made her way down the path that led to the water. She went down it with a hammering heart, wondering if Madame Constantinos was right that Nikolas truly loved her. Thinking back, it seemed to her that he did—or had. If only she hadn't ruined it!

Nikolas had beached the rowboat and was securing it against the tide when she walked across the sand up to him. He wore only a pair of blue cut-off jeans and his nearly nude, muscular body rippled with lithe grace as he moved. She caught her breath in sheer admiration and stopped in her tracks.

Nikolas straightened and saw her. His black eyes were impossible to read as he stood there looking at her, and she drew in a quivering breath. He wouldn't make the first move, she knew; she'd have to do it. Taking her courage in both hands, she said quietly, "Nikolas, I love you. Can you possibly forgive me?"

Something flickered in the black depths of his eyes, then was gone. "Of course," he said simply, and walked toward her.

When he was so close that she could smell the clean sweat of his body, he stopped and asked, "Why?"

"Your mother opened my eyes," she said, swallowing with some difficulty. Her heart was lodged in her throat and was pounding so hard she could barely speak. He wasn't going to make it easy for her, she could see. "She made me realize that I've been allowing my pride to ruin my life. I—I love you, and even if you don't love me, I want to spend the rest of my life with you. I hope you love me; Maman thinks you do, but even if you c-can't love me, it doesn't matter."

He shoved his fingers through his black hair, his face suddenly grim and impatient. "Are you blind?" he demanded roughly. "All of Europe knew I took one look at you and went mad. Do you think I'm such a slave to lust that I'd have pursued you so single-mindedly if I'd only wanted you for sex?"

Her heart leaped wildly as he spoke words that were so similar to those his mother had used. So Madame Constantinos did know her son! And as she'd said, Niko was much like his father. She reached out shaking hands and her fingers clutched at the warm skin that covered his ribs. "I love you," she whispered shakily. "How can you ever forgive me for being so blind and stupid?"

A quiver ran through his entire body, and with a deep groan, he snatched her to him, burying his face in her tangled hair. "There's no question of forgiving you," he muttered fiercely. "If you can forgive me, if you can still love me after the way I've hounded you so mercilessly, how can I hold a grudge against you? Besides, my life won't be worth living if I let you go. I love you." Then he lifted his head and repeated, "I love you."

Her entire body began to quiver as she heard his deep voice at last saying those words, and once he had admitted it, he kept on saying it, over and over, while she clung to him with desperate strength, her face buried in the warm, curly hair that covered his chest. He cupped her chin in his palm and turned her face up to his and she was engulfed in his hungry, possessive kiss. Wild little tingles began to shoot along her nerves and she stood on tiptoe to press herself against him, her arms sliding up to twine about his neck. His firm, warm skin beneath her fingers made her feel drunk and now she no longer wanted to resist him; she responded to him without reserve. At last she could indulge her own need to touch him; to stroke his darkly tanned skin and bite sensuously at his lips. A deep groan came from his chest as she did exactly that, and the next moment he had scooped her up in his arms and was striding across the sand.

"Where are you taking me?" she whispered, trailing her lips across his shoulder, and he answered her in a strained voice.

"Over here, to where the rocks hide us from view." And in a moment they were surrounded by the rocks and he carefully placed her on the sun-warmed sand. Despite the urgency she sensed in him, he was gentle as he made love to her, holding himself back, as if he feared hurting her. His skilled, patient attention carried her to rapture, and when she floated back to earth, she knew that their lovemaking and been clean and healing, wiping out all of the pain and anger of the past months. It had sealed the pact of their confessed love, made them truly man and wife. Clasped tightly in his arms, her face buried against his heaving chest, she whispered, "All of this time wasted! If only I'd told you—"

"Shhh," he interrupted, stroking her hair. "No self-recriminations, darling, because I'm not free from guilt either, and I'm not good at admitting when I'm wrong." His strong mouth curved into a wry smile and he moved his hand to her back, the stroking motion continuing as if she was a cat. "I understand now why you were so wary of me, but at the time every rejection was like a slap in the face," he continued softly. "I wanted to leave you alone;

you'll never know how much I wanted to be able to walk away and forget about you, and it made me furious that I couldn't. I'm not used to anyone having that kind of power over me," he confessed in self-mockery. "I couldn't admit that I'd finally been defeated; I did everything I could to get the upper hand again, to try to manage my emotions, but nothing worked, not even Diana."

Jessica gasped at his audacity in even mentioning that name to her and she raised her head from his chest to glare at him jealously. "Yes, what about Diana?" she asked sharply.

"Ouch," he winced, flicking the tip of her nose with a long brown finger. "I've opened my bloody mouth when I should've kept it shut, haven't I?" But his black eyes sparkled and she knew that he was enjoying her jealousy.

To get back at him, she refused to be put off. "Yes, you did," she agreed. "Tell me about Diana. That night you said you'd only kissed her once, is that true?"

"Within reason," he hedged.

Furious, she clenched her fist and struck him in the stomach with all her strength, which wasn't enough to really hurt him but which made him grunt. "Hey!" he protested, grabbing her fist and holding it. But he was laughing, a carefree laugh that she'd never heard from him before. He looked exultant, he looked happy, and that made her even more jealous. "Niko," she bit out, "tell me!"

"All right," he said, his laughter fading to a faint smile. His black eyes watched her sharply as he admitted, "I meant to take her. She was willing, and she was balm to a battered ego. Diana and I had a brief affair some months before I met you, and she made it clear that she wanted to resume our relationship. You had me so confused, so frustrated, that I couldn't think of anything but trying to break the hold you had on me. You wouldn't let me have you, but I kept coming back for more of that delicate cold shoulder and I was furious with myself. You acted as if you couldn't stand my touch, while Diana made it obvious that she wanted me. And I wanted a responsive woman in my arms, but when I began kissing her, it just wasn't right. She wasn't you, and I didn't want her. I wanted only you, even if I couldn't admit to myself just then that I loved you."

His explanation hardly mollified her, but as he still held her fist and her other arm was effectively pinned to her side by his encircling arm, she couldn't take out her anger on him physically. She still glared at him as she ordered, "You're not to kiss another woman again, do you hear? I won't stand for it!"

"I promise," he murmured. "I'm all yours, darling; I have been from the moment you walked across my office toward me, if you'd only wanted me. But I admit that I like that green fire in your eyes; you're beautiful when you're jealous."

His words were accompanied by a wickedly charming grin that accomplished its purpose, for she melted at the look of loving ownership he gave her. "I suppose it tickles your ego that I'm jealous?" she asked, letting herself relax against him.

"Of course. I went through torture, I've been so jealous of you; it's only fair that you be a little jealous, too."

He followed his admission with a searching kiss that had her flowing against him; it was as if her desire for him, so long denied, had burst out of control and she couldn't hold back her pleasure. Like an animal he sensed that and took advantage of it, deepening his kiss, stroking her body with sure, knowing hands. "You're beautiful," he whispered raggedly. "I've dreamed so many times of having you like this; I don't want to let you go for even a minute."

"But we have to," Jessica replied dreamily, her green eyes sleepy with love and need. "Maman will be waiting for us."

"Then I suppose we'd better return," Nikolas growled, sitting up and raising her with an arm behind her back. "I wouldn't like for her to send someone looking for us. And you *are* sleepy, aren't you?"

"Sleepy?" she asked, startled.

"You won't be able to stay awake, will you?" he continued, his black eyes sparkling. "You'll have to take a nap."

"Oh!" she exclaimed, her eyes widening as understanding dawned. "I believe you're right; I'm so sleepy I won't be able to stay awake until lunch."

He laughed and helped her dress, and hand in hand they walked up the path. Holding his strong hand tightly, Jessica felt the golden glow of love inside her expand until it included the whole world. For the first time in her life everything was as it should be; she loved Nikolas and he loved her, and already she carried his child. She would tell him the full story of her marriage, explain why she had hidden behind the lies others had told, even from him, but it would make no difference to their love, she knew. In deep contentment she asked, "When did you admit to yourself that you love me?"

"When you were in Cornwall," he admitted gruffly, his fingers tightening. He stopped and turned to face her and his dark face had a grim expression as he remembered. "It was two days before Charles deigned to tell me where you'd gone, and I was on the verge of insanity before he decided I'd been punished enough. I'd spent two days trying to get you on the phone, waiting hours outside your house for you to come home. I kept thinking of the things I'd said to you, remembering the look in your eyes as you left, and I was in a cold sweat thinking I'd lost you. That was when I knew I loved you, because the thought of not seeing you again was agony."

She looked at him in surprise. If he'd loved her that early, why had he insisted on those insulting conditions in the prenuptial agreement? She asked him as much, her voice troubled, and in response to the echo of pain he saw in her eyes, he pulled her into his arms and laid his cheek on her head.

"I was in pain, and I lashed out," he muttered. "I'm sorry, darling, I'll have that damned thing torn up. But I kept thinking that you were holding out for a ring so you could get your hands on my money, and it drove me wild because I loved you so much I had to have you, even thinking all you wanted was money."

"I've never wanted your money. I'm even glad you took control of my money, because I was furious with you for bullying me into taking such a large sum for the shares of ConTech when I didn't want it."

"I know that now, but at the time I thought that that was *exactly* what you wanted. My eyes were opened on our wedding night, and when I woke up and you were gone—" He broke off the sentence and closed his eyes, his expression tormented.

"Don't think of that," she said gently. "I love you."

His eyes opened and he looked at her, the clear depths of her eyes shining with the love she felt. "Even when I'm mad with jealousy and frustration, I still have a spark of sanity left," he said, his mouth curving in amusement. "I still had the sense to make you my wife." He leaned down and swept her up in his arms. "Maman is waiting for us. Let's give her the good news, then take that nap. I'll take you home, love"—and he started up the path to their home, his stride long and effortless as he carried her. Jessica curled her arms about his neck and rested against him, knowing she was safe in the strength of his love.

**Silhouette Books
is proud to present
our best authors,
their best books...
and the best in
your reading pleasure!**

Throughout 1993, look for exciting books
by these top names in contemporary
romance:

CATHERINE COULTER—
Aftershocks in February

FERN MICHAELS—
Nightstar in March

DIANA PALMER—
Heather's Song in March

ELIZABETH LOWELL
Love Song for a Raven in April

SANDRA BROWN
(previously published under
the pseudonym Erin St. Claire)—
Led Astray in April

LINDA HOWARD—
All That Glitters in May

When it comes to passion,
we wrote the book.

Silhouette®   BOBT1RR

A romantic collection that
will touch your heart....

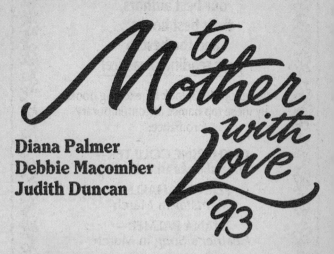

to Mother with Love '93

Diana Palmer
Debbie Macomber
Judith Duncan

As part of your annual tribute to
motherhood, join three of Silhouette's
best-loved authors as they celebrate the
joy of one of our most precious gifts—
mothers.

Available in May at your favorite retail outlet.

Only from 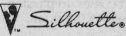 *Silhouette*®

—where passion lives.

If you've been looking for something a little bit different,
a little bit spooky, let Silhouette Books take you on
a journey to the dark side of love with

Every month, Silhouette will bring you two romantic,
spine-tingling Shadows novels, written by some of your
favorite authors, such as *New York Times* bestseller
Heather Graham Pozzessere, Anne Stuart, Helen R. Myers
and Rachel Lee—to name just a few.

In May, look for:
FLASHBACK by Terri Herrington
WAITING FOR THE WOLF MOON by Evelyn Vaughn

In June, look for:
BREAK THE NIGHT by Anne Stuart
IMMINENT THUNDER by Rachel Lee

Come into the world of Shadows and prepare
to tremble with fear—and passion....

SHAD2

WHERE WERE YOU WHEN THE LIGHTS WENT OUT?

SILHOUETTE

SUMMER Sizzlers '93

This summer, Silhouette turns up the heat when a midsummer blackout leaves the entire Eastern seaboard in the dark. Who could ask for a more romantic atmosphere? And who can deliver it better than:

**LINDA HOWARD
CAROLE BUCK
SUZANNE CAREY**

Look for it this June at your favorite retail outlet.

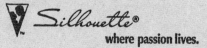

Silhouette®

where passion lives.

SS93

INTIMATE MOMENTS®

10TH Anniversary

Celebrate our anniversary with a fabulous collection of firsts....

The first Intimate Moments titles written by three of your favorite authors:

NIGHT MOVES   Heather Graham Pozzessere
LADY OF THE NIGHT   Emilie Richards
A STRANGER'S SMILE Kathleen Korbel

Silhouette Intimate Moments is proud to present a FREE hardbound collection of our authors' firsts—titles that you will treasure in the years to come, from some of the line's founding writers.

This collection will not be sold in retail stores and is available only through this exclusive offer. Look for details in Silhouette Intimate Moments titles available in retail stores in May, June and July.

SIMANN-R-R